Praise for the Percy Jackson series:

'A fantastic blend of myth and modern. Rick Riordan takes the reader back to the stories we love, then shakes the cobwebs out of them' – Eoin Colfer, author of *Artemis Fowl*

'Funny . . . very exciting . . . but it's the storytelling that will get readers hooked. After all, this is the stuff of legends' – *Guardian*

'It's *Buffy* meets *Artemis Fowl*. Thumbs up' – *Sunday Times*

'One of the books of the year . . . vastly entertaining' – *Independent*

'Funny, clever and exciting' – *The Times*

'Riordan delivers puns, jokes and subtle wit, alongside a gripping storyline' – *Sunday Telegraph*

'Unputdownable' – *Irish Times*

Books by Rick Riordan

The Percy Jackson series:

PERCY JACKSON AND THE LIGHTNING THIEF

PERCY JACKSON AND THE SEA OF MONSTERS

PERCY JACKSON AND THE TITAN'S CURSE

PERCY JACKSON AND THE BATTLE OF THE LABYRINTH

PERCY JACKSON AND THE LAST OLYMPIAN

THE DEMIGOD FILES

PERCY JACKSON AND THE GREEK GODS

PERCY JACKSON AND THE GREEK HEROES

For more about Percy Jackson, try:

PERCY JACKSON: THE ULTIMATE GUIDE

The Heroes of Olympus series:

THE LOST HERO

THE SON OF NEPTUNE

THE MARK OF ATHENA

THE HOUSE OF HADES

THE BLOOD OF OLYMPUS

THE DEMIGOD DIARIES

The Kane Chronicles series:

THE RED PYRAMID

THE THRONE OF FIRE

THE SERPENT'S SHADOW

For more about the Kane Chronicles, try:

THE KANE CHRONICLES: SURVIVAL GUIDE

Percy Jackson/Kane Chronicles Adventures (ebooks):

THE SON OF SOBEK

THE STAFF OF SERAPIS

THE CROWN OF PTOLEMY

www.rickriordan.co.uk

RICK RIORDAN

PUFFIN

To Topher Bradfield, a camper who made all the difference

PUFFIN BOOKS

UK | USA | Canada | Ireland | Australia
India | New Zealand | South Africa

Puffin Books is part of the Penguin Random House group of companies
whose addresses can be found at global.penguinrandomhouse.com.

puffinbooks.com

First published in the USA by Hyperion Books for Children 2007
Published in Great Britain by Puffin Books 2007
This edition published 2013

020

Percy Jackson and the Battle of the Labyrinth: first published in the USA by
Hyperion Books for Children and in Great Britain by Puffin Books 2008

Set in Centaur MT
Printed in Great Britain by Clays Ltd, St Ives plc

A CIP catalogue record for this book is available from the British Library

ISBN: 978–0–141–34681–6

www.greenpenguin.co.uk

Penguin Random House is committed to a
sustainable future for our business, our readers
and our planet. This book is made from Forest
Stewardship Council® certified paper.

CONTENTS

I MY RESCUE OPERATION GOES VERY WRONG

The Friday before winter break, my mom packed me an overnight bag and a few deadly weapons, and took me to a new boarding school. We picked up my friends Annabeth and Thalia on the way.

It was an eight-hour drive from New York to Bar Harbor, Maine. Sleet and snow pounded the highway. Annabeth, Thalia and I hadn't seen each other in months, but between the blizzard and the thought of what we were about to do, we were too nervous to talk much. Except for my mom. She talks *more* when she's nervous. By the time we finally got to Westover Hall, it was getting dark, and she'd told Annabeth and Thalia every embarrassing baby story there was to tell about me.

Thalia wiped the fog off the car window and peered outside. 'Oh, yeah. This'll be fun.'

Westover Hall looked like an evil knight's castle. It was all black stone, with towers and slit windows and a big set of wooden double doors. It stood on a snowy cliff overlooking this big frosty forest on one side and the grey churning ocean on the other.

'Are you sure you don't want me to wait?' my mother asked.

'No, thanks, Mom,' I said. 'I don't know how long it will take. We'll be okay.'

'But how will you get back? I'm worried, Percy.'

I hoped I wasn't blushing. It was bad enough I had to depend on my mom to drive me to my battles.

'It's okay, Ms Jackson.' Annabeth smiled reassuringly. Her blonde hair was tucked into a ski cap and her grey eyes were the same colour as the ocean. 'We'll keep him out of trouble.'

My mom seemed to relax a little. She thinks Annabeth is the most level-headed demigod ever to hit eighth grade. She's sure Annabeth often keeps me from getting killed. She's right, but that doesn't mean I have to like it.

'All right, dears,' my mom said. 'Do you have everything you need?'

'Yes, Ms Jackson,' Thalia said. 'Thanks for the ride.'

'Extra sweaters? You have my cell phone number?'

'Mom –'

'Your ambrosia and nectar, Percy? And a golden drachma in case you need to contact camp?'

'Mom, seriously! We'll be fine. Come on, guys.'

She looked a little hurt, and I was sorry about that, but I was ready to be out of that car. If my mom told one more story about how cute I looked in the bath when I was three years old, I was going to burrow into the snow and freeze myself to death.

Annabeth and Thalia followed me outside. The wind blew straight through my coat like ice daggers.

Once my mother's car was out of sight, Thalia said, 'Your mom is so cool, Percy.'

'She's pretty okay,' I admitted. 'What about you? You ever get in touch with your mom?'

As soon as I said it, I wished I hadn't. Thalia was great

at giving evil looks, what with the punk clothes she always wears – the ripped-up army jacket, black leather trousers and chain jewellery, the black eyeliner and those intense blue eyes. But the look she gave me now was a perfect evil 'ten'. 'If that was any of your business, Percy –'

'We'd better get inside,' Annabeth interrupted. 'Grover will be waiting.'

Thalia looked at the castle and shivered. 'You're right. I wonder what he found here that made him send the distress call.'

I stared up at the dark towers of Westover Hall. 'Nothing good,' I guessed.

The oak doors groaned open, and the three of us stepped into the entry hall in a swirl of snow.

All I could say was, 'Whoa.'

The place was huge. The walls were lined with battle flags and weapon displays: antique rifles, battleaxes and a bunch of other stuff. I mean, I knew Westover was a military school and all, but the decorations seemed like overkill. Literally.

My hand went to my pocket, where I kept my lethal ballpoint pen, Riptide. I could already sense something wrong in this place. Something dangerous. Thalia was rubbing her silver bracelet, her favourite magic item. I knew we were thinking the same thing. A fight was coming.

Annabeth started to say, 'I wonder where –'

The doors slammed shut behind us.

'Oo-kay,' I mumbled. 'Guess we'll stay a while.'

I could hear music echoing from the other end of the hall. It sounded like dance music.

We stashed our overnight bags behind a pillar and started down the hall. We hadn't gone very far when I heard footsteps on the stone floor, and a man and woman marched out of the shadows to intercept us.

They both had short grey hair and black military-style uniforms with red trim. The woman had a wispy moustache, and the guy was clean-shaven, which seemed kind of backwards to me. They both walked stiffly, like they had broomsticks taped to their spines.

'Well?' the woman demanded. 'What are you doing here?'

'Um . . .' I realized I hadn't planned for this. I'd been so focused on getting to Grover and finding out what was wrong, I hadn't considered that someone might question three kids sneaking into the school at night. We hadn't talked at all in the car about how we would get inside. I said, 'Ma'am, we're just –'

'Ha!' the man snapped, which made me jump. 'Visitors are not allowed at the dance! You shall be *eee-jected!*'

He had an accent – French, maybe. He pronounced his *J* like in *Jacques*. He was tall, with a hawkish face. His nostrils flared when he spoke, which made it really hard not to stare up his nose, and his eyes were two different colours – one brown, one blue – like an alley cat's.

I figured he was about to toss us into the snow, but then Thalia stepped forward and did something very weird.

She snapped her fingers. The sound was sharp and loud. Maybe it was just my imagination, but I felt a gust of wind ripple out from her hand, across the room. It washed over all of us, making the banners rustle on the walls.

'Oh, but we're not visitors, sir,' Thalia said. 'We go to

school here. You remember: I'm Thalia. And this is Annabeth and Percy. We're in the eighth grade.'

The male teacher narrowed his two-coloured eyes. I didn't know what Thalia was thinking. Now we'd probably get punished for lying *and* thrown into the snow. But the man seemed to be hesitating.

He looked at his colleague. 'Ms Gottschalk, do you know these students?'

Despite the danger we were in, I had to bite my tongue to keep from laughing. A teacher named *Got Chalk*? He had to be kidding.

The woman blinked, like someone had just woken her up from a trance. 'I . . . yes. I believe I do, sir.' She frowned at us. 'Annabeth. Thalia. Percy. What are you doing away from the gymnasium?'

Before we could answer, I heard more footsteps, and Grover ran up, breathless. 'You made it! You –'

He stopped short when he saw the teachers. 'Oh, Mrs Gottschalk. Dr Thorn! I, uh –'

'What *is* it, Mr Underwood?' said the man. His tone made it clear that he detested Grover. 'What do you mean they made it? These students live here.'

Grover swallowed. 'Yes, sir. Of course, Dr Thorn. I just meant I'm so glad they made . . . the punch for the dance! The punch is great. And they made it!'

Dr Thorn glared at us. I decided one of his eyes had to be fake. The brown one? The blue one? He looked like he wanted to pitch us off the castle's highest tower, but then Mrs Gottschalk said dreamily, 'Yes, the punch is excellent. Now run along, all of you. You are not to leave the gymnasium again!'

We didn't wait to be told twice. We left with a lot of 'Yes, ma'ams' and 'Yes, sirs' and a couple of salutes, just because it seemed like the thing to do.

Grover hustled us down the hall in the direction of the music.

I could feel the teachers' eyes on my back, but I walked closely to Thalia and asked in a low voice, 'How did you do that finger-snap thing?'

'You mean the Mist? Hasn't Chiron shown you how to do that yet?'

An uncomfortable lump formed in my throat. Chiron was our head trainer at camp, but he'd never shown me anything like that. Why had he shown Thalia and not me?

Grover hurried us to a door that had GYM written on the glass. Even with my dyslexia, I could read that much.

'That was close!' Grover said. 'Thank the gods you got here!'

Annabeth and Thalia both hugged Grover. I gave him a big high five.

It was good to see him after so many months. He'd got a little taller and had sprouted a few more whiskers, but otherwise he looked like he always did when he passed for human – a red cap on his curly brown hair to hide his goat horns, baggy jeans and trainers with fake feet to hide his furry legs and hooves. He was wearing a black T-shirt that took me a few seconds to read. It said WESTOVER HALL: GRUNT. I wasn't sure whether that was, like, Grover's rank or maybe just the school motto.

'So what's the emergency?' I asked.

Grover took a deep breath. 'I found two.'

'Two half-bloods?' Thalia asked, amazed. 'Here?'

Grover nodded.

Finding one half-blood was rare enough. This year, Chiron had put the satyrs on emergency overtime and sent them all over the country, scouring schools from fourth grade through high school for possible recruits. These were desperate times. We were losing campers. We needed all the new fighters we could find. The problem was, there just weren't that many demigods out there.

'A brother and a sister,' he said. 'They're ten and twelve. I don't know their parentage, but they're strong. We're running out of time, though. I need help.'

'Monsters?'

'One.' Grover looked nervous. 'He suspects. I don't think he's positive yet, but this is the last day of term. I'm sure he won't let them leave campus without finding out. It may be our last chance! Every time I try to get close to them, he's always there, blocking me. I don't know what to do!'

Grover looked at Thalia desperately. I tried not to feel upset by that. Grover used to look to me for answers, but Thalia had seniority. Not just because her dad was Zeus. Thalia had more experience than any of us with fending off monsters in the real world.

'Right,' she said. 'These half-bloods are at the dance?'

Grover nodded.

'Then let's dance,' Thalia said. 'Who's the monster?'

'Oh,' Grover said, and looked around nervously. 'You just met him. The vice-principal, Dr Thorn.'

Weird thing about military schools: the kids go absolutely nuts when there's a special event and they get to be out of uniform. I guess it's because everything's so strict the rest of the time, they feel like they've got to overcompensate or something.

There were black and red balloons all over the gym floor, and guys were kicking them in each other's faces, or trying to strangle each other with the crêpe-paper streamers taped to the walls. Girls moved around in football huddles, the way they always do, wearing lots of makeup and spaghetti-strap tops and brightly coloured trousers and shoes that looked like torture devices. Every once in a while they'd surround some poor guy like a pack of piranhas, shrieking and giggling, and when they finally moved on, the guy would have ribbons in his hair and a bunch of lipstick graffiti all over his face. Some of the older guys looked more like me – uncomfortable, hanging out at the edges of the gym and trying to hide, like any minute they might have to fight for their lives. Of course, in my case, it was true . . .

'There they are.' Grover nodded towards a couple of younger kids arguing in the bleachers. 'Bianca and Nico di Angelo.'

The girl wore a floppy green cap, like she was trying to hide her face. The boy was obviously her little brother. They both had dark silky hair and olive skin, and they used their hands a lot as they talked. The boy was shuffling some kind of trading cards. His sister seemed to be scolding him about something. She kept looking around like she sensed something was wrong.

Annabeth said, 'Do they . . . I mean, have you told them?'

Grover shook his head. 'You know how it is. That could

put them in more danger. Once they realize who they are, their scent becomes stronger.'

He looked at me, and I nodded. I'd never really understood what half-bloods 'smell' like to monsters and satyrs, but I knew that your scent could get you killed. And the more powerful a demigod you became, the more you smelled like a monster's lunch.

'So let's grab them and get out of here,' I said.

I started forward, but Thalia put her hand on my shoulder. The vice-principal, Dr Thorn, had slipped out of a doorway near the bleachers and was standing near the di Angelo siblings. He nodded coldly in our direction. His blue eye seemed to glow.

Judging from his expression, I guessed Thorn hadn't been fooled by Thalia's trick with the Mist after all. He suspected who we were. He was just waiting to see why we were here.

'Don't look at the kids,' Thalia ordered. 'We have to wait for a chance to get them. We need to pretend we're not interested in them. Throw him off the scent.'

'How?'

'We're three powerful half-bloods. Our presence should confuse him. Mingle. Act natural. Do some dancing. But keep an eye on those kids.'

'Dancing?' Annabeth asked.

Thalia nodded. She cocked her ear to the music and made a face. 'Ugh. Who chose the Jesse McCartney?'

Grover looked hurt. 'I did.'

'Oh my gods, Grover. That is so lame. Can't you play, like, Green Day or something?'

'Green who?'

'Never mind. Let's dance.'

'But I can't dance!'

'You can if I'm leading,' Thalia said. 'Come on, goat boy.'

Grover yelped as Thalia grabbed his hand and led him onto the dance floor.

Annabeth smiled.

'What?' I asked.

'Nothing. It's just cool to have Thalia back.'

Annabeth had grown taller than me since last summer, which I found kind of disturbing. She used to wear no jewellery except for her Camp Half-Blood bead necklace, but now she wore little silver earrings shaped like owls – the symbol of her mother, Athena. She pulled off her ski cap, and her long blonde hair tumbled down her shoulders. It made her look older, for some reason.

'So . . .' I tried to think of something to say. *Act natural,* Thalia had told us. When you're a half-blood on a dangerous mission, what the heck is natural? 'Um, design any good buildings lately?'

Annabeth's eyes lit up, the way they always did when she talked about architecture. 'Oh my gods, Percy. At my new school, I get to take 3-D design, and there's this cool computer program . . .'

She went on to explain how she'd designed this huge monument that she wanted to build at Ground Zero in Manhattan. She talked about structural supports and facades and stuff, and I tried to listen. I knew she wanted to be a super architect when she grew up – she loves maths and historical buildings and all that – but I hardly understood a word she was saying.

The truth was I was kind of disappointed to hear that she liked her new school so much. It was the first time she'd gone to school in New York. I'd been hoping to see her more often. It was a boarding school in Brooklyn, which she and Thalia were both attending, close enough to Camp Half-Blood that Chiron could help if they got into any trouble. Because it was an all-girls school, and I was going to MS-54 in Manhattan, I hardly ever saw them.

'Yeah, uh, cool,' I said. 'So you're staying there the rest of the year, huh?'

Her face got dark. 'Well, maybe, if I don't –'

'Hey!' Thalia called to us. She was slow dancing with Grover, who was tripping all over himself, kicking Thalia in the shins, and looking like he wanted to die. At least his feet were fake. Unlike me, he had an excuse for being clumsy.

'Dance, you guys!' Thalia ordered. 'You look stupid just standing there.'

I looked nervously at Annabeth, then at the groups of girls who were roaming the gym.

'Well?' Annabeth said.

'Um, who should I ask?'

She punched me in the gut. '*Me*, Seaweed Brain.'

'Oh. Oh, right.'

So we went onto the dance floor, and I looked over to see how Thalia and Grover were doing things. I put one hand on Annabeth's hip, and she clasped my other hand like she was about to judo throw me.

'I'm not going to bite,' she told me. 'Honestly, Percy. Don't you guys have dances at your school?'

I didn't answer. The truth was we did. But I'd never,

like, actually *danced* at one. I was usually one of the guys playing basketball in the corner.

We shuffled around for a few minutes. I tried to concentrate on little things, like the crêpe-paper streamers and the punch bowl – anything but the fact that Annabeth was taller than me, and my hands were sweaty and probably gross, and I kept stepping on her toes.

'What were you saying earlier?' I asked. 'Are you having trouble at school or something?'

She pursed her lips. 'It's not that. It's my dad.'

'Uh-oh.' I knew Annabeth had a rocky relationship with her father. 'I thought it was getting better with you two. Is it your stepmom again?'

Annabeth sighed. 'He decided to move. Just when I was getting settled in New York, he took this stupid new job researching for a World War I book. In *San Francisco*.'

She said this the same way she might say *Fields of Punishment* or *Hades's gym shorts*.

'So he wants you to move out there with him?' I asked.

'To the other side of the country,' she said miserably. 'And half-bloods can't live in San Francisco. He should know that.'

'What? Why not?'

Annabeth rolled her eyes. Maybe she thought I was kidding. 'You know. It's right *there*.'

'Oh,' I said. I had no idea what she was talking about, but I didn't want to sound stupid. 'So . . . you'll go back to living at camp or what?'

'It's more serious than that, Percy. I . . . I probably should tell you something.'

Suddenly she froze. 'They're gone.'

'What?'

I followed her gaze. The bleachers. The two half-blood kids, Bianca and Nico, were no longer there. The door next to the bleachers was wide open. Dr Thorn was nowhere in sight.

'We have to get Thalia and Grover!' Annabeth looked around frantically. 'Oh, where'd they dance off to? Come on!'

She ran through the crowd. I was about to follow when a mob of girls got in my way. I manoeuvred round them to avoid getting the ribbon-and-lipstick treatment, and by the time I was free Annabeth had disappeared. I turned, looking for her or Thalia and Grover. Instead, I saw something that chilled my blood.

About fifteen metres away, lying on the gym floor, was a floppy green cap just like the one Bianca di Angelo had been wearing. Near it were a few scattered trading cards. Then I caught a glimpse of Dr Thorn. He was hurrying out a door at the opposite end of the gym, steering the di Angelo kids by the scruffs of their necks, like kittens.

I still couldn't see Annabeth, but I knew she'd be heading the other way, looking for Thalia and Grover.

I almost ran after her, and then I thought, *Wait.*

I remembered what Thalia had said to me in the entry hall, looking at me all puzzled when I asked about the finger-snap trick: *Hasn't Chiron shown you how to do that yet?* I thought about the way Grover had turned to her, expecting her to save the day.

Not that I resented Thalia. She was cool. It wasn't her fault her dad was Zeus and she got all the attention . . . Still, I didn't need to run after her to solve every problem.

Besides, there wasn't time. The di Angelos were in danger. They might be long gone by the time I found my friends. I knew monsters. I could handle this myself.

I took Riptide out of my pocket and ran after Dr Thorn.

The door led into a dark hallway. I heard sounds of scuffling up ahead, then a painful grunt. I uncapped Riptide.

The pen grew in my hands until I held a bronze Greek sword about a metre long with a leather-bound grip. The blade glowed faintly, casting a golden light on the rows of lockers.

I jogged down the corridor, but when I got to the other end, no one was there. I opened a door and found myself back in the main entry hall. I had gone full circle. I didn't see Dr Thorn anywhere, but there on the opposite side of the room were the di Angelo kids. They stood frozen in horror, staring right at me.

I advanced slowly, lowering the tip of my sword. 'It's okay. I'm not going to hurt you.'

They didn't answer. Their eyes were full of fear. What was wrong with them? Where was Dr Thorn? Maybe he'd sensed the presence of Riptide and retreated. Monsters hated celestial bronze weapons.

'My name's Percy,' I said, trying to keep my voice level. 'I'm going to take you out of here, get you somewhere safe.'

Bianca's eyes widened. Her fists clenched. Only too late did I realize what her look meant. She wasn't afraid of me. She was trying to warn me.

I whirled round and something went *WHIIISH!* Pain

exploded in my shoulder. A force like a huge hand yanked me backwards and slammed me to the wall.

I slashed with my sword but there was nothing to hit.

A cold laugh echoed through the hall.

'Yes, Perseus *Jackson*,' Dr Thorn said. His accent mangled the *J* in my last name. 'I know who you are.'

I tried to free my shoulder. My coat and shirt were pinned to the wall by some kind of spike – a black daggerlike projectile about half a metre long. It had grazed the skin of my shoulder as it passed through my clothes, and the cut burned. I'd felt something like this before. Poison.

I forced myself to concentrate. I would *not* pass out.

A dark silhouette now moved towards us. Dr Thorn stepped into the dim light. He still looked human, but his face was ghoulish. He had perfect white teeth and his brown/blue eyes reflected the light of my sword.

'Thank you for coming out of the gym,' he said. 'I hate middle-school dances.'

I tried to swing my sword again, but he was just out of reach.

WHIIIISH! A second projectile shot from somewhere behind Dr Thorn. He didn't appear to move. It was as if someone invisible were standing behind him, throwing knives.

Next to me, Bianca yelped. The second thorn impaled itself in the stone wall, a millimetre from her face.

'All three of you will come with me,' Dr Thorn said. 'Quietly. Obediently. If you make a single noise, if you call out for help or try to fight, I will show you just how accurately I can throw.'

2 THE VICE-PRINCIPAL GETS A MISSILE LAUNCHER

I didn't know what kind of monster Dr Thorn was, but he was fast.

Maybe I could defend myself if I could get my shield activated. All that it would take was a touch of my wristwatch. But defending the di Angelo kids was another matter. I needed help, and there was only one way I could think to get it.

I closed my eyes.

'What are you doing, Jackson?' hissed Dr Thorn. 'Keep moving!'

I opened my eyes and kept shuffling forward. 'It's my shoulder,' I lied, trying to sound miserable, which wasn't hard. 'It burns.'

'Bah! My poison causes pain. It will not kill you. Walk!'

Thorn herded us outside, and I tried to concentrate. I pictured Grover's face. I focused on my feelings of fear and danger. Last summer, Grover had created an empathy link between us. He'd sent me visions in my dreams to let me know when he was in trouble. As far as I knew, we were still linked, but I'd never tried to contact Grover before. I didn't even know if it would work while Grover was awake.

Hey, Grover! I thought. *Thorn's kidnapping us! He's a poisonous spike-throwing maniac! Help!*

Thorn marched us into the woods. We took a snowy

path dimly lit by old-fashioned lamplights. My shoulder ached. The wind blowing through my ripped clothes was so cold that I felt like a Percysicle.

'There is a clearing ahead,' Thorn said. 'We will summon your ride.'

'What ride?' Bianca demanded. 'Where are you taking us?'

'Silence, you insufferable girl!'

'Don't talk to my sister that way!' Nico said. His voice quavered, but I was impressed that he had the guts to say anything at all.

Dr Thorn made a growling sound that definitely wasn't human. It made the hairs on the back of my neck stand up, but I forced myself to keep walking and pretend I was being a good little captive. Meanwhile, I projected my thoughts like crazy – anything to get Grover's attention: Grover! Apples! Tin cans! Get your furry goat behind out here and bring some heavily armed friends!

'Halt,' Thorn said.

The woods had opened up. We'd reached a cliff overlooking the sea. At least, I *sensed* the sea was down there, about a hundred metres below. I could hear the waves churning and I could smell the cold salty froth. But all I could see was mist and darkness.

Dr Thorn pushed us towards the edge. I stumbled, and Bianca caught me.

'Thanks,' I murmured.

'What *is* he?' she whispered. 'How do we fight him?'

'I . . . I'm working on it.'

'I'm scared,' Nico mumbled. He was fiddling with something – a little metal toy soldier of some kind.

'Stop talking!' Dr Thorn said. 'Face me!'

We turned.

Thorn's two-tone eyes glittered hungrily. He pulled something from under his coat. At first I thought it was a switchblade, but it was only a phone. He pressed the side button and said, 'The package – it is ready to deliver.'

There was a garbled reply, and I realized Thorn was in walkie-talkie mode. This seemed way too modern and creepy – a monster using a cell phone.

I glanced behind me, wondering how far the drop was.

Dr Thorn laughed. 'By all means, Son of Poseidon. *Jump!* There is the sea. Save yourself.'

'What did he call you?' Bianca muttered.

'I'll explain later,' I said.

'You do have a plan, right?'

Grover! I thought desperately. Come to me!

Maybe I could get both the di Angelos to jump with me into the ocean. If we survived the fall, I could use the water to protect us. I'd done things like that before. If my dad was in a good mood, and listening, he might help. Maybe.

'I would kill you before you ever reached the water,' Dr Thorn said, as if reading my thoughts. 'You do not realize who I am, do you?'

A flicker of movement behind him, and another missile whistled so close to me that it nicked my ear. Something had sprung up behind Dr Thorn – like a catapult, but more flexible . . . almost like a tail.

'Unfortunately,' Thorn said, 'you are wanted alive, if possible. Otherwise you would already be dead.'

'Who wants us?' Bianca demanded. 'Because if you think you'll get a ransom, you're wrong. We don't have any family.

Nico and I . . .' Her voice broke a little. 'We've got no one but each other.'

'Aww,' Dr Thorn said. 'Do not worry, little brats. You will be meeting my employer soon enough. Then you will have a brand-new family.'

'Luke,' I said. 'You work for Luke.'

Dr Thorn's mouth twisted with distaste when I said the name of my old enemy – a former friend who'd tried to kill me several times. 'You have no idea what is happening, Perseus Jackson. I will let the General enlighten you. You are going to do him a great service tonight. He is looking forward to meeting you.'

'The General?' I asked. Then I realized I'd said it with a French accent. 'I mean . . . who's the General?'

Thorn looked towards the horizon. 'Ah, here we are. Your transportation.'

I turned and saw a light in the distance, a searchlight over the sea. Then I heard the chopping of helicopter blades getting louder and closer.

'Where are you taking us?' Nico said.

'You should feel honoured, my boy. You will have the opportunity to join a great army! Just like that silly game you play with cards and dolls.'

'They're not dolls! They're figurines! And you can take your great army and –'

'Now, now,' Dr Thorn warned. 'You will change your mind about joining us, my boy. And, if you do not, well . . . there are other uses for half-bloods. We have many monstrous mouths to feed. The Great Stirring is underway.'

'The Great what?' I asked. Anything to keep him talking while I tried to figure out a plan.

'The stirring of monsters.' Dr Thorn smiled evilly. 'The worst of them, the most powerful, are now waking. Monsters that have not been seen in thousands of years. They will cause death and destruction the likes of which mortals have never known. And soon we shall have the most important monster of all – the one that shall bring about the downfall of Olympus!'

'Okay,' Bianca whispered to me. 'He's completely nuts.'

'We have to jump off the cliff,' I told her quietly. 'Into the sea.'

'Oh, super idea. You're completely nuts, too.'

I never got the chance to argue with her, because just then an invisible force slammed into me.

Looking back on it, Annabeth's move was brilliant. Wearing her cap of invisibility, she ploughed into the di Angelos and me, knocking us to the ground. For a split second, Dr Thorn was taken by surprise, so his first volley of missiles zipped harmlessly over our heads. This gave Thalia and Grover a chance to advance from behind – Thalia wielding her magic shield, Aegis.

If you've never seen Thalia run into battle, you have never been truly frightened. She uses a huge spear that expands from this collapsible Mace canister she carries in her pocket, but that's not the scary part. Her shield is modelled on one her dad Zeus uses – also called Aegis – a gift from Athena. The shield has the head of the gorgon Medusa moulded into the bronze, and even though it won't turn you to stone it's so horrible most people will panic and run at the sight of it.

Even Dr Thorn winced and growled when he saw it.

Thalia moved in with her spear. 'For Zeus!'

I thought Dr Thorn was a goner. Thalia jabbed at his head, but he snarled and swatted the spear aside. His hand changed into an orange paw with enormous claws that sparked against Thalia's shield as he slashed. If it hadn't been for Aegis, Thalia would've been sliced like a loaf of bread. As it was, she managed to roll backwards and land on her feet.

The sound of the helicopter was getting louder behind me, but I didn't dare look.

Dr Thorn launched another volley of missiles at Thalia, and this time I could see how he did it. He had a tail – a leathery, scorpionlike tail that bristled with spikes at the tip. The missiles deflected off Aegis, but the force of their impact knocked Thalia down.

Grover sprang forward. He put his reed pipes to his lips and began to play – a frantic jig that sounded like something pirates would dance to. Grass broke through the snow. Within seconds, rope-thick weeds were wrapping round Dr Thorn's legs, entangling him.

Dr Thorn roared and began to change. He grew larger until he was in his true form – his face still human, but his body that of a huge lion. His leathery, spiky tail whipped deadly thorns in all directions.

'A manticore!' Annabeth said, now visible. Her magical New York Yankees cap had come off when she'd ploughed into us.

'Who *are* you people?' Bianca di Angelo demanded. 'And what is *that*?'

'A manticore?' Nico gasped. 'He's got three thousand attack power and plus five to saving throws!'

I didn't know what he was talking about, but I didn't have time to worry about it. The manticore clawed Grover's magic weeds to shreds then turned towards us with a snarl.

'Get down!' Annabeth pushed the di Angelos flat into the snow. At the last second, I remembered my own shield. I hit my wristwatch, and metal plating spiralled out into a thick bronze shield. Not a moment too soon. The thorns impacted against it with such force they dented the metal. The beautiful shield, a gift from my brother, was badly damaged. I wasn't sure it would even stop a second volley.

I heard a *thwack* and a yelp, and Grover landed next to me with a thud.

'Yield!' the monster roared.

'Never!' Thalia yelled from across the field. She charged the monster and, for a second, I thought she would run him through. But then there was a thunderous noise and a blaze of light from behind us. The helicopter appeared out of the mist, hovering just beyond the cliffs. It was a sleek black military-style gunship, with attachments on the sides that looked like laser-guided rockets. The helicopter had to be manned by mortals, but what was it doing here? How could mortals be working with a monster? The searchlights blinded Thalia, and the manticore swatted her away with its tail. Her shield flew off into the snow. Her spear flew in the other direction.

'No!' I ran out to help her. I parried away a spike just before it would've hit her chest. I raised my shield over us, but I knew it wouldn't be enough.

Dr Thorn laughed. 'Now do you see how hopeless it is? Yield, little heroes.'

We were trapped between a monster and a fully armed helicopter. We had no chance.

Then I heard a clear, piercing sound: the call of a hunting horn blowing in the woods.

The manticore froze. For a moment, no one moved. There was only the swirl of snow and wind and the chopping of the helicopter blades.

'No,' Dr Thorn said. 'It cannot be –'

His sentence was cut short when something shot past me like a streak of moonlight. A glowing silver arrow sprouted from Dr Thorn's shoulder.

He staggered backwards, wailing in agony.

'Curse you!' Thorn cried. He unleashed his spikes, dozens of them at once, into the woods where the arrow had come from, but just as fast, silvery arrows shot back in reply. It almost looked like the arrows had intercepted the thorns in mid-air and sliced them in two, but my eyes must've been playing tricks on me. No one, not even Apollo's kids at camp, could shoot with that much accuracy.

The manticore pulled the arrow out of his shoulder with a howl of pain. His breathing was heavy. I tried to swipe at him with my sword, but he wasn't as injured as he looked. He dodged my attack and slammed his tail into my shield, knocking me aside.

Then the archers came from the woods. They were girls, about a dozen of them. The youngest was maybe ten. The oldest, about fourteen, like me. They wore silvery ski parkas and jeans, and they were all armed with bows. They advanced on the manticore with determined expressions.

'The Hunters!' Annabeth cried.

Next to me, Thalia muttered, 'Oh, wonderful.'

I didn't have a chance to ask what she meant.

One of the older archers stepped forward with her bow drawn. She was tall and graceful with coppery coloured skin. Unlike the other girls, she had a silver circlet braided into the top of her long dark hair, so she looked like some kind of Persian princess. 'Permission to kill, my lady?'

I couldn't tell who she was talking to, because she kept her eyes on the manticore.

The monster wailed. 'This is not fair! Direct interference! It is against the Ancient Laws.'

'Not so,' another girl said. This one was a little younger than me, maybe twelve or thirteen. She had auburn hair gathered back in a ponytail and strange eyes, silvery yellow like the moon. Her face was so beautiful it made me catch my breath, but her expression was stern and dangerous. 'The hunting of all wild beasts is within my sphere. And you, foul creature, are a wild beast.' She looked at the older girl with the circlet. 'Zoë, permission granted.'

The manticore growled. 'If I cannot have these alive, I shall have them dead!'

He lunged at Thalia and me, knowing we were weak and dazed.

'No!' Annabeth yelled, and she charged at the monster.

'Get back, half-blood!' the girl with the circlet said. 'Get out of the line of fire!'

But Annabeth leaped onto the monster's back and drove her knife into his mane. The manticore howled, turning in circles with his tail flailing as Annabeth hung on for dear life.

'Fire!' Zoë ordered.

'No!' I screamed.

But the Hunters let their arrows fly. The first caught the manticore in the neck. Another hit his chest. The manticore staggered backwards, wailing, 'This is not the end, Huntress! You shall pay!'

And before anyone could react, the monster, with Annabeth still on his back, leaped over the cliff and tumbled into the darkness.

'Annabeth!' I yelled.

I started to run after her, but our enemies weren't done with us. There was a *snap-snap-snap* from the helicopter – the sound of gunfire.

Most of the Hunters scattered as tiny holes appeared in the snow at their feet, but the girl with auburn hair just looked up calmly at the helicopter.

'Mortals,' she announced, 'are not allowed to witness my hunt.'

She thrust out her hand, and the helicopter exploded into dust – no, not dust. The black metal dissolved into a flock of birds – ravens, which scattered into the night.

The Hunters advanced on us.

The one called Zoë stopped short when she saw Thalia. 'You,' she said with distaste.

'Zoë Nightshade.' Thalia's voice trembled with anger. 'Perfect timing, as usual.'

Zoë scanned the rest of us. 'Four half-bloods and a satyr, my lady.'

'Yes,' the younger girl said. 'Some of Chiron's campers, I see.'

'Annabeth!' I yelled. 'You have to let us save her!'

The auburn-haired girl turned towards me. 'I'm sorry, Percy Jackson, but your friend is beyond help.'

I tried to struggle to my feet, but a couple of the girls held me down.

'You are in no condition to be hurling yourself off cliffs,' the auburn-haired girl said.

'Let me go!' I demanded. 'Who do you think you are?'

Zoë stepped forward as if to slap me.

'No,' the other girl ordered. 'I sense no disrespect, Zoë. He is simply distraught. He does not understand.'

The young girl looked at me, her eyes colder and brighter than the winter moon. 'I am Artemis,' she said. 'Goddess of the Hunt.'

3 BIANCA DI ANGELO MAKES A CHOICE

After seeing Dr Thorn turn into a monster and plummet off the edge of a cliff with Annabeth, you'd think nothing else could shock me. But when this twelve-year-old girl told me she was the goddess Artemis, I said something really intelligent like, 'Um . . . okay.'

That was nothing compared to Grover. He gasped, then knelt hastily in the snow and started yammering, 'Thank you, Lady Artemis! You're so . . . you're so . . . Wow!'

'Get up, goat boy!' Thalia snapped. 'We have other things to worry about. Annabeth is gone!'

'Whoa,' Bianca di Angelo said. 'Hold up. Time out.'

Everybody looked at her. She pointed her finger at all of us in turn, like she was trying to connect the dots. 'Who . . . who are you people?'

Artemis's expression softened. 'It might be a better question, my dear girl, to ask who are *you*? Who are your parents?'

Bianca glanced nervously at her brother, who was still staring in awe at Artemis.

'Our parents are dead,' Bianca said. 'We're orphans. There's a bank trust that pays for our school, but . . .'

She faltered. I guess she could tell from our faces that we didn't believe her.

'What?' she demanded. 'I'm telling the truth.'

'You are a half-blood,' Zoë Nightshade said. Her accent was hard to place. It seemed old-fashioned, like she was reading from a really old book. 'One of thy parents was mortal. The other was an Olympian.'

'An Olympian . . . athlete?'

'No,' Zoë said. 'One of the gods.'

'Cool!' said Nico.

'No!' Bianca's voice quavered. 'This is not cool!'

Nico danced around like he needed to use the restroom. 'Does Zeus really have lightning bolts that do six hundred damage? Does he get extra movement points for –'

'Nico, shut up!' Bianca put her hands to her face. 'This is not your stupid Mythomagic game, okay? There are no gods!'

As anxious as I felt about Annabeth – all I wanted to do was search for her – I couldn't help feeling sorry for the di Angelos. I remembered what it was like for me when I first learned I was a demigod.

Thalia must've been feeling something similar, because the anger in her eyes subsided a little bit. 'Bianca, I know it's hard to believe. But the gods are still around. Trust me. They're immortal. And whenever they have kids with regular humans, kids like us, well . . . Our lives are dangerous.'

'Dangerous,' Bianca said, 'like the girl who fell.'

Thalia turned away. Even Artemis looked pained.

'Do not despair for Annabeth,' the goddess said. 'She was a brave maiden. If she can be found, I shall find her.'

'Then why won't you let us go and look for her?' I asked.

'She is gone. Can't you sense it, Son of Poseidon? Some

magic is at work. I do not know exactly how or why, but your friend has vanished.'

I still wanted to jump off the cliff and search for her, but I had a feeling that Artemis was right. Annabeth was gone. If she'd been down there in the sea, I thought, I'd be able to feel her presence.

'Oo!' Nico raised his hand. 'What about Dr Thorn? That was awesome how you shot him with arrows! Is he dead?'

'He was a manticore,' Artemis said. 'Hopefully, he is destroyed for now, but monsters never truly die. They re-form over and over again, and they must be hunted whenever they reappear.'

'Or they'll hunt us,' Thalia said.

Bianca di Angelo shivered. 'That explains . . . Nico, you remember last summer, those guys who tried to attack us in the alley in D.C.?'

'And that bus driver,' Nico said. 'The one with the ram's horns. I *told* you that was real.'

'That's why Grover has been watching you,' I said. 'To keep you safe, if you turned out to be half-bloods.'

'Grover?' Bianca stared at him. 'You're a demigod?'

'Well, a satyr, actually.' He kicked off his shoes and displayed his goat hooves. I thought Bianca was going to faint right there.

'Grover, put your shoes back on,' Thalia said. 'You're freaking her out.'

'Hey, my hooves are clean!'

'Bianca,' I said, 'we came here to help you. You and Nico need training to survive. Dr Thorn won't be the last monster you meet. You need to come to camp.'

'Camp?' she asked.

'Camp Half-Blood,' I said. 'It's where half-bloods learn to survive and stuff. You can join us, stay there year round if you like.'

'Sweet, let's go!' said Nico.

'Wait.' Bianca shook her head. 'I don't –'

'There *is* another option,' Zoë said.

'No, there isn't!' Thalia said.

Thalia and Zoë glared at each other. I didn't know what they were talking about, but I could tell there was bad history between them. For some reason, they seriously hated each other.

'We've burdened these children enough,' Artemis announced. 'Zoë, we will rest here for a few hours. Raise the tents. Treat the wounded. Retrieve our guests' belongings from the school.'

'Yes, my lady.'

'And, Bianca, come with me. I would like to speak with you.'

'What about me?' Nico asked.

Artemis considered the boy. 'Perhaps you can show Grover how to play that card game you enjoy. I'm sure Grover would be happy to entertain you for a while . . . as a favour to me?'

Grover just about tripped over himself getting up. 'You bet! Come on, Nico!'

Nico and Grover walked off towards the woods, talking about hit points and armour ratings and a bunch of other geeky stuff. Artemis led a confused-looking Bianca along the cliff. The Hunters began unpacking their backpacks and making camp.

Zoë gave Thalia one more evil look, then left to oversee things.

As soon as she was gone, Thalia stamped her foot in frustration. 'The nerve of those Hunters! They think they're so . . . Argh!'

'I'm with you,' I said. 'I don't trust –'

'Oh, you're with me?' Thalia turned on me furiously. 'What were you thinking back there in the gym, Percy? You'd take on Dr Thorn all by yourself? You *knew* he was a monster!'

'I –'

'If we'd stuck together, we could've taken him without the Hunters getting involved. Annabeth might still be here. Did you think of that?'

My jaw clenched. I thought of some harsh things to say, and I might've said them, too, but then I looked down and saw something navy blue lying in the snow at my feet. Annabeth's New York Yankees baseball cap.

Thalia didn't say another word. She wiped a tear from her cheek, turned and marched off, leaving me alone with a trampled cap in the snow.

The Hunters set up their campsite in a matter of minutes. Seven large tents, all of silver silk, curved in a crescent round one side of a bonfire. One of the girls blew a silver dog whistle, and a dozen white wolves appeared out of the woods. They began circling the camp like guard dogs. The Hunters walked among them and fed them treats, completely unafraid, but I decided I would stick close to the tents. Falcons watched us from the trees, their eyes flashing in the firelight, and I got the feeling they were on guard duty, too. Even the weather seemed to bend to the goddess's will. The air was still cold, but the wind died down and the snow stopped falling, so it was almost pleasant sitting by the fire.

Almost . . . Except for the pain in my shoulder and the guilt weighing me down. I couldn't believe Annabeth was gone. And, as angry as I was at Thalia, I had a sinking feeling that she was right. It *was* my fault.

What had Annabeth wanted to tell me in the gym? *Something serious,* she'd said. Now I might never find out. I thought about how we'd danced together for half a song, and my heart felt even heavier.

I watched Thalia pacing in the snow at the edge of camp, walking among the wolves without fear. She stopped and looked back at Westover Hall, which was now completely dark, looming on the hillside beyond the woods. I wondered what she was thinking.

Seven years ago, Thalia had been turned into a pine tree by her father, to prevent her from dying. She'd stood her ground against an army of monsters on top of Half-Blood Hill in order to give her friends Luke and Annabeth time to escape. She'd only been back as a human for a few months now, and once in a while she would stand so motionless you'd think she was still a tree.

Finally, one of the Hunters brought me my backpack. Grover and Nico returned from their walk, and Grover helped me fix up my wounded arm.

'It's green!' Nico said with delight.

'Hold still,' Grover told me. 'Here, eat some ambrosia while I clean that out.'

I winced as he dressed the wound, but the ambrosia

square helped. It tasted like homemade brownie, dissolving in my mouth and sending a warm feeling through my whole body. Between that and the magic salve Grover used, my shoulder felt better within a couple of minutes.

Nico rummaged through his own bag, which the Hunters had apparently packed for him, though how they'd snuck into Westover Hall unseen, I didn't know. Nico laid out a bunch of figurines in the snow – little battle replicas of Greek gods and heroes. I recognized Zeus with a lightning bolt, Ares with a spear, Apollo with his sun chariot.

'Big collection,' I said.

Nico grinned. 'I've got almost all of them, plus their holographic cards! Well, except for a few really rare ones.'

'You've been playing this game a long time?'

'Just this year. Before that . . .' He knitted his eyebrows.

'What?' I asked.

'I forgot. That's weird.'

He looked unsettled, but it didn't last long. 'Hey, can I see that sword you were using?'

I showed him Riptide, and explained how it turned from a pen into a sword just by uncapping it.

'Cool! Does it ever run out of ink?'

'Um, well, I don't actually write with it.'

'Are you really the son of Poseidon?'

'Well, yeah.'

'Can you surf really well, then?'

I looked at Grover, who was trying hard not to laugh.

'Jeez, Nico,' I said. 'I've never really tried.'

He went on asking questions. Did I fight a lot with Thalia, since she was a daughter of Zeus? (I didn't answer that one.) If Annabeth's mother was Athena, the goddess of wisdom, then why didn't Annabeth know better than to fall off a cliff? (I tried not to strangle Nico for asking that one.) Was Annabeth my girlfriend? (At this point, I was ready to stick the kid in a meat-flavoured sack and throw him to the wolves.)

I figured any second he was going to ask me how many hit points I had, and I'd lose my cool completely, but then Zoë Nightshade came up to us.

'Percy Jackson.'

She had dark brown eyes and a slightly upturned nose. With her silver circlet and her proud expression, she looked so much like royalty that I had to resist the urge to sit up straight and say 'Yes, ma'am.' She studied me distastefully, like I was a bag of dirty laundry she'd been sent to fetch.

'Come with me,' she said. 'Lady Artemis wishes to speak with thee.'

Zoë led me to the last tent, which looked no different from the others, and waved me inside. Bianca di Angelo was seated next to the auburn-haired girl, who I still had trouble thinking of as Artemis.

The inside of the tent was warm and comfortable. Silk rugs and pillows covered the floor. In the centre, a golden brazier of fire seemed to burn without fuel or smoke. Behind the goddess, on a polished oak display stand, was her huge silver bow, carved to resemble gazelle horns. The walls were hung with animal pelts – black bear, tiger and several others I didn't recognize. I figured an animal-rights activist would've had a heart attack looking at all those rare skins, but maybe, since Artemis was the goddess of the hunt, she could replenish whatever she shot. I thought she had another animal pelt lying next to her, and then I realized it was alive – a deer with glittering fur and silver horns, its head resting contentedly in Artemis's lap.

'Join us, Percy Jackson,' the goddess said.

I sat across from her on the tent floor. The goddess studied me, which made me uncomfortable. She had such old eyes for a young girl.

'Are you surprised by my age?' she asked.

'Uh . . . a little.'

'I could appear as a grown woman, or a blazing fire, or anything else I want, but this is what I prefer. This is the average age of my Hunters, and all young maidens for whom I am patron, before they go astray.'

'Go astray?' I asked.

'Grow up. Become smitten with boys. Become silly, preoccupied, insecure. Forget themselves.'

'Oh.'

Zoë sat down to Artemis's right. She glared at me as if all the stuff Artemis had just said was my fault, like I'd invented the idea of being a guy.

'You must forgive my Hunters if they do not welcome you,' Artemis said. 'It is very rare that we would have boys in this camp. Boys are usually forbidden to have any contact with the Hunters. The last one to see this camp . . .' She looked at Zoë. 'Which one was it?'

'That boy in Colorado,' Zoë said. 'You turned him into a jackalope.'

'Ah, yes.' Artemis nodded, satisfied. 'I enjoy making jackalopes. At any rate, Percy, I've asked you here so that you might tell me more of the manticore. Bianca has reported some of the . . . mmm, disturbing things the monster said. But she may not have understood them. I'd like to hear them from you.'

And so I told her.

When I was done, Artemis put her hand thoughtfully on her silver bow. 'I feared this was the answer.'

Zoë sat forward. 'The scent, my lady?'

'Yes.'

'What scent?' I asked.

'Things are stirring that I have not hunted in millennia,' Artemis murmured. 'Prey so old I have nearly forgotten.'

She stared at me intently. 'We came here tonight sensing the manticore, but he was not the one I seek. Tell me again, exactly what Dr Thorn said.'

'Um, "I hate middle school dances."'

'No, no. After that.'

'He said somebody called the General was going to explain things to me.'

Zoë's face paled. She turned to Artemis and started to say something, but Artemis raised her hand.

'Go on, Percy,' the goddess said.

'Well, then Thorn was talking about the Great Stir Pot –'

'Stirring,' Bianca corrected.

'Yeah. And he said, "Soon we shall have the most important monster of all – the one that shall bring about the downfall of Olympus."'

The goddess was so still she could've been a statue.

'Maybe he was lying,' I said.

Artemis shook her head. 'No. He was not. I've been too slow to see the signs. I must hunt this monster.'

Zoë looked like she was trying very hard not to be

afraid, but she nodded. 'We will leave right away, my lady.'

'No, Zoë. I must do this alone.'

'But, Artemis –'

'This task is too dangerous even for the Hunters. You know where I must start my search. You cannot go there with me.'

'As . . . as you wish, my lady.'

'I will find this creature,' Artemis vowed. 'And I shall bring it back to Olympus by winter solstice. It will be all the proof I need to convince the Council of the Gods of how much danger we are in.'

'You know what the monster is?' I asked.

Artemis gripped her bow. 'Let us pray I am wrong.'

'Can goddesses pray?' I asked, because I'd never really thought about that.

A flicker of a smile played across Artemis's lips. 'Before I go, Percy Jackson, I have a small task for you.'

'Does it involve getting turned into a jackalope?'

'Sadly, no. I want you to escort the Hunters back to Camp Half-Blood. They can stay there in safety until I return.'

'What?' Zoë blurted out. 'But, Artemis, we hate that place. The last time we stayed there –'

'Yes, I know,' Artemis said. 'But I'm sure Dionysus will not hold a grudge just because of a little, ah, misunderstanding. It's your right to use Cabin Eight whenever you are in need. Besides, I hear they rebuilt the cabins you burned down.'

Zoë muttered something about foolish campers.

'And now there is one last decision to make.' Artemis turned to Bianca. 'Have you made up your mind, my girl?'

Bianca hesitated. 'I'm still thinking about it.'

'Wait,' I said. 'Thinking about what?'

'They . . . they've invited me to join the Hunt.'

'What? But you can't! You have to come to Camp Half-Blood so Chiron can train you. It's the only way you can learn to survive.'

'It is *not* the only way for a girl,' Zoë said.

I couldn't believe I was hearing this. 'Bianca, camp is cool! It's got a pegasus stable and a sword-fighting arena and . . . I mean, what do you get by joining the Hunters?'

'To begin with,' Zoë said, 'immortality.'

I stared at her, then at Artemis. 'She's kidding, right?'

'Zoë rarely kids about anything,' Artemis said. 'My Hunters follow me on my adventures. They are my maidservants, my companions, my sisters-in-arms. Once they swear loyalty to me, they are indeed immortal . . . unless they fall in battle, which is unlikely. Or break their oath.'

'What oath?' I said.

'To forswear romantic love forever,' Artemis said. 'To never grow up, never get married. To be a maiden eternally.'

'Like you?'

The goddess nodded.

I tried to imagine what she was saying. Being immortal. Hanging out with only middle-school girls forever. I couldn't get my mind round it. 'So you just go around the country recruiting half-bloods –'

'Not just half-bloods,' Zoë interrupted. 'Lady Artemis does not discriminate by birth. All who honour the goddess may join. Half-bloods, nymphs, mortals –'

'Which are you, then?'

Anger flashed in Zoë's eyes. 'That is not thy concern, boy. The point is Bianca may join if she wishes. It is her choice.'

'Bianca, this is crazy,' I said. 'What about your brother? Nico can't be a Hunter.'

'Certainly not,' Artemis agreed. 'He will go to camp. Unfortunately, that's the best boys can do.'

'Hey!' I protested.

'You can see him from time to time,' Artemis assured Bianca. 'But you will be free of responsibility. He will have the camp counsellors to take care of him. And you will have a new family. Us.'

'A new family,' Bianca repeated dreamily. 'Free of responsibility.'

'Bianca, you can't do this,' I said. 'It's nuts.'

She looked at Zoë. 'Is it worth it?'

Zoë nodded. 'It is.'

'What do I have to do?'

'Say this,' Zoë told her, '"I pledge myself to the goddess Artemis."'

'I . . . I pledge myself to the goddess Artemis.'

'"I turn my back on the company of men, accept eternal maidenhood and join the Hunt."'

Bianca repeated the lines. 'That's it?'

Zoë nodded. 'If Lady Artemis accepts thy pledge, then it is binding.'

'I accept it,' Artemis said.

The flames in the brazier brightened, casting a silver glow over the room. Bianca looked no different, but she took a deep breath and opened her eyes wide. 'I feel . . . stronger.'

'Welcome, sister,' Zoë said.

'Remember your pledge,' Artemis said. 'It is now your life.'

I couldn't speak. I felt like a trespasser. And a complete failure. I couldn't believe I'd come all this way and suffered so much only to lose Bianca to some eternal girls' club.

'Do not despair, Percy Jackson,' Artemis said. 'You will still get to show the di Angelos your camp. And if Nico so chooses, he can stay there.'

'Great,' I said, trying not to sound surly. 'How are we supposed to get there?'

Artemis closed her eyes. 'Dawn is approaching. Zoë, break camp. You must get to Long Island quickly and safely. I shall summon a ride from my brother.'

Zoë didn't look very happy about this idea, but she nodded and told Bianca to follow her. As she was leaving, Bianca paused in front of me. 'I'm sorry, Percy. But I want this. I really, really do.'

Then she was gone, and I was left alone with the twelve-year-old goddess.

'So,' I said glumly. 'We're going to get a ride from your brother, huh?'

Artemis's silver eyes gleamed. 'Yes, boy. You see, Bianca di Angelo is not the only one with an annoying brother. It's time for you to meet my irresponsible twin, Apollo.'

4 THALIA TORCHES NEW ENGLAND

Artemis assured us that dawn was coming, but you could've fooled me. It was colder and darker and snowier than ever. Up on the hill, Westover Hall's windows were completely lightless. I wondered if the teachers had even noticed the di Angelos and Dr Thorn were missing yet. I didn't want to be around when they did. With my luck, the only name Mrs Gottschalk would remember would be 'Percy Jackson', and then I'd be the subject of a nationwide manhunt . . . again.

The Hunters broke camp as quickly as they'd set it up. I stood shivering in the snow (unlike the Hunters, who didn't seem to feel at all uncomfortable), and Artemis stared into the east like she was expecting something. Bianca sat off to one side, talking with Nico. I could tell from his gloomy face that she was explaining her decision to join the Hunt. I couldn't help thinking how selfish it was of her, abandoning her brother like that.

Thalia and Grover came up and huddled around me, anxious to hear what had happened during my audience with the goddess.

When I told them, Grover turned pale. 'The last time the Hunters visited camp, it didn't go well.'

'How'd they even show up here?' I wondered. 'I mean, they just appeared out of nowhere.'

'And Bianca *joined* them,' Thalia said, disgusted. 'It's all Zoë's fault. That stuck-up, no good –'

'Who can blame her?' Grover said. 'Eternity with Artemis?' He heaved a big sigh.

Thalia rolled her eyes. 'You satyrs. You're all in love with Artemis. Don't you get that she'll never love you back?'

'But she's so . . . into nature,' Grover swooned.

'You're nuts,' said Thalia.

'Nuts and berries,' Grover said dreamily. 'Yeah.'

Finally the sky began to lighten. Artemis muttered, 'About time. He's so-o-o lazy during the winter.'

'You're, um, waiting for sunrise?' I asked.

'For my brother. Yes.'

I didn't want to be rude. I mean, I knew the legends about Apollo – or sometimes Helios – driving a big sun chariot across the sky. But I also knew that the sun was really a star about a zillion miles away. I'd got used to some of the Greek myths being true, but still . . . I didn't see how Apollo could drive the sun.

'It's not exactly as you think,' Artemis said, like she was reading my mind.

'Oh, okay.' I started to relax. 'So, it's not like he'll be pulling up in a –'

There was a sudden burst of light on the horizon. A blast of warmth.

'Don't look,' Artemis advised. 'Not until he parks.'

Parks?

I averted my eyes, and saw that the other kids were doing the same. The light and warmth intensified until my winter coat felt like it was melting off me. Then suddenly the light died.

I looked. And I couldn't believe it. It was *my* car. Well, the car I wanted, anyway. A red convertible Maserati Spyder. It was so awesome it glowed. Then I realized it was glowing because the metal was hot. The snow had melted round the Maserati in a perfect circle, which explained why I was now standing on green grass and my shoes were wet.

The driver got out, smiling. He looked about seventeen or eighteen, and, for a second, I had the uneasy feeling it was Luke, my old enemy. This guy had the same sandy hair and outdoorsy good looks. But it wasn't Luke. This guy was taller, with no scar on his face like Luke's. His smile was brighter and more playful. (Luke didn't do much more than scowl and sneer these days.) The Maserati driver wore jeans and loafers and a sleeveless T-shirt.

'Wow,' Thalia muttered. 'Apollo is hot.'

'He's the sun god,' I said.

'That's not what I meant.'

'Little sister!' Apollo called. If his teeth were any whiter he could've blinded us without the sun car. 'What's up? You never call. You never write. I was getting worried!'

Artemis sighed. 'I'm fine, Apollo. And I am not your *little* sister.'

'Hey, I was born first.'

'We're twins! How many millennia do we have to argue –'

'So what's up?' he interrupted. 'Got the girls with you, I see. You all need some tips on archery?'

Artemis gritted her teeth. 'I need a favour. I have some

hunting to do, *alone*. I need you to take my companions to Camp Half-Blood.'

'Sure, sis!' Then he raised his hands in a *stop everything* gesture. 'I feel a haiku coming on.'

The Hunters all groaned. Apparently they'd met Apollo before.

He cleared his throat and held up one hand dramatically.

> '*Green grass breaks through snow.*
> *Artemis pleads for my help.*
> *I am so cool.*'

He grinned at us, waiting for applause.

'That last line was only four syllables,' Artemis said.

Apollo frowned. 'Was it?'

'Yes. What about *I am so big-headed*?'

'No, no, that's six syllables. Hmm.' He started muttering to himself.

Zoë Nightshade turned to us. 'Lord Apollo has been going through this haiku phase ever since he visited Japan. 'Tis not as bad as the time he visited Limerick. If I'd had to hear one more poem that started with, *There once was a goddess from Sparta* –'

'I've got it!' Apollo announced. '*I am so awesome*. That's five syllables!' He bowed, looking very pleased with himself. 'And now, sis. Transportation for the Hunters, you say? Good timing. I was just about ready to roll.'

'These demigods will also need a ride,' Artemis said, pointing to us. 'Some of Chiron's campers.'

'No problem!' Apollo checked us out. 'Let's see . . . Thalia, right? I've heard all about you.'

Thalia blushed. 'Hi, Lord Apollo.'

'Zeus's girl, yes? Makes you my half-sister. Used to be a tree, didn't you? Glad you're back. I hate it when pretty girls turn into trees. Man, I remember one time –'

'Brother,' Artemis said. 'You should get going.'

'Oh, right.' Then he looked at me, and his eyes narrowed. 'Percy Jackson?'

'Yeah. I mean . . . yes, sir.'

It seemed weird calling a teenager 'sir', but I'd learned to be careful with immortals. They tended to get offended easily. Then they blew stuff up.

Apollo studied me, but he didn't say anything, which I found a little creepy.

'Well!' he said at last. 'We'd better load up, huh? Ride only goes one way – west. And if you miss it, you miss it.'

I looked at the Maserati, which would seat two people max. There were about twenty of us.

'Cool car,' Nico said.

'Thanks, kid,' Apollo said.

'But how will we all fit?'

'Oh.' Apollo seemed to notice the problem for the first time. 'Well, yeah. I hate to change out of sports-car mode, but I suppose . . .'

He took out his car keys and beeped the security alarm button. *Chirp, chirp.*

For a moment, the car glowed brightly again. When the glare died, the Maserati had been replaced by one of those small buses just like we used for school basketball games.

'Right,' he said. 'Everybody in.'

Zoë ordered the Hunters to start loading. She picked

up her camping pack, and Apollo said, 'Here, sweetheart. Let me get that.'

Zoë recoiled. Her eyes flashed murderously.

'Brother,' Artemis chided. 'You do not help my Hunters. You do not look at, talk to, or flirt with my Hunters. And you do *not* call them sweetheart.'

Apollo spread his hands. 'Sorry. I forgot. Hey, sis, where are you off to, anyway?'

'Hunting,' Artemis said. 'It's none of your business.'

'I'll find out. I see all. Know all.'

Artemis snorted. 'Just drop them off, Apollo. And no messing around!'

'No, no! I never mess around.'

Artemis rolled her eyes, then looked at us. 'I will see you by winter solstice. Zoë, you are in charge of the Hunters. Do well. Do as I would do.'

Zoë straightened. 'Yes, my lady.'

Artemis knelt and touched the ground as if looking for tracks. When she rose, she looked troubled. 'So much danger. The beast must be found.'

She sprinted towards the woods and melted into the snow and shadows.

Apollo turned and grinned, jangling the car keys on his finger. 'So,' he said. 'Who wants to drive?'

The Hunters piled into the van. They all crammed into the back so they'd be as far away as possible from Apollo and the rest of us highly infectious males. Bianca sat with them, leaving her little brother to hang in the front with us, which seemed cold to me, but Nico didn't seem to mind.

'This is so cool!' Nico said, jumping up and down in

the driver's seat. 'Is this really the sun? I thought Helios and Selene were the sun and moon gods. How come sometimes it's them and sometimes it's you and Artemis?'

'Downsizing,' Apollo said. 'The Romans started it. They couldn't afford all those temple sacrifices, so they laid off Helios and Selene and folded their duties into our job descriptions. My sis got the moon. I got the sun. It was pretty annoying at first, but at least I got this cool car.'

'But how does it work?' Nico asked. 'I thought the sun was a big fiery ball of gas!'

Apollo chuckled and ruffled Nico's hair. 'That rumour probably got started because Artemis used to call me a big fiery ball of gas. Seriously, kid, it depends on whether you're talking astronomy or philosophy. You want to talk astronomy? Bah, what fun is that? You want to talk about how humans *think* about the sun? Ah, now that's more interesting. They've got a lot riding on the sun . . . er, so to speak. It keeps them warm, grows their crops, powers engines, makes everything look, well, sunnier. This chariot is built out of human *dreams* about the sun, kid. It's as old as Western Civilization. Every day, it drives across the sky from east to west, lighting up all those puny little mortal lives. The chariot is a manifestation of the sun's power, the way mortals perceive it. Make sense?'

Nico shook his head. 'No.'

'Well then, just think of it as a really powerful, really dangerous solar car.'

'Can I drive?'

'No. Too young.'

'Oo! Oo!' Grover raised his hand.

'Mm, no,' Apollo said. 'Too furry.' He looked past me and focused on Thalia.

'Daughter of Zeus!' he said. 'Lord of the sky. Perfect.'

'Oh, no.' Thalia shook her head. 'No, thanks.'

'C'mon,' Apollo said. 'How old are you?'

Thalia hesitated. 'I don't know.'

It was sad, but true. She'd been turned into a tree when she was twelve, but that had been seven years ago. So she should be nineteen, if you went by years. But she still felt like she was twelve. If you looked at her, though, she seemed somewhere in between. The best Chiron could work out, she had kept aging while in tree form, but much more slowly.

Apollo tapped his finger to his lips. 'You're fifteen, almost sixteen.'

'How do you know that?'

'Hey, I'm the god of prophecy. I know stuff. You'll turn sixteen in about a week.'

'That's my birthday! December twenty-second.'

'Which means you're old enough now to drive with a learner's permit!'

Thalia shifted her feet nervously. 'Uh –'

'I know what you're going to say,' Apollo said. 'You don't deserve an honour like driving the sun chariot.'

'That's not what I was going to say.'

'Don't sweat it! Maine to Long Island is a really short trip, and don't worry about what happened to the last kid I trained. You're Zeus's daughter. He's not going to blast *you* out of the sky.'

Apollo laughed good-naturedly. The rest of us didn't join him.

Thalia tried to protest, but Apollo was absolutely not going to take 'no' for an answer. He hit a button on the dashboard, and a sign popped up along the top of the windscreen. I had to read it backwards (which, for a dyslexic really isn't that different to reading forward). I was pretty sure it said WARNING: STUDENT DRIVER.

'Take it away!' Apollo told Thalia. 'You're gonna be a natural!'

I'll admit I was jealous. I couldn't wait to start driving. A couple of times that autumn, my mom had taken me out to Montauk when the beach road was empty, and she'd let me try out her Mazda. I mean, yeah, that was a Japanese compact, and this was the sun chariot, but how different could it be?

'Speed equals heat,' Apollo advised. 'So start slowly, and make sure you've got good altitude before you really open her up.'

Thalia gripped the wheel so tightly her knuckles turned white. She looked like she was going to be sick.

'What's wrong?' I asked her.

'Nothing,' she said shakily. 'N-nothing is wrong.'

She pulled back on the wheel. It tilted and the bus lurched upwards so fast I fell back and crashed against something soft.

'Ow,' Grover said.

'Sorry.'

'Slower!' Apollo said.

'Sorry!' Thalia said. 'I've got it under control!'

I managed to get to my feet. Looking out of the window, I saw a smoking ring of trees from the clearing where we'd taken off.

'Thalia,' I said, 'lighten up on the accelerator.'

'I've *got* it, Percy,' she said, gritting her teeth. But she kept it floored.

'Loosen up,' I told her.

'I'm loose!' Thalia said. She was so stiff she looked like she was made out of plywood.

'We need to veer south for Long Island,' Apollo said. 'Hang a left.'

Thalia jerked the wheel and again threw me into Grover, who yelped.

'The other left,' Apollo suggested.

I made the mistake of looking out of the window again. We were at aeroplane height now – so high the sky was starting to look black.

'Ah . . .' Apollo said, and I got the feeling he was forcing himself to sound calm. 'A little lower, sweetheart. Cape Cod is freezing over.'

Thalia tilted the wheel. Her face was chalk white, her forehead beaded with sweat. Something was definitely wrong. I'd never seen her like this.

The bus pitched down and somebody screamed. Maybe it was me. Now we were heading straight towards the Atlantic Ocean at a thousand miles an hour, the New England coastline off to our left. And it was getting hot in the bus.

Apollo had been thrown somewhere in the back of the bus, but he started climbing up the rows of seats.

'Take the wheel!' Grover begged him.

'No worries,' Apollo said. He looked plenty worried. 'She just has to learn to – WHOA!'

I saw what he was seeing. Down below us was a little

snow-covered New England town. At least, it used to be snow-covered. As I watched, the snow melted off the trees and the roofs and the lawns. The white steeple on a church turned brown and started to smolder. Little plumes of smoke, like birthday candles, were popping up all over the town. Trees and rooftops were catching fire.

'Pull up!' I yelled.

There was a wild light in Thalia's eyes. She yanked back on the wheel, and I held on this time. As we zoomed up, I could see through the back window that the fires in the town were being snuffed out by the sudden blast of cold.

'There!' Apollo pointed. 'Long Island, dead ahead. Let's slow down, dear. 'Dead' is only an expression.'

Thalia was thundering towards the coastline of northern Long Island. There was Camp Half-Blood: the valley, the woods, the beach. I could see the dining pavilion and cabins and the amphitheatre.

'I'm under control,' Thalia muttered. 'I'm under control.'

We were only a few hundred metres away now.

'Brake,' Apollo said.

'I can do this.'

'BRAKE!'

Thalia slammed her foot on the brake, and the sun bus pitched forward at a forty-five-degree angle, slamming into the Camp Half-Blood canoe lake with a huge *FLOOOOOOSH!* Steam billowed up, sending several frightened naiads scrambling out of the water with half-woven wicker baskets.

The bus bobbed to the surface along with a couple of capsized, half-melted canoes.

5 I MAKE AN UNDERWATER PHONE CALL

I'd never seen Camp Half-Blood in winter before, and the snow surprised me.

See, the camp has the ultimate magic climate control. Nothing gets inside the borders unless the director, Mr D, wants it to. I thought it would be warm and sunny, but instead the snow had been allowed to fall lightly. Frost covered the chariot track and the strawberry fields. The cabins were decorated with tiny flickering lights, like Christmas lights, except they seemed to be balls of real fire. More lights glowed in the woods, and, weirdest of all, a fire flickered in the attic window of the Big House, where the Oracle dwelt, imprisoned in an old mummified body. I wondered if the spirit of Delphi was roasting marshmallows up there or something.

'Whoa,' Nico said as he climbed off the bus. 'Is that a climbing wall?'

'Yeah,' I said.

'Why is there lava pouring down it?'

'Little extra challenge. Come on. I'll introduce you to Chiron. Zoë, have you met –'

'I know Chiron,' Zoë said stiffly. 'Tell him we will be in Cabin Eight. Hunters, follow me.'

'I'll show you the way,' Grover offered.

'We know the way.'

'Oh, really, it's no trouble. It's easy to get lost here, if you don't –' he tripped over a canoe and came up still talking – 'like my old daddy goat used to say! Come on!'

Zoë rolled her eyes, but I guess she figured there was no getting rid of Grover. The Hunters shouldered their packs and their bows and headed off towards the cabins. As Bianca di Angelo was leaving, she leaned over and whispered something in her brother's ear. She looked at him for an answer, but Nico just scowled and turned away.

'Take care, sweethearts!' Apollo called after the Hunters. He winked at me. 'Watch out for those prophecies, Percy. I'll see you soon.'

'What do you mean?'

Instead of answering, he hopped back in the bus. 'Later, Thalia,' he called. 'And, uh, be good!'

He gave her a wicked smile, as if he knew something she didn't. Then he closed the doors and revved the engine. I turned aside as the sun chariot took off in a blast of heat. When I looked back, the lake was steaming. A red Maserati soared over the woods, glowing brighter and climbing higher until it disappeared in a ray of sunlight.

Nico was still looking grumpy. I wondered what his sister had told him.

'Who's Chiron?' he asked. 'I don't have his figurine.'

'Our activities director,' I said. 'He's . . . well, you'll see.'

'If those Hunter girls don't like him,' Nico grumbled, 'that's good enough for me. Let's go.'

The second thing that surprised me about camp was how empty it was. I mean, I knew most half-bloods only trained during the summer. Just the year-rounders would be here

– the ones who didn't have homes to go to, or would get attacked by monsters too much if they left. But there didn't even seem to be many of them, either.

I spotted Charles Beckendorf from the Hephaestus cabin stoking the forge outside the camp armoury. The Stoll brothers, Travis and Connor, from the Hermes cabin, were picking the lock on the camp store. A few kids from the Ares cabin were having a snowball fight with the wood nymphs at the edge of the forest. That was about it. Even my old rival from the Ares cabin, Clarisse, didn't seem to be around.

The Big House was decorated with strings of red and yellow fireballs that warmed the porch but didn't seem to set anything alight. Inside, flames crackled in the hearth. The air smelled like hot chocolate. Mr D, the camp director, and Chiron were playing a quiet game of cards in the parlour.

Chiron's brown beard was shaggier for the winter. His curly hair had grown a little longer. He wasn't posing as a teacher this year, so I guess he could afford to be casual. He wore a fuzzy sweater with a hoof-print design on it, and he had a blanket on his lap that almost hid his wheelchair completely.

He smiled when he saw us. 'Percy! Thalia! Ah, and this must be –'

'Nico di Angelo,' I said. 'He and his sister are half-bloods.'

Chiron breathed a sigh of relief. 'You succeeded, then.'

'Well . . .'

His smile melted. 'What's wrong? And where is Annabeth?'

'Oh, dear,' Mr D said in a bored voice. 'Not another one lost.'

I'd been trying not to pay attention to Mr D, but he was kind of hard to ignore in his neon-orange leopard-skin warm-up suit and his purple running shoes. (Like Mr D had ever run a day in his immortal life.) A golden laurel wreath was tilted sideways on his curly black hair, which must've meant he'd won the last hand of cards.

'What do you mean?' Thalia asked. 'Who else is lost?'

Just then, Grover trotted into the room, grinning like crazy. He had a black eye and red lines on his face that looked like a slap mark. 'The Hunters are all moved in!'

Chiron frowned. 'The Hunters, eh? I see we have much to talk about.' He glanced at Nico. 'Grover, perhaps you should take our young friend to the den and show him our orientation film.'

'But . . . Oh, right. Yes, sir.'

'Orientation film?' Nico asked. 'Is it G or PG? 'Cause Bianca is kinda strict –'

'It's PG-13,' Grover said.

'Cool!' Nico happily followed him out of the room.

'Now,' Chiron said to Thalia and me, 'perhaps you two should sit down and tell us the whole story.'

When we were done, Chiron turned to Mr D. 'We should launch a search for Annabeth immediately.'

'I'll go,' Thalia and I said at the same time.

Mr D sniffed. 'Certainly not!'

Thalia and I both started complaining, but Mr D held up his hand. He had that purplish angry fire in his eyes that usually meant something bad and godly was going to happen if we didn't shut up.

'From what you have told me,' Mr D said, 'we have broken even on this escapade. We have, ah, regrettably lost Annie Bell –'

'Annabeth,' I snapped. She'd gone to camp since she was seven, and still Mr D pretended not to know her name.

'Yes, yes,' he said. 'And you procured a small annoying boy to replace her. So I see no point risking further half-bloods on a ridiculous rescue. The possibility is very great that this Annie girl is dead.'

I wanted to strangle Mr D. It wasn't fair Zeus had sent him here to dry out as camp director for a hundred years. It was meant to be a punishment for Mr D's bad behavior on Olympus, but it ended up being a punishment for all of us.

'Annabeth may be alive,' Chiron said, but I could tell he was having trouble sounding upbeat. He'd practically raised Annabeth all those years she was a year-round camper, before she'd given living with her dad and stepmom a second try. 'She's very bright. If . . . if our enemies have her, she will try to play for time. She may even pretend to cooperate.'

'That's right,' Thalia said. 'Luke would want her alive.'

'In which case,' said Mr D, 'I'm afraid she will have to be smart enough to escape on her own.'

I got up from the table.

'Percy.' Chiron's tone was full of warning. In the back of my mind, I knew Mr D was not somebody to mess with. Even if you were an impulsive ADHD kid like me, he wouldn't give you any slack. But I was so angry I didn't care.

'You're glad to lose another camper,' I said. 'You'd like it if we all disappeared!'

Mr D stifled a yawn. 'You have a point?'

'Yeah,' I growled. 'Just because you were sent here as a punishment doesn't mean you have to be a lazy jerk! This is your civilization, too. Maybe you could try helping out a little!'

For a second, there was no sound except the crackle of the fire. The light reflected in Mr D's eyes, giving him a sinister look. He opened his mouth to say something – probably a curse that would blast me to smithereens – when Nico burst into the room, followed by Grover.

'SO COOL!' Nico yelled, holding his hands out to Chiron. 'You're . . . you're a centaur!'

Chiron managed a nervous smile. 'Yes, Mr di Angelo, if you please. Though, I prefer to stay in human form in this wheelchair for, ah, first encounters.'

'And, whoa!' He looked at Mr D. 'You're the wine dude? No way!'

Mr D turned his eyes away from me and gave Nico a look of loathing. 'The wine dude?'

'Dionysus, right? Oh, wow! I've got your figurine.'

'My figurine.'

'In my game, Mythomagic. And a holofoil card, too! And even though you've only got like five hundred attack points and everybody thinks you're the lamest god card, I totally think your powers are sweet!'

'Ah.' Mr D seemed truly perplexed, which probably saved my life. 'Well, that's . . . gratifying.'

'Percy,' Chiron said quickly, 'you and Thalia go down

to the cabins. Inform the campers we'll be playing capture the flag tomorrow evening.'

'Capture the flag?' I asked. 'But we don't have enough –'

'It is a tradition,' Chiron said. 'A friendly match, whenever the Hunters visit.'

'Yeah,' Thalia muttered. 'I bet it's real friendly.'

Chiron jerked his head towards Mr D, who was still frowning as Nico talked about how many defence points all the gods had in his game. 'Run along now,' Chiron told us.

'Oh, right,' Thalia said. 'Come on, Percy.'

She hauled me out of the Big House before Dionysus could remember that he wanted to kill me.

'You've already got Ares on your bad side,' Thalia reminded me as we trudged towards the cabins. 'You need another immortal enemy?'

She was right. My first summer as a camper, I'd got in a fight with Ares, and now he and all his children wanted to kill me. I didn't need to make Dionysus mad, too.

'Sorry,' I said. 'I couldn't help it. It's just so unfair.'

She stopped by the armoury and looked out across the valley, towards the top of Half-Blood Hill. Her pine tree was still there, the Golden Fleece glittering in its lowest branch. The tree's magic still protected the borders of camp, but it no longer used Thalia's spirit for power.

'Percy, everything is unfair,' Thalia muttered. 'Sometimes I wish . . .'

She didn't finish, but her tone was so sad I felt sorry for her. With her ragged black hair and her black punk clothes, an old wool overcoat wrapped round her, she looked like some kind of huge raven, completely out of place in the white landscape.

'We'll get Annabeth back,' I promised. 'I just don't know how yet.'

'First I found out that Luke is lost,' she said. 'Now Annabeth –'

'Don't think like that.'

'You're right.' She straightened up. 'We'll find a way.'

Over at the basketball court, a few of the Hunters were shooting hoops. One of them was arguing with a guy from the Ares cabin. The Ares kid had his hand on his sword and the Hunter girl looked like she was going to exchange her basketball for a bow and arrow any second.

'I'll break that up,' Thalia said. 'You circulate round the cabins. Tell everybody about capture the flag tomorrow.'

'All right. You should be team captain.'

'No, no,' she said. 'You've been at camp longer. You do it.'

'We can, uh . . . co-captain or something.'

She looked about as comfortable with that as I felt, but she nodded.

As she headed for the court, I said, 'Hey, Thalia.'

'Yeah?'

'I'm sorry about what happened at Westover. I should've waited for you guys.'

''S okay, Percy. I probably would've done the same thing.' She shifted from foot to foot, like she was trying to decide whether or not to say more. 'You know, you asked about my mom and I kinda snapped at you. It's just . . . I went back to find her after seven years, and I found out she died in Los Angeles. She, um . . . she was a heavy drinker, and apparently she was out driving late one night about two years ago, and . . .' Thalia blinked hard.

'I'm sorry.'

'Yeah, well. It's . . . it's not like we were ever close. I ran away when I was ten. Best two years of my life were when I was running around with Luke and Annabeth. But still –'

'That's why you had trouble with the sun van.'

She gave me a wary look. 'What do you mean?'

'The way you stiffened up. You must've been thinking about your mom, not wanting to get behind the wheel.'

I was sorry I'd said anything. Thalia's expression was dangerously close to Zeus's, the one time I'd seen him get angry – like any minute, her eyes would shoot a million volts.

'Yeah,' she muttered. 'Yeah, that must've been it.'

She trudged off towards the court, where the Ares camper and the Hunter were trying to kill each other with a sword and a basketball.

The cabins were the weirdest collection of buildings you've ever seen. Zeus and Hera's big white-columned buildings, Cabins One and Two, stood in the middle, with five gods' cabins on the left and five goddesses' cabins on the right, so they all made a U round the central green and the barbecue hearth.

I made the rounds, telling everybody about capture the flag. I woke up some Ares kid from his midday nap and he yelled at me to go away. When I asked him where Clarisse was he said, 'Went on a quest for Chiron. Top secret!'

'Is she okay?'

'Haven't heard from her in a month. She's missing in action. Like your butt's gonna be if you don't get outta here!'

I decided to let him go back to sleep.

Finally I got to Cabin Three, the cabin of Poseidon. It was a low grey building hewn from sea stone, with shells and coral fossils imprinted in the rock. Inside, it was just as empty as always, except for my bunk. A Minotaur horn hung on the wall next to my pillow.

I took Annabeth's baseball cap out of my backpack and set it on my nightstand. I'd give it to her when I found her. And I *would* find her.

I took off my wristwatch and activated the shield. It creaked noisily as it spiralled out. Dr Thorn's spikes had dented the brass in a dozen places. One gash kept the shield from opening all the way, so it looked like a pizza with two slices missing. The beautiful metal pictures that my brother had crafted were all banged up. In the picture of me and Annabeth fighting the Hydra, it looked like a meteor had made a crater in my head. I hung the shield on its hook, next to the Minotaur horn, but it was painful to look at now. Maybe Beckendorf from the Hephaestus cabin could fix it for me. He was the best armoursmith in the camp. I'd ask him at dinner.

I was staring at the shield when I noticed a strange sound – water gurgling – and I realized there was something new in the room. At the back of the cabin was a big basin of grey sea rock, with a spout like the head of a fish carved in stone. Out of its mouth burst a stream of water, a saltwater spring that trickled into the pool. The water must've been hot, because it sent mist into the cold winter air like a sauna. It made the room feel warm and summery, fresh with the smell of the sea.

I stepped up to the pool. There was no note attached or anything, but I knew it could only be a gift from Poseidon.

I looked into the water and said, 'Thanks, Dad.'

The surface rippled. At the bottom of the pool, coins shimmered – a dozen or so golden drachma. I realized what the fountain was for. It was a reminder to keep in touch with my family.

I opened the nearest window, and the wintry sunlight made a rainbow in the mist. Then I fished a coin out of the hot water.

'Iris, O Goddess of the Rainbow,' I said, 'accept my offering.'

I tossed a coin into the mist and it disappeared. Then I realized I didn't know who to contact first.

My mom? That would've been the 'good son' thing to do, but she wouldn't be worried about me yet. She was used to me disappearing for days or weeks at a time.

My father? It had been way too long, almost two years, since I'd actually talked to him. But could you even send an Iris-message to a god? I'd never tried. Would it make them mad, like a sales call or something?

I hesitated. Then I made up my mind.

'Show me Tyson,' I requested. 'At the forges of the Cyclopes.'

The mist shimmered, and the image of my half-brother appeared. He was surrounded by fire, which would've been a problem if he weren't a Cyclops. He was bent over an anvil, hammering a red-hot sword blade. Sparks flew and flames swirled around his body. There was a marble-framed window behind him, and it looked out onto dark blue water – the bottom of the ocean.

'Tyson!' I yelled.

He didn't hear me at first because of the hammering and the roar of the flames.

'TYSON!'

He turned, and his one enormous eye widened. His face broke into a crooked yellow grin. 'Percy!'

He dropped the sword blade and ran at me, trying to give me a hug. The vision blurred and I instinctively lurched back. 'Tyson, it's an Iris-message. I'm not really here.'

'Oh.' He came back into view, looking embarrassed. 'Oh, I knew that. Yes.'

'How are you?' I asked. 'How's the job?'

His eye lit up. 'Love the job! Look!' He picked up the hot sword blade with his bare hands. 'I made this!'

'That's really cool.'

'I wrote my name on it. Right there.'

'Awesome. Listen, do you talk to Dad much?'

Tyson's smile faded. 'Not much. Daddy is busy. He is worried about the war.'

'What do you mean?'

Tyson sighed. He stuck the sword blade out the window, where it made a cloud of boiling bubbles. When Tyson brought it back in, the metal was cool. 'Old sea spirits making trouble. Aigaios. Oceanus. Those guys.'

I sort of knew what he was talking about. He meant the immortals who ruled the oceans back in the days of the Titans. Before the Olympians took over. The fact that they were back now, with the Titan Lord Kronos and his allies gaining strength, was not good.

'Is there anything I can do?' I asked.

Tyson shook his head sadly. 'We are arming the mermaids. They need a thousand more swords by tomorrow.' He looked at his sword blade and sighed. 'Old spirits are protecting the bad boat.'

'The *Princess Andromeda*?' I said. 'Luke's boat?'

'Yes. They make it hard to find. Protect it from Daddy's storms. Otherwise he would smash it.'

'Smashing it would be good.'

Tyson perked up, as if he'd just had another thought. 'Annabeth! Is she there?'

'Oh, well . . .' My heart felt like a bowling ball. Tyson thought Annabeth was just about the coolest thing since peanut butter (and he seriously loved peanut butter). I didn't have the heart to tell him she was missing. He'd start crying so bad he'd probably put out his fires. 'Well, no . . . she's not here right now.'

'Tell her hello!' He beamed. 'Hello to Annabeth!'

'Okay.' I fought back a lump in my throat. 'I'll do that.'

'And, Percy, don't worry about the bad boat. It is going away.'

'What do you mean?'

'Panama Canal! Very far away.'

I frowned. Why would Luke take his demon-infested cruise ship all the way down there? The last time we'd seen him, he'd been cruising along the East Coast, recruiting half-bloods and training his monstrous army.

'All right,' I said, not feeling reassured. 'That's . . . good. I guess.'

In the forges, a deep voice bellowed something I couldn't make out. Tyson flinched. 'Got to get back to work! Boss will get mad. Good luck, brother!'

'Okay, tell Dad –'

But before I could finish the vision shimmered and faded. I was alone again in my cabin, feeling even lonelier than before.

I was pretty miserable at dinner that night.

I mean, the food was excellent as usual. You can't go wrong with barbecue, pizza and never-empty soda goblets. The torches and braziers kept the outdoor pavilion warm, but we all had to sit with our cabin mates, which meant I was alone at the Poseidon table. Thalia sat alone at the Zeus table, but we couldn't sit together. Camp rules. At least the Hephaestus, Ares and Hermes cabins had a few people each. Nico sat with the Stoll brothers, since new campers always got stuck in the Hermes cabin if their Olympian parent was unknown. The Stoll brothers seemed to be trying to convince Nico that poker was a much better game than Mythomagic. I hoped Nico didn't have any money to lose.

The only table that really seemed to be having a good time was the Artemis table. The Hunters drank and ate and laughed like one big happy family. Zoë sat at the head like she was the mama. She didn't laugh as much as the others, but she did smile from time to time. Her silver lieutenant's band glittered in the dark braids of her hair. I thought she looked a lot nicer when she smiled. Bianca di Angelo seemed to be having a great time. She was trying to learn how to arm wrestle from the big girl who'd picked a fight with the Ares kid on the basketball court. The bigger girl was beating her every time, but Bianca didn't seem to mind.

When we'd finished eating, Chiron made the customary toast to the gods and formally welcomed the Hunters of Artemis. The clapping was pretty half-hearted. Then he announced the 'goodwill' capture-the-flag game for tomorrow night, which got a much better reception.

Afterwards, we all trailed back to our cabins for an early, winter lights out. I was exhausted, which meant I fell asleep easily. That was the good part. The bad part was I had a nightmare, and even by my standards it was a whopper.

Annabeth was on a dark hillside, shrouded in fog. It almost seemed like the Underworld, because I immediately felt claustrophobic and I couldn't see the sky above – just a close heavy darkness, as if I were in a cave.

Annabeth struggled up the hill. Old broken Greek columns of black marble were scattered around, as though something had blasted a huge building to ruins.

'Thorn!' Annabeth cried. 'Where are you? Why did you bring me here?' She scrambled over a section of broken wall and came to the crest of the hill.

She gasped.

There was Luke. And he was in pain.

He was crumpled on the rocky ground, trying to rise. The blackness seemed to be thicker around him, fog swirling hungrily. His clothes were in tatters and his face was scratched and drenched with sweat.

'Annabeth!' he called. 'Help me! Please!'

She ran forward.

I tried to cry out: *He's a traitor! Don't trust him!*

But my voice didn't work in the dream.

Annabeth had tears in her eyes. She reached down like she wanted to touch Luke's face, but at the last second she hesitated.

'What happened?' she asked.

'They left me here,' Luke groaned. 'Please. It's killing me.'

I couldn't see what was wrong with him. He seemed to be struggling against some invisible curse, as though the fog were squeezing him to death.

'Why should I trust you?' Annabeth asked. Her voice was filled with hurt.

'You shouldn't,' Luke said. 'I've been terrible to you. But, if you don't help me, I'll die.'

Let him die, I wanted to scream. Luke had tried to kill us in cold blood too many times. He didn't deserve anything from Annabeth.

Then the darkness above Luke began to crumble, like a cavern roof in an earthquake. Huge chunks of black rock began falling. Annabeth rushed in just as a crack appeared, and the whole ceiling dropped. She held it somehow – tons of rock. She kept it from collapsing on her and Luke just with her own strength. It was impossible. She shouldn't have been able to do that.

Luke rolled free, gasping. 'Thanks,' he managed.

'Help me hold it,' Annabeth groaned.

Luke caught his breath. His face was covered in grime and sweat. He rose unsteadily.

'I knew I could count on you.' He began to walk away as the trembling blackness threatened to crush Annabeth.

'HELP ME!' she pleaded.

'Oh, don't worry,' Luke said. 'Your help is on the way. It's all part of the plan. In the meantime, try not to die.'

The ceiling of darkness began to crumble more, pushing Annabeth against the ground.

I sat bolt upright in bed, clawing at the sheets. There was no sound in my cabin except the gurgle of the saltwater spring. The clock on my nightstand read just after midnight.

Only a dream, but I was sure of two things: Annabeth was in terrible danger. And Luke was responsible.

6 AN OLD DEAD FRIEND COMES TO VISIT

The next morning after breakfast, I told Grover about my dream. We sat in the meadow watching the satyrs chase the wood nymphs through the snow. The nymphs had promised to kiss the satyrs if they got caught, but they hardly ever did. Usually the nymph would let the satyr get up a full head of steam, then she'd turn into a snow-covered tree and the poor satyr would slam into it head first and get a pile of snow dumped on him.

When I told Grover my nightmare, he started twirling his finger in his shaggy leg fur.

'A cave ceiling collapsed on her?' he asked.

'Yeah. What the heck does that mean?'

Grover shook his head. 'I don't know. But after what Zoë dreamed –'

'Whoa. What do you mean? Zoë had a dream like that?'

'I . . . I don't know, exactly. About three in the morning she came to the Big House and demanded to talk to Chiron. She looked really panicked.'

'Wait, how do you know this?'

Grover blushed. 'I was sort of camped outside the Artemis cabin.'

'What for?'

'Just to be, you know, near them.'

'You're a stalker with hooves.'

'I am not! Anyway, I followed her to the Big House and hid in a bush and watched the whole thing. She got really upset when Argus wouldn't let her in. It was kind of a dangerous scene.'

I tried to imagine that. Argus was the head of security for camp – a big blond dude with eyes all over his body. He rarely showed himself unless something serious was going on. I wouldn't want to place bets on a fight between him and Zoë Nightshade.

'What did she say?' I asked.

Grover grimaced. 'Well, she starts talking really old-fashioned when she gets upset, so it was kind of hard to understand. But something about Artemis being in trouble and needing the Hunters. And then she called Argus a boil-brained lout . . . I think that's a bad thing. And then he called her –'

'Whoa, wait. How could Artemis be in trouble?'

'I . . . well, finally Chiron came out in his pyjamas and his horse tail in curlers and –'

'He wears curlers in his tail?'

Grover covered his mouth.

'Sorry,' I said. 'Go on.'

'Well, Zoë said she needed permission to leave camp immediately. Chiron refused. He reminded Zoë that the Hunters were supposed to stay here until they received orders from Artemis. And she said . . .' Grover gulped. 'She said, "How are we to get orders from Artemis if Artemis is lost?"'

'What do you mean lost? Like she needs directions?'

'No. I think she meant gone. Taken. Kidnapped.'

'*Kidnapped?*' I tried to get my mind round that idea.

'How would you kidnap an immortal goddess? Is that even possible?'

'Well, yeah. I mean, it happened to Persephone.'

'But she was like, the goddess of *flowers*.'

Grover looked offended. 'Springtime.'

'Whatever. Artemis is a lot more powerful than that. Who could kidnap her? And why?'

Grover shook his head miserably. 'I don't know. Kronos?'

'He can't be that powerful already. Can he?'

The last time we'd seen Kronos, he'd been in tiny pieces. Well . . . we hadn't actually *seen* him. Thousands of years ago, after the big Titan-God war, the gods had sliced him to bits with his own scythe and scattered his remains in Tartarus, which is like the gods' bottomless recycling bin for their enemies. Two summers ago, Kronos had tricked us to the very edge of the pit and almost pulled us in. Then last summer, on board Luke's demon cruise ship, we'd seen a golden coffin, where Luke claimed he was summoning the Titan Lord out of the abyss, bit by bit, every time someone new joined their cause. Kronos could influence people with dreams and trick them, but I didn't see how he could physically overcome Artemis if he were still like a pile of evil bark mulch.

'I don't know,' Grover said. 'I think somebody would know if Kronos had re-formed. The gods would be more nervous. But, still, it's weird – you having a nightmare the same night as Zoë. It's almost like –'

'They're connected,' I said.

Over in the frozen meadow, a satyr skidded on his hooves as he chased after a redheaded tree nymph. She giggled and held out her arms as he ran towards her. *Pop!*

She turned into a Scotch pine and he kissed the trunk at top speed.

'Ah, love,' Grover said dreamily.

I thought about Zoë's nightmare, which she'd had only a few hours after mine.

'I've got to talk to Zoë,' I said.

'Um, before you do . . .' Grover took something out of his coat pocket. It was a three-fold display like a travel brochure. 'You remember what you said – about how it was weird the Hunters just happened to show up at Westover Hall? I think they might've been scouting us.'

'Scouting us? What do you mean?'

He gave me the brochure. It was about the Hunters of Artemis. The front read, A WISE CHOICE FOR YOUR FUTURE! Inside were pictures of young maidens doing hunter stuff, chasing monsters, shooting bows. There were captions like: HEALTH BENEFITS: IMMORTALITY AND WHAT IT MEANS FOR YOU! And A BOY-FREE TOMORROW!

'I found that in Annabeth's backpack,' Grover said.

I stared at him. 'I don't understand.'

'Well, it seems to me . . . maybe Annabeth was thinking about joining.'

I'd like to say I took the news well.

The truth was I wanted to strangle the Hunters of Artemis one eternal maiden at a time. The rest of the day I tried to keep busy, but I was worried sick about Annabeth. I went to javelin-throwing class, but the Ares camper in charge yelled at me after I got distracted and threw the javelin at the target before he got out of the way. I apologized for the hole in his trousers, but he still sent me packing.

I visited the pegasus stables, but Silena Beauregard from the Aphrodite cabin was having an argument with one of the Hunters, and I decided I'd better not get involved.

After that, I sat in the empty chariot stands and sulked. Down at the archery fields, Chiron was conducting target practice. I knew he'd be the best person to talk to. Maybe he could give me some advice, but something held me back. I had a feeling Chiron would try to protect me, like he always did. He might not tell me everything he knew.

I looked in the other direction. At the top of Half-Blood Hill, Mr D and Argus were feeding the baby dragon that guarded the Golden Fleece.

Then it occurred to me: no one would be in the Big House. There was someone else . . . some*thing* else I could ask for guidance.

My blood was humming in my ears as I ran into the house and took the stairs. I'd only done this once before, and I still had nightmares about it. I opened the trapdoor and stepped into the attic.

The room was dark and dusty and cluttered with junk, just like I remembered. There were shields with monster bites out of them, and swords bent in the shapes of daemon heads, and a bunch of taxidermy, like a stuffed harpy and a bright orange python.

Over by the window, sitting on a three-legged stool, was the shrivelled-up mummy of an old lady in a tie-dyed hippie dress. The Oracle.

I made myself walk towards her. I waited for green mist to billow from the mummy's mouth, like it had before, but nothing happened.

'Hi,' I said. 'Uh, what's up?'

I winced at how stupid that sounded. Not much could be 'up' when you're dead and stuck in the attic. But I knew the spirit of the Oracle was in there somewhere. I could feel a cold presence in the room, like a coiled sleeping snake.

'I have a question,' I said a little louder. 'I need to know about Annabeth. How can I save her?'

No answer. The sun slanted through the dirty attic window, making the dust motes dance in the air.

I waited longer.

Then I got angry. I was being stonewalled by a corpse.

'All right,' I said. 'Fine. I'll figure it out myself.'

I turned and bumped into a big table full of souvenirs. It seemed more cluttered than the last time I was here. Heroes stored all kinds of stuff in the attic: quest trophies they no longer wanted to keep in their cabins, or stuff that held painful memories. I knew Luke had stored a dragon claw somewhere up here – the one that had scarred his face. There was a broken sword hilt labelled: *This broke and Leroy got killed. 1999.*

Then I noticed a pink silk scarf with a label attached to it. I picked up the tag and tried to read it:

SCARF OF THE GODDESS APHRODITE
Recovered at Waterland, Denver, Co.,
by Annabeth Chase and Percy Jackson

I stared at the scarf. I'd totally forgotten about it. Two years ago, Annabeth had ripped this scarf out of my hands and said something like, *Oh, no. No love magic for you!*

I'd just assumed she'd thrown it away. And yet here it

was. She'd kept it all this time? And why had she stashed it in the attic?

I turned to the mummy. She hadn't moved, but the shadows across her face made it look like she was smiling gruesomely.

I dropped the scarf and tried not to run towards the exit.

That night after dinner, I was seriously ready to beat the Hunters at capture the flag. It was going to be a small game. Only thirteen Hunters, including Bianca di Angelo, and about the same number of campers.

Zoë Nightshade looked pretty upset. She kept glancing resentfully at Chiron, like she couldn't believe he was making her do this. The other Hunters didn't look too happy either. Unlike last night, they weren't laughing or joking around. They just huddled together in the dining pavilion, whispering nervously to each other as they strapped on their armour. Some of them even looked like they'd been crying. I guess Zoë had told them about her nightmare.

On our team, we had Beckendorf and two other Hephaestus guys, a few from the Ares cabin (though it still seemed strange that Clarisse wasn't around), the Stoll brothers and Nico from Hermes cabin, and a few Aphrodite kids. It was weird that the Aphrodite cabin wanted to play. Usually they sat on the sidelines, chatted and checked their reflections in the river and stuff, but when they heard we were fighting the Hunters, they were raring to go.

'I'll show them "love is worthless",' Silena Beauregard

grumbled as she strapped on her armour. 'I'll pulverize them!'

That left Thalia and me.

'I'll take the offence,' Thalia volunteered. 'You take defence.'

'Oh.' I hesitated, because I'd been about to say the exact same thing, only reversed. 'Don't you think, with your shield and all, you'd be better defence?'

Thalia already had Aegis on her arm, and even our own teammates were giving her a wide berth, trying not to cower before the bronze head of Medusa.

'Well, I was thinking it would make better offence,' Thalia said. 'Besides, you've had more practice at defence.'

I wasn't sure if she was teasing me. I'd had some pretty bad experiences with defence on capture the flag. My first year, Annabeth had put me out as a kind of bait, and I'd almost been gored to death with spears and killed by a hellhound.

'Yeah, no problem,' I lied.

'Cool.' Thalia turned to help some of the Aphrodite kids, who were having trouble suiting up their armour without breaking their nails. Nico di Angelo ran up to me with a big grin on his face.

'Percy, this is awesome!' His blue-feathered bronze helmet was falling in his eyes, and his breastplate was about six sizes too big. I wondered if there was any way I'd looked that ridiculous when I'd first arrived. Unfortunately, I probably had.

Nico lifted his sword with effort. 'Do we get to kill the other team?'

'Well . . . no.'

'But the Hunters are immortal, right?'

'That's only if they don't fall in battle. Besides –'

'It would be awesome if we just, like, resurrected as soon as we were killed, so we could keep fighting, and –'

'Nico, this is serious. Real swords. These can hurt.'

He stared at me, a little disappointed, and I realized that I'd just sounded like my mother. Whoa. Not a good sign.

I patted Nico on the shoulder. 'Hey, it's cool. Just follow the team. Stay out of Zoë's way. We'll have a blast.'

Chiron's hoof thundered on the pavilion floor.

'Heroes!' he called. 'You know the rules! The river is the boundary line. Blue team, Camp Half-Blood, shall take the west woods. Hunters of Artemis, red team, shall take the east woods. I will serve as referee and battlefield medic. No intentional maiming, please! All magic items are allowed. To your positions!'

'Sweet,' Nico whispered next to me. 'What kind of magic items? Do I get one?'

I was about to break it to him that he didn't, when Thalia said, 'Blue team! Follow me!'

They cheered and followed. I had to run to catch up, and tripped over somebody's shield, so I didn't look much like a co-captain. More like an idiot.

We set our flag at the top of Zeus's Fist. It's this cluster of boulders in the middle of the west woods that, if you look at it just the right way, looks like a huge fist sticking out of the ground. If you look at it from any other side, it looks like a pile of enormous deer droppings, but Chiron wouldn't let us call the place the Poop Pile, especially after it had been named for Zeus, who doesn't have much of a sense of humor.

Anyway, it was a good place to set the flag. The top boulder was six metres tall and really hard to climb, so the flag was clearly visible, like the rules said it had to be, and it didn't matter that the guards weren't allowed to stand within ten metres of it.

I set Nico on guard duty with Beckendorf and the Stoll brothers, figuring he'd be safely out of the way.

'We'll send out a decoy to the left,' Thalia told the team. 'Silena, you lead that.'

'Got it!'

'Take Laurel and Jason. They're good runners. Make a wide arc round the Hunters, attract as many as you can. I'll take the main raiding party round to the right and catch them by surprise.'

Everybody nodded. It sounded good, and Thalia said it with such confidence you couldn't help but believe it would work.

Thalia looked at me. 'Anything to add, Percy?'

'Um, yeah. Keep sharp on defence. We've got four guards, two scouts. That's not much for a big forest. I'll be roving. Yell if you need help.'

'And don't leave your post!' Thalia said.

'Unless you see a golden opportunity,' I added.

Thalia scowled. 'Just don't leave your post.'

'Right, unless –'

'Percy!' She touched my arm and shocked me. I mean, everybody can give static shocks in the winter, but when Thalia does, it hurts. I guess it's because her dad is the god of lightning. She's been known to fry off people's eyebrows.

‘Sorry,’ Thalia said, though she didn’t sound particularly sorry. ‘Now, is everybody clear?’

Everybody nodded. We broke into our smaller groups. The horn sounded, and the game began.

Silena’s group disappeared into the woods on the left. Thalia’s group gave it a few seconds, then darted off towards the right.

I waited for something to happen. I climbed Zeus’s Fist and had a good view over the forest. I remembered how the Hunters had stormed out of the woods when they fought the manticore, and I was prepared for something like that – one huge charge that could overwhelm us. But nothing happened.

I caught a glimpse of Silena and her two scouts. They ran through a clearing, followed by five of the Hunters, leading them deep into the woods and away from Thalia. The plan seemed to be working. Then I spotted another clump of Hunters heading to the right, bows ready. They must’ve spotted Thalia.

‘What’s happening?’ Nico demanded, trying to climb up next to me.

My mind was racing. Thalia would never get through, but the Hunters were divided. With that many on either flank, their centre had to be wide open. If I moved fast . . .

I looked at Beckendorf. ‘Can you guys hold the fort?’

Beckendorf snorted. ‘Of course.’

‘I’m going in.’

The Stoll brothers and Nico cheered as I raced towards the boundary line.

I was running at top speed and I felt great. I leaped over the creek into enemy territory. I could see their silver flag up ahead, only one guard, who wasn't even looking in my direction. I heard fighting to my left and right, somewhere in the woods. I had it made.

The guard turned at the last minute. It was Bianca di Angelo. Her eyes widened as I slammed into her and she went sprawling in the snow.

'Sorry!' I yelled. I ripped down the silver silk flag from the tree and took off.

I was ten metres away before Bianca managed to yell for help. I thought I was home free.

ZIP! A silvery cord raced across my ankles and fastened to the tree next to me. A trip wire, fired from a bow! Before I could even think about stopping I went down hard, sprawling in the snow.

'Percy!' Thalia yelled, off to my left. 'What are you *doing*?'

Before she reached me, an arrow exploded at her feet and a cloud of yellow smoke billowed around her team. They started coughing and gagging. I could smell the gas from across the woods – the horrible smell of sulphur.

'No fair!' Thalia gasped. 'Fart arrows are unsportsmanlike!'

I got up and started running again. Only a few more metres to the river and I had the game. More arrows whizzed past my ears. A Hunter came out of nowhere and slashed at me with her knife, but I parried and kept running.

I heard yelling from our side of the river. Beckendorf and Nico were running towards me. I thought they were coming to welcome me back, but then I saw they were chasing someone – Zoë Nightshade, racing towards me like a cheetah, dodging campers with no trouble. And she had our flag in her hands.

'No!' I yelled, and poured on the speed.

I was a metre from the water when Zoë bolted across to her own side, slamming into me for good measure. The Hunters cheered as both sides converged on the creek. Chiron appeared out of the woods, looking grim. He had the Stoll brothers on his back, and it looked as if both of them had taken some nasty whacks to the head. Connor Stoll had two arrows sticking out of his helmet like antennae.

'The Hunters win!' Chiron announced without pleasure. Then he muttered, 'For the fifty-sixth time in a row.'

'Perseus Jackson!' Thalia yelled, storming towards me. She smelled like rotten eggs, and she was so mad that blue sparks flickered on her armour. Everybody cringed and backed up because of Aegis. It took all my willpower not to cower.

'What in the name of the gods were you THINKING?' she bellowed.

I balled my fists. I'd had enough bad stuff happen to me for one day. I didn't need this. 'I got the flag, Thalia!' I shook it in her face. 'I saw a chance and I took it!'

'I WAS AT THEIR BASE!' Thalia yelled. 'But the flag was gone. If you hadn't butted in, we would've won.'

'You had too many on you!'

'Oh, so it's my fault?'

'I didn't say that.'

'Argh!' Thalia pushed me, and a shock went through my body that blew me backwards three metres into the water. Some of the campers gasped. A couple of the Hunters stifled laughs.

'Sorry!' Thalia said, turning pale. 'I didn't mean to –'

Anger roared in my ears. A wave erupted from the river, blasting into Thalia's face and dousing her from head to toe.

I stood up. 'Yeah,' I growled. 'I didn't mean to either.'

Thalia was breathing heavily.

'Enough!' Chiron ordered.

But Thalia held out her spear. 'You want some, Seaweed Brain?'

Somehow, it was okay when Annabeth called me that – at least, I'd got used to it – but hearing it from Thalia was not cool.

'Bring it on, Pinecone Face!'

I raised Riptide, but before I could even defend myself, Thalia yelled, and a blast of lightning came down from the sky, hit her spear like a lightning rod, and slammed into my chest.

I sat down hard. There was a burning smell; I had a feeling it was my clothes.

'Thalia!' Chiron said. 'That is *enough!*'

I got to my feet and willed the entire river to rise. It swirled up, hundreds of gallons of water in a massive icy funnel cloud.

'Percy!' Chiron pleaded.

I was about to hurl it at Thalia when I saw something in the woods. I lost my anger and my concentration all at once. The water splashed back into the riverbed. Thalia was so surprised she turned to see what I was looking at.

Someone . . . something was approaching. It was shrouded in a murky green mist, but as it got closer, the campers and Hunters gasped.

'This is impossible,' Chiron said. I'd never heard him sound so nervous. 'It . . . she has never left the attic. Never.'

And yet the withered mummy that held the Oracle shuffled forward until she stood in the centre of the group. Mist curled around our feet, turning the snow a sickly shade of green.

None of us dared move. Then her voice hissed inside my head. Apparently everyone could hear it, because several clutched their hands over the ears.

I am the spirit of Delphi, the voice said. *Speaker of the prophecies of Phoebus Apollo, slayer of the mighty Python.*

The Oracle regarded me with its cold, dead eyes. Then she turned unmistakably towards Zoë Nightshade. *Approach, Seeker, and ask.*

Zoë swallowed. 'What must I do to help my goddess?'

The Oracle's mouth opened, and green mist poured out. I saw the vague image of a mountain, and a girl standing at the barren peak. It was Artemis, but she was wrapped in chains, fettered to the rocks. She was kneeling, her hands raised as if to fend off an attacker, and it looked like she was in pain. The Oracle spoke:

Five shall go west to the goddess in chains,
One shall be lost in the land without rain,
The bane of Olympus shows the trail,
Campers and Hunters combined prevail,
The Titan's curse must one withstand,
And one shall perish by a parent's hand.

Then, as we were watching, the Mist swirled and retreated like a great green serpent into the mummy's mouth. The

Oracle sat down on a rock and became as still as she'd been in the attic, as if she might sit by this creek for a hundred years.

7 EVERYBODY HATES ME BUT THE HORSE

The least the Oracle could've done was walk back to the attic by herself.

Instead, Grover and I were elected to carry her. I didn't figure that was because we were the most popular.

'Watch her head!' Grover warned as we went up the stairs. But it was too late.

Bonk! I whacked her mummified face against the trapdoor frame and dust flew.

'Ah, man.' I set her down and checked for damage. 'Did I break anything?'

'I can't tell,' Grover admitted.

We hauled her up and set her on her tripod stool, both of us huffing and sweating. Who knew a mummy could weigh so much?

I assumed she wouldn't talk to me, and I was right. I was relieved when we finally got out of there and slammed the attic door shut.

'Well,' Grover said, 'that was gross.'

I knew he was trying to keep things light for my sake, but I still felt really down. The whole camp would be mad at me for losing the game to the Hunters, and then there was the new prophecy from the Oracle. It was like the spirit of Delphi had gone out of her way to exclude me. She'd ignored my question and walked half a mile to talk to Zoë. *And* she'd said nothing, not even a hint, about Annabeth.

'What will Chiron do?' I asked Grover.

'I wish I knew.' He looked wistfully out of the second-floor window at the rolling hills covered in snow. 'I want to be out there.'

'Searching for Annabeth?'

He had a little trouble focusing on me. Then he blushed. 'Oh, right. That too. Of course.'

'Why?' I asked. 'What were you thinking?'

He clopped his hooves uneasily. 'Just something the manticore said, about the Great Stirring. I can't help but wonder . . . if all those ancient powers are waking up, maybe . . . maybe not all of them are evil.'

'You mean Pan.'

I felt kind of selfish, because I'd totally forgotten about Grover's life ambition. The nature god had gone missing two thousand years ago. He was rumoured to have died, but the satyrs didn't believe that. They were determined to find him. They'd been searching in vain for centuries, and Grover was convinced he'd be the one to succeed. This year, with Chiron putting all the satyrs on emergency duty to find half-bloods, Grover hadn't been able to continue his search. It must've been driving him nuts.

'I've let the trail go cold,' he said. 'I feel restless, like I'm missing something really important. He's out there somewhere. I can just feel it.'

I didn't know what to say. I wanted to encourage him, but I didn't know how. My optimism had pretty much been trampled into the snow out there in the woods, along with our capture-the-flag hopes.

Before I could respond, Thalia tromped up the stairs. She was officially not talking to me now, but she looked at Grover and said, 'Tell Percy to get his butt downstairs.'

'Why?' I asked.

'Did he say something?' Thalia asked Grover.

'Um, he asked why.'

'Dionysus is calling a council of cabin leaders to discuss the prophecy,' she said. 'Unfortunately, that includes Percy.'

The council was held round a ping-pong table in the rec room. Dionysus waved his hand and supplied snacks: Cheez Whiz, crackers and several bottles of red wine. Then Chiron reminded him that wine was against his restrictions and most of us were underage. Mr D sighed. With a snap of his fingers the wine turned to Diet Coke. Nobody drank that either.

Mr D and Chiron (in wheelchair form) sat at one end of the table. Zoë and Bianca di Angelo (who had kind of become Zoë's personal assistant) took the other end. Thalia and Grover and I sat along the right, and the other head councillors, Beckendorf, Silena Beauregard, and the Stoll brothers, sat on the left. The Ares kids were supposed to send a representative, too, but all of them had got broken limbs (accidentally) during capture the flag, courtesy of the Hunters. They were resting up in the infirmary.

Zoë started the meeting off on a positive note. 'This is pointless.'

'Cheez Whiz!' Grover gasped. He began scooping up crackers and ping-pong balls and spraying them with topping.

'There is no time for talk,' Zoë continued. 'Our goddess

needs us. The Hunters must leave immediately.'

'And go where?' Chiron asked.

'West!' Bianca said. I was amazed at how different she looked after just a few days with the Hunters. Her dark hair was braided like Zoë's now, so you could actually see her face. She had a splash of freckles across her nose, and her dark eyes vaguely reminded me of someone famous, but I couldn't think who. She looked like she'd been working out, and her skin glowed faintly, like the other Hunters, as if she'd been taking showers in liquid moonlight. 'You heard the prophecy. '*Five shall go west to the goddess in chains.*' We can get five hunters and go.'

'Yes,' Zoë agreed. 'Artemis is being held hostage! We must find her and free her.'

'You're missing something, as usual,' Thalia said. '*Campers and Hunters combined prevail.* We're supposed to do this together.'

'No!' Zoë said. 'The Hunters do not need thy help.'

'*Your*,' Thalia grumbled. 'Nobody has said *thy* in like three hundred years, Zoë. Get with the times.'

Zoë hesitated, like she was trying to form the word correctly. '*Yerrr.* We do not need *yerrr* help.'

Thalia rolled her eyes. 'Forget it.'

'I fear the prophecy says you *do* need our help,' Chiron said. 'Campers and Hunters must cooperate.'

'Or do they?' Mr D mused, swirling his Diet Coke under his nose like it had a fine bouquet. '*One shall be lost. One shall perish.* That sounds rather nasty, doesn't it? What if you fail *because* you try to cooperate?'

'Mr D,' Chiron sighed, 'with all due respect, whose side are you on?'

Dionysus raised his eyebrows. 'Sorry, my dear centaur. Just trying to be helpful.'

'We're supposed to work together,' Thalia said stubbornly. 'I don't like it either, Zoë, but you know prophecies. You want to fight against one?'

Zoë grimaced, but I could tell Thalia had scored a point.

'We must not delay,' Chiron warned. 'Today is Sunday. This very Friday, December twenty-first, is the winter solstice.'

'Oh, joy,' Dionysus muttered. 'Another dull annual meeting.'

'Artemis must be present at the solstice,' Zoë said. 'She has been one of the most vocal on the council arguing for action against Kronos's minions. If she is absent, the gods will decide nothing. We will lose another year of war preparations.'

'Are you suggesting that the gods have trouble acting together, young lady?' Dionysus asked.

'Yes, Lord Dionysus.'

Mr D nodded. 'Just checking. You're right, of course. Carry on.'

'I must agree with Zoë,' said Chiron. 'Artemis's presence at the winter council is critical. We have only a week to find her. And possibly even more important: to locate the monster she was hunting. Now, we must decide who goes on this quest.'

'Three and two,' I said.

Everybody looked at me. Even Thalia forgot to ignore me.

'We're supposed to have five,' I said, feeling self-conscious. 'Three Hunters, two from Camp Half-Blood. That's more than fair.'

Thalia and Zoë exchanged looks.

'Well,' Thalia said. 'It does make sense.'

Zoë grunted. 'I would prefer to take *all* the Hunters. We will need strength of numbers.'

'You'll be retracing the goddess's path,' Chiron reminded her. 'Moving quickly. No doubt Artemis tracked the scent of this rare monster, whatever it is, as she moved west. You will have to do the same. The prophecy was clear: *The bane of Olympus shows the trail.* What would your mistress say? "Too many Hunters spoil the scent." A small group is best.'

Zoë picked up a ping-pong paddle and studied it like she was deciding who she wanted to whack first. 'This monster – the bane of Olympus. I have hunted at Lady Artemis's side for many years, yet I have no idea what this beast might be.'

Everybody looked at Dionysus, I guess because he was the only god present and gods are supposed to know things. He was flipping through a wine magazine, but when everyone got silent he glanced up. 'Well, don't look at me. I'm a *young* god, remember? I don't keep track of all those ancient monsters and dusty Titans. They make for terrible party conversation.'

'Chiron,' I said, 'you don't have any ideas about the monster?'

Chiron pursed his lips. 'I have several ideas, none of them good. And none of them quite make sense. Typhon, for instance, could fit this description. He was truly a bane of Olympus. Or the sea monster Ketos. But if either of these were stirring, we would know it. They are ocean monsters the size of skyscrapers. Your father Poseidon would already have sounded the alarm. I fear this monster may be more elusive. Perhaps even more powerful.'

'That's some serious danger you're facing,' Connor Stoll said. (I liked how he said *you* and not *we*.) 'It sounds like at least two of the five are going to die.'

'*One shall be lost in the land without rain*,' Beckendorf said. 'If I were you, I'd stay out of the desert.'

There was a muttering of agreement.

'And *the Titan's curse must one withstand*,' Silena said. 'What could that mean?'

I saw Chiron and Zoë exchange a nervous look, but whatever they were thinking, they didn't share it.

'*One shall perish by a parent's hand*,' Grover said in between bites of Cheez Whiz and ping-pong balls. 'How is that possible? Whose parent would kill them?'

There was a heavy silence round the table.

I glanced at Thalia and wondered if she was thinking the same thing I was. Years ago, Chiron had had a prophecy about the next child of the Big Three – Zeus, Poseidon or Hades – who turned sixteen. Supposedly, that kid would make a decision that would save or destroy the gods forever. Because of that, the Big Three had taken an oath after World War II not to have any more kids. But Thalia and I had been born anyway, and now we were both getting close to sixteen.

I remembered a conversation I'd had last year with Annabeth. I'd asked her if I was so potentially dangerous, why the gods didn't just kill me.

Some of the gods would like to kill you, she'd said. *But they're afraid of offending Poseidon.*

Could an Olympian parent turn against his half-blood child? Would it sometimes be easier just to let them die?

If there were ever any half-bloods who needed to worry about that, it was Thalia and me. I wondered if maybe I should've sent Poseidon that seashell-pattern tie for Father's Day after all.

'There will be deaths,' Chiron decided. 'That much we know.'

'Oh, goody!' Dionysus said.

Everyone looked at him. He glanced up innocently from the pages of *Wine Connoisseur* magazine. 'Ah, Pinot Noir is making a comeback. Don't mind me.'

'Percy is right,' Silena Beauregard said. 'Two campers should go.'

'Oh, I see,' Zoë said sarcastically. 'And I suppose you wish to volunteer?'

Silena blushed. 'I'm not going anywhere with the Hunters. Don't look at me!'

'A daughter of Aphrodite does not wish to be looked at,' Zoë scoffed. 'What would thy mother say?'

Silena started to get out of her chair, but the Stoll brothers pulled her back.

'Stop it,' Beckendorf said. He was a big guy with a bigger voice. He didn't talk much, but when he did people tended to listen. 'Let's start with the Hunters. Which three of you will go?'

Zoë stood. 'I shall go, of course, and I will take Phoebe. She is our best tracker.'

'The big girl who likes to hit people on the head?' Travis Stoll asked cautiously.

Zoë nodded.

'The one who put the arrows in my helmet?' Connor added.

'Yes,' Zoë snapped. 'Why?'

'Oh, nothing,' Travis said. 'Just we have a T-shirt for her from the camp store.' He held up a big silver T-shirt that said ARTEMIS THE MOON GODDESS, HUNTING TOUR 2002, with a huge list of national parks and stuff underneath. 'It's a collector's item. She was admiring it. You want to give it to her?'

I knew the Stolls were up to something. They always were. But I guess Zoë didn't know them as well as I did. She just sighed and took the T-shirt. 'As I was saying, I will take Phoebe. And I wish Bianca to go.'

Bianca looked stunned. 'Me? But . . . I'm so new. I wouldn't be any good.'

'You will do fine,' Zoë insisted. 'There is no better way to prove thyself.'

Bianca closed her mouth. I felt kind of sorry for her. I remembered my first quest when I was twelve. I had felt totally unprepared. A little honoured, maybe, but a lot resentful and plenty scared. I figured the same things were running around in Bianca's head right now.

'And for campers?' Chiron asked. His eyes met mine, but I couldn't tell what he was thinking.

'Me!' Grover stood up so fast he bumped the ping-pong table. He brushed cracker crumbs and ping-pong ball scraps off his lap. 'Anything to help Artemis!'

Zoë wrinkled her nose. 'I think not, satyr. You are not even a half-blood.'

'But he *is* a camper,' Thalia said. 'And he's got a satyr's senses and woodland magic. Can you play a tracker's song yet, Grover?'

'Absolutely!'

Zoë wavered. I didn't know what a tracker's song was, but apparently Zoë thought it was a good thing.

'Very well,' Zoë said. 'And the second camper?'

'I'll go.' Thalia stood and looked around, daring anyone to question her.

Now, okay, maybe my maths skills weren't the best. But it suddenly occurred to me that we'd reached the number five, and I wasn't in the group.

'Whoa, wait a sec,' I said. 'I want to go, too.'

Thalia said nothing. Chiron was still studying me, his eyes sad.

'Oh,' Grover said, suddenly aware of the problem. 'Whoa, yeah, I forgot! Percy has to go. I didn't mean . . . I'll stay. Percy should go in my place.'

'He cannot,' Zoë said. 'He is a boy. I won't have Hunters travelling with a boy.'

'You travelled here with me,' I reminded her.

'That was a short-term emergency, and it was ordered by the goddess. I will not go across country and fight many dangers in the company of a boy.'

'What about Grover?' I demanded.

Zoë shook her head. 'He does not count. He's a satyr. He is not technically a boy.'

'Hey!' Grover protested.

'I *have* to go,' I said. 'I need to be on this quest.'

'Why?' Zoë asked. 'Because of thy friend Annabeth?'

I felt myself blushing. I hated that everyone was looking at me. 'No! I mean, partly. I just feel like I'm supposed to go!'

Nobody rose to my defence. Mr D looked bored, still reading his magazine. Silena, the Stoll brothers and

Beckendorf were staring at the table. Bianca gave me a look of pity.

'No,' Zoë said flatly. 'I insist upon this. I will take a satyr if I must, but not a male hero.'

Chiron sighed. 'The quest is for Artemis. The Hunters should be allowed to approve their companions.'

My ears were ringing as I sat down. I knew Grover and some of the others were looking at me sympathetically, but I couldn't meet their eyes. I just sat there as Chiron concluded the council.

'So be it,' he said. 'Thalia and Grover will accompany Zoë, Bianca and Phoebe. You shall leave at first light. And may the gods –' he glanced at Dionysus – 'present company included, we hope – be with you.'

I didn't show up for dinner that night, which was a mistake, because Chiron and Grover came looking for me.

'Percy, I'm so sorry!' Grover said, sitting next to me on the bunk. 'I didn't know they'd – that you'd – Honest!'

He started to sniffle, and I figured if I didn't cheer him up he'd either start bawling or chewing up my mattress. He tends to eat inanimate objects whenever he gets upset.

'It's okay,' I lied. 'Really. It's fine.'

Grover's lower lip trembled. 'I wasn't even thinking . . . I was so focused on helping Artemis. But, I promise, I'll look everywhere for Annabeth. If I can find her, I will.'

I nodded and tried to ignore the big crater that was opening in my chest.

'Grover,' Chiron said, 'perhaps you'd let me have a word with Percy?'

'Sure,' he sniffled.

Chiron waited.

'Oh,' Grover said. 'You mean alone. Sure, Chiron.' He looked at me miserably. 'See? Nobody needs a goat.'

He trotted out the door, blowing his nose on his sleeve.

Chiron sighed and knelt on his horse legs. 'Percy, I don't pretend to understand prophecies.'

'Yeah,' I said. 'Well, maybe that's because they don't make any sense.'

Chiron gazed at the saltwater spring gurgling in the corner of the room. 'Thalia would not have been my first choice to go on this quest. She's too impetuous. She acts without thinking. She is too sure of herself.'

'Would you have chosen me?'

'Frankly, no,' he said. 'You and Thalia are much alike.'

'Thanks a lot.'

He smiled. 'The difference is that you are less sure of yourself than Thalia. That could be good or bad. But one thing I can say: both of you together would be a dangerous thing.'

'We could handle it.'

'The way you handled it at the creek tonight?'

I didn't answer. He'd nailed me.

'Perhaps it is for the best,' Chiron mused. 'You can go home to your mother for the holidays. If we need you, we can call.'

'Yeah,' I said. 'Maybe.'

I pulled Riptide out of my pocket and set in on my nightstand. It didn't seem that I'd be using it for anything but writing Christmas cards.

When he saw the pen, Chiron grimaced. 'It's no wonder

Zoë doesn't want you along, I suppose. Not while you're carrying that particular weapon.'

I didn't understand what he meant. Then I remembered something he'd told me a long time ago, when he first gave me the magic sword: *It has a long and tragic history, which we need not go into.*

I wanted to ask him about that, but then he pulled a golden drachma from his saddlebag and tossed it to me. 'Call your mother, Percy. Let her know you're coming home in the morning. And, ah, for what it's worth . . . I almost volunteered for this quest myself. I would have gone, if not for the last line.'

'*One shall perish by a parent's hand.* Yeah.'

I didn't need to ask. I knew Chiron's dad was Kronos, the evil Titan Lord himself. The line would make perfect sense if Chiron went on the quest. Kronos didn't care for anyone, including his own children.

'Chiron,' I said. 'You know what this Titan's curse is, don't you?'

His face darkened. He made a claw over his heart and pushed outwards – an ancient gesture for warding off evil. 'Let us hope the prophecy does not mean what I think. Now, goodnight, Percy. And your time will come. I'm convinced of that. There's no need to rush.'

He said *your time* the way people did when they meant *your death.* I didn't know if Chiron meant it that way, but the look in his eyes made me scared to ask.

I stood at the saltwater spring, rubbing Chiron's coin in my hand and trying to figure out what to say to my mom. I really wasn't in the mood to have one more adult tell me that doing nothing was the greatest thing I could do, but I figured my mom deserved an update.

Finally, I took a deep breath and threw in the coin. 'O goddess, accept my offering.'

The mist shimmered. The light from the bathroom was just enough to make a faint rainbow.

'Show me Sally Jackson,' I said. 'Upper East Side, Manhattan.'

And there in the mist was a scene I did not expect. My mom was sitting at our kitchen table with some . . . guy. They were laughing hysterically. There was a big stack of textbooks between them. The man was, I don't know, thirty-something, with longish salt-and-pepper hair and a brown jacket over a black T-shirt. He looked like an actor – like a guy who might play an undercover cop on television.

I was too stunned to say anything, and, fortunately, my mom and the guy were too busy laughing to notice my Iris-message.

The guy said, 'Sally, you're a riot. You want some more wine?'

'Ah, I shouldn't. You go ahead if you want.'

'Actually, I'd better use your bathroom. May I?'

'Down the hall,' she said, trying not to laugh.

The actor dude smiled and got up and left.

'Mom!' I said.

She jumped so hard she almost knocked her textbooks off the table. Finally she focused on me. 'Percy! Oh, honey! Is everything okay?'

'What are you doing?' I demanded.

She blinked. 'Homework.' Then she seemed to

understand the look on my face. 'Oh, honey, that's just Paul – um, Mr Blofis. He's in my writing seminar.'

'Mr Blowfish?'

'*Blofis*. He'll be back in a minute, Percy. Tell me what's wrong.'

She always knew when something was wrong. I told her about Annabeth. The other stuff, too, but mostly it boiled down to Annabeth.

My mother's eyes teared up. I could tell she was trying hard to keep it together for my sake. 'Oh, Percy . . .'

'Yeah. So they tell me there's nothing I can do. I guess I'll be coming home.'

She turned her pencil round in her fingers. 'Percy, as much as I want you to come home –' she sighed like she was mad at herself – 'as much as I want you to be safe, I want you to understand something. You need to do whatever you think you have to.'

I stared at her. 'What do you mean?'

'I mean, do you really, deep down, believe that you have to help save her? Do you think it's the right thing to do? Because I know one thing about you, Percy. Your heart is always in the right place. Listen to it.'

'You're . . . you're telling me to go?'

My mother pursed her lips. 'I'm telling you that . . . you're getting too old for me to tell you what to do. I'm telling you that I'll support you, even if what you decide to do is dangerous. I can't believe I'm saying this.'

'Mom –'

The toilet flushed down the hall in our apartment.

'I don't have much time,' my mom said. 'Percy, whatever

you decide, I love you. And I *know* you'll do what's best for Annabeth.'

'How can you be sure?'

'Because she'd do the same for you.'

And, with that, my mother waved her hand over the mist, and the connection dissolved, leaving me with one final image of her new friend Mr Blowfish smiling down at her.

I don't remember falling asleep, but I remember the dream.

I was back in that barren cave, the ceiling heavy and low above me. Annabeth was kneeling under the weight of a dark mass like a pile of boulders. She was too tired even to cry out. Her legs trembled. Any second, I knew she would run out of strength and the cavern ceiling would collapse on top of her.

'How is our mortal guest?' a male voice boomed.

It wasn't Kronos. Kronos's voice was raspy and metallic, like a knife scraped across stone. I'd heard it taunting me many times before in my dreams. *This* voice was deeper and lower, like a bass guitar. Its force made the ground vibrate.

Luke emerged from the shadows. He ran to Annabeth, knelt beside her, then looked back at the unseen man. 'She's fading. We must hurry.'

The hypocrite. Like he really cared what happened to her.

The deep voice chuckled. It belonged to someone in the shadows, at the edge of my dream. Then a meaty hand thrust someone forward into the light – Artemis – her hands and feet bound in celestial bronze chains.

I gasped. Her silvery dress was torn and tattered. Her face and arms were cut in several places, and she was bleeding ichor, the golden blood of the gods.

'You heard the boy,' said the man in the shadows. 'Decide!'

Artemis's eyes flashed with anger. I didn't know why she just didn't will the chains to burst, or make herself disappear, but she didn't seem able to. Maybe the chains prevented her, or some magic about this dark, horrible place.

The goddess looked at Annabeth, and her expression changed to concern and outrage. 'How dare you torture a maiden like this!'

'She will die soon,' Luke said. 'You can save her.'

Annabeth made a weak sound of protest. My heart felt like it was being twisted into a knot. I wanted to run to her, but I couldn't move.

'Free my hands,' Artemis said.

Luke brought out his sword, Backbiter. With one expert strike, he broke the goddess's handcuffs.

Artemis ran to Annabeth and took the burden from her shoulders. Annabeth collapsed on the ground and lay there shivering. Artemis staggered, trying to support the weight of the black rocks.

The man in the shadows chuckled. 'You are as predictable as you were easy to beat, Artemis.'

'You surprised me,' the goddess said, straining under her burden. 'It will not happen again.'

'Indeed it will not,' the man said. 'Now you are out of the way for good! I knew you could not resist helping a young maiden. That is, after all, your speciality, my dear.'

Artemis groaned. 'You know nothing of mercy, you swine.'

'On that,' the man said, 'we can agree. Luke, you may kill the girl now.'

'No!' Artemis shouted.

Luke hesitated. 'She – she may yet be useful, sir. Further bait.'

'Bah! You truly believe that?'

'Yes, General. They will come for her. I'm sure.'

The man considered. 'Then the *dracaenae* can guard her here. Assuming she does not die from her injuries, you may keep her alive until winter solstice. After that, if our sacrifice goes as planned, her life will be meaningless. The lives of *all* mortals will be meaningless.'

Luke gathered up Annabeth's listless body and carried her away from the goddess.

'You will never find the monster you seek,' Artemis said. 'Your plan will fail.'

'How little you know, my young goddess,' the man in the shadows said. 'Even now, your darling attendants begin their quest to find you. They shall play directly into my hands. Now, if you'll excuse us, we have a long journey to make. We must greet your Hunters and make sure their quest is . . . challenging.'

The man's laughter echoed in the darkness, shaking the ground until it seemed the whole cavern ceiling would collapse.

I woke with a start. I was sure I'd heard a loud banging.

I looked around the cabin. It was dark outside. The salt spring still gurgled. No other sounds but the hoot of an owl in the woods and the distant surf on the beach. In the moonlight, on my nightstand, was Annabeth's New York Yankees cap. I stared at it for a second, and then: *BANG. BANG.*

Someone, or something, was pounding on my door.

I grabbed Riptide and got out of bed.

'Hello?' I called.

THUMP. THUMP.

I crept to the door.

I uncapped the blade, flung open the door, and found myself face to face with a black pegasus.

Whoa, boss! Its voice spoke in my mind as it clopped away from the sword blade. *I don't wanna be a horse-ke-bob!*

Its black wings spread in alarm, and the wind buffeted me back a step.

'Blackjack,' I said, relieved but a little irritated. 'It's the middle of the night!'

Blackjack huffed. *Ain't either, boss. It's five in the morning. What you still sleeping for?*

'How many times have I told you? Don't call me boss.'

Whatever you say, boss. You're the man. You're my number one.

I rubbed the sleep out of my eyes and tried not to let the pegasus read my thoughts. That's the problem with being Poseidon's son: since he created horses out of sea foam, I can understand most equestrian animals, but they can understand me, too. Sometimes, like in Blackjack's case, they kind of adopt me.

See, Blackjack had been a captive on board Luke's ship last summer, until we'd caused a little distraction that allowed him to escape. I'd really had very little to do with it, seriously, but Blackjack credited me with saving him.

'Blackjack,' I said, 'you're supposed to stay in the stables.'

Meh, the stables. You see Chiron staying in the stables?

'Well . . . no.'

Exactly. Listen, we got another little sea friend needs your help.

'Again?'

Yeah. I told the hippocampi I'd come get you.

I groaned. Anytime I was anywhere near the beach, the hippocampi would ask me to help them with their problems. And they had a lot of problems. Beached whales, porpoises caught in fishing nets, mermaids with hangnails – they'd call me to come underwater and help.

'All right,' I said. 'I'm coming.'

You're the best, boss.

'And don't call me boss!'

Blackjack whinnied softly. It might've been a laugh.

I looked back at my comfortable bed. My bronze shield still hung on the wall, dented and unusable. And on my nightstand was Annabeth's magic Yankees cap. On an impulse, I stuck the cap in my pocket. I guess I had a feeling, even then, that I wasn't coming back to my cabin for a long, long time.

8 I MAKE A DANGEROUS PROMISE

Blackjack gave me a ride down the beach, and I have to admit it was cool. Being on a flying horse, skimming over the waves at a hundred miles an hour with the wind in my hair and the sea spray in my face – hey, it beats waterskiing any day.

Here. Blackjack slowed and turned in a circle. *Straight down.*

'Thanks.' I tumbled off his back and plunged into the icy sea.

I'd got more comfortable doing stunts like that the past couple of years. I could pretty much move however I wanted to underwater, just by willing the ocean currents to change around me and propel me along. I could breathe underwater, no problem, and my clothes never got wet unless I wanted them to.

I shot down into the darkness.

Eight, ten, twelve metres. The pressure wasn't uncomfortable. I'd never tried to push it – to see if there was a limit to how deep I could dive. I knew most regular humans couldn't go past sixty-five metres without crumpling like a tin can. I should've been blind, too, this deep in the water at night, but I could see the heat from living forms, and the cold of the currents. It's hard to describe. It wasn't like regular seeing, but I could tell where everything was.

As I got closer to the bottom, I saw three hippocampi – fish-tailed horses – swimming in a circle round an overturned boat. The hippocampi were beautiful to watch. Their fish tails shimmered in rainbow colours, glowing phosphorescent. Their manes were white, and they were galloping through the water the way nervous horses do in a thunderstorm. Something was upsetting them.

I got closer and saw the problem. A dark shape – some kind of animal – was wedged halfway under the boat and tangled in a fishing net, one of those big nets they use on trawlers to catch everything at once. I hated those things. It was bad enough they drowned porpoises and dolphins, but they also occasionally caught mythological animals. When the nets got tangled, some lazy fishermen would just cut them loose and let the trapped animals die.

Apparently this poor creature had been mucking around on the bottom of Long Island Sound and had somehow got itself tangled in the net of this sunken fishing boat. It had tried to get out and managed to get even more hopelessly stuck, shifting the boat in the process. Now the wreckage of the hull, which was resting against a big rock, was teetering and threatening to collapse on top of the tangled animal.

The hippocampi were swimming around frantically, wanting to help but not sure how. One was trying to chew the net, but hippocampi teeth just aren't meant for cutting rope. Hippocampi are really strong, but they don't have hands, and they're not (shhh) all that smart.

Free it, lord! A hippocampus said when it saw me. The others joined in, asking the same thing.

I swam in for a closer look at the tangled creature. At

first I thought it was a young hippocampus. I'd rescued several of them before. But then I heard a strange sound, something that did not belong underwater:

'Mooooooo!'

I got next to the thing and saw that it was a cow. I mean . . . I'd heard of sea cows, like manatees and stuff, but this really was a cow with the back end of a serpent. The front half was a calf – a baby, with black fur and big, sad brown eyes and a white muzzle – and its back half was a black-and-brown snaky tail with fins running down the top and bottom, like an enormous eel.

'Whoa, little one,' I said. 'Where did you come from?'

The creature looked at me sadly. 'Moooo!'

But I couldn't understand its thoughts. I only speak horse.

We don't know what it is, lord, one of the hippocampus said. *Many strange things are stirring.*

'Yeah,' I murmured. 'So I've heard.'

I uncapped Riptide, and the sword grew to full-length in my hands, its bronze blade gleaming in the dark.

The cow serpent freaked out and started struggling against the net, its eyes full of terror. 'Whoa!' I said. 'I'm not going to hurt you! Just let me cut the net.'

But the cow serpent thrashed around and got even more tangled. The boat started to tilt, stirring up the muck on the sea bottom and threatening to topple onto the cow serpent. The hippocampi whinnied in a panic and thrashed in the water, which didn't help.

'Okay, okay!' I said. I put away the sword and started speaking as calmly as I could so the hippocampi and the cow serpent would stop panicking. I didn't know if it was possible to get stampeded underwater, but I didn't really want to find out. 'It's cool. No sword. See? No sword. Calm thoughts. Sea grass. Mama cows. Vegetarianism.'

I doubted the cow serpent understood what I was saying, but it responded to the tone of my voice. The hippocampi were still skittish, but they stopped swirling around me quite so fast.

Free it, lord! they pleaded.

'Yeah,' I said. 'I got that part. I'm thinking.'

But how could I free the cow serpent when she (I decided it was probably a 'she') panicked at the sight of a blade? It was like she'd seen swords before and knew how dangerous they were.

'All right,' I told the hippocampi. 'I need all of you to push exactly the way I tell you.'

First we started with the boat. It wasn't easy but, with the strength of three horsepower, we managed to shift the wreckage so it was no longer threatening to collapse on the baby cow serpent. Then I went to work on the net, untangling it section by section, getting lead weights and fishing hooks straightened out, yanking out knots round the cow serpent's hooves. It took forever – I mean, it was worse than the time I'd had to untangle all my video game controller wires. The whole time, I kept talking to the cow fish, telling her everything was okay while she mooed and moaned.

'It's okay, Bessie,' I said. Don't ask me why I started calling her that. It just seemed like a good cow name. 'Good cow. Nice cow.'

Finally, the net came off and the cow serpent zipped through the water and did a happy somersault.

The hippocampi whinnied with joy. *Thank you, lord!*

'Moooo!' The cow serpent nuzzled me and gave me the big brown eyes.

'Yeah,' I said. 'That's okay. Nice cow. Well . . . stay out of trouble.'

Which reminded me, I'd been underwater how long? An hour, at least. I had to get back to my cabin before Argus or the harpies discovered I was breaking curfew.

I shot to the surface and broke through. Immediately, Blackjack zoomed down and let me catch hold of his neck. He lifted me into the air and took me back towards the shore.

Success, boss?

'Yeah. We rescued a baby . . . something or other. Took forever. Almost got stampeded.'

Good deeds are always dangerous, boss. You saved my sorry mane, didn't you?

I couldn't help thinking about Annabeth in my dream, crumpled and lifeless in Luke's arms. Here I was rescuing baby monsters, but I couldn't save my friend.

As Blackjack flew back towards my cabin, I happened to glance at the dining pavilion. I saw a figure – a boy hunkered down behind a Greek column, like he was hiding from someone.

It was Nico, but it wasn't even dawn yet. Nowhere near time for breakfast. What was he doing up there?

I hesitated. The last thing I wanted was more time for Nico to tell me about his Mythomagic game. But something was wrong. I could tell by the way he was crouching.

'Blackjack,' I said, 'set me down over there, will you? Behind that column.'

* * *

I almost blew it.

I was coming up the steps behind Nico. He didn't see me at all. He was behind a column, peeking round the corner, all his attention focused on the dining area. I was two metres away from him, and I was about to say *What are you doing*, really loud, when it occurred to me that he was pulling a Grover: he was spying on the Hunters.

There were voices – two girls talking at one of the dining tables. At this ungodly hour of the morning? Well, unless you're the goddess of dawn, I guess.

I took Annabeth's cap out of my pocket and put it on.

I didn't feel any different, but when I raised my arms I couldn't see them. I was invisible.

I crept up to Nico and sneaked round him. I couldn't see the girls very well in the dark, but I knew their voices: Zoë and Bianca. It sounded like they were arguing.

'It *cannot* be cured,' Zoë was saying. 'Not quickly, at any rate.'

'But how did it happen?' Bianca asked.

'A foolish prank,' Zoë growled. 'Those Stoll boys from the Hermes cabin. Centaur blood is like acid. Everyone knows that. They sprayed the inside of that Artemis Hunting Tour T-shirt with it.'

'That's terrible!'

'She will live,' Zoë said. 'But she'll be bedridden for weeks with horrible hives. There is no way she can go. It's up to me . . . and thee.'

'But the prophecy,' Bianca said. 'If Phoebe can't go, we only have four. We'll have to pick another.'

'There is no time,' Zoë said. 'We must leave at first

light. That's immediately. Besides, the prophecy said we would lose one.'

'In the land without rain,' Bianca said, 'but that can't be here.'

'It might be,' Zoë said, though she didn't sound convinced. 'The camp has magic borders. Nothing, not even weather, is allowed in without permission. It *could* be a land without rain.'

'But –'

'Bianca, hear me.' Zoë's voice was strained. 'I . . . I can't explain, but I have a sense that we should *not* pick someone else. It would be too dangerous. They would meet an end worse than Phoebe's. I don't want Chiron choosing a camper as our fifth companion. And . . . I don't want to risk another Hunter.'

Bianca was silent. 'You should tell Thalia the rest of your dream.'

'No. It would not help.'

'But if your suspicions are correct, about the General –'

'I have thy word not to talk about that,' Zoë said. She sounded really anguished. 'We will find out soon enough. Now come. Dawn is breaking.'

Nico scooted out of their way. He was faster than me. As the girls sprinted down the steps, Zoë almost ran into me. She froze, her eyes narrowing. Her hand crept towards her bow, but then Bianca said, 'The lights of the Big House are on. Hurry!'

And Zoë followed her out of the pavilion.

I could tell what Nico was thinking. He took a deep breath and was about to run after his sister when I took off the invisibility cap and said, 'Wait.'

He almost slipped on the icy steps as he spun round to find me. 'Where did you come from?'

'I've been here the whole time. Invisible.'

He mouthed the word *invisible*. 'Wow. Cool.'

'How did you know Zoë and your sister were here?'

He blushed. 'I heard them walk by the Hermes cabin. I don't . . . I don't sleep too well at camp. So I heard footsteps, and them whispering. And so I kind of followed.'

'And now you're thinking about following them on the quest,' I guessed.

'How did you know that?'

'Because if it was my sister, I'd probably be thinking the same thing. But you can't.'

He looked defiant. 'Because I'm too young?'

'Because they won't let you. They'll catch you and send you back here. And . . . yeah, because you're too young. You remember the manticore? There will be lots more like that. More dangerous. Some of the heroes will die.'

His shoulders sagged. He shifted from foot to foot. 'Maybe you're right. But, but *you* can go for me.'

'Say what?'

'You can turn invisible. You can go!'

'The Hunters don't like boys,' I reminded him. 'If they find out –'

'Don't let them find out. Follow them invisibly. Keep an eye on my sister! You have to. Please?'

'Nico –'

'You're planning to go anyway, aren't you?'

I wanted to say no. But he looked me in the eyes, and I somehow couldn't lie to him.

'Yeah,' I said. 'I have to find Annabeth. I have to help, even if they don't want me to.'

'I won't tell on you,' he said. 'But you have to promise to keep my sister safe.'

'I . . . that's a big thing to promise, Nico, on a trip like this. Besides, she's got Zoë, Grover and Thalia –'

'Promise,' he insisted.

'I'll do my best. I promise that.'

'Get going, then!' he said. 'Good luck!'

It was crazy. I wasn't packed. I had nothing but the cap and the sword and the clothes I was wearing. I was supposed to be going home to Manhattan this morning. 'Tell Chiron –'

'I'll make something up.' Nico smiled crookedly. 'I'm good at that. Go on!'

I ran, putting on Annabeth's cap. As the sun came up, I turned invisible. I hit the top of Half-Blood Hill in time to see the camp's van disappearing down the farm road, probably Argus taking the quest group into the city. After that they would be on their own.

I felt a twinge of guilt, and stupidity, too. How was I supposed to keep up with them. Run?

Then I heard the beating of huge wings. Blackjack landed next to me. He began casually nuzzling a few tufts of grass that stuck through the ice.

If I was guessing, boss, I'd say you need a getaway horse. You interested?

A lump of gratitude stuck in my throat, but I managed to say, 'Yeah. Let's fly.'

9 I LEARN HOW TO GROW ZOMBIES

The thing about flying on a pegasus during the daytime is that, if you're not careful, you can cause a serious traffic accident on the Long Island Expressway. I had to keep Blackjack up in the clouds, which were fortunately pretty low in the winter. We darted around, trying to keep the white Camp Half-Blood van in sight. And if it was cold on the ground, it was seriously cold in the air, with icy rain stinging my skin.

I was wishing I'd brought some of that Camp Half-Blood orange thermal underwear they sold in the camp store but, after the story about Phoebe and the centaur-blood T-shirt, I wasn't sure I trusted their products any more.

We lost the van twice, but I had a pretty good sense that they would go into Manhattan first, so it wasn't too difficult to pick up their trail again.

Traffic was bad with the holidays and all. It was mid morning before they got into the city. I landed Blackjack near the top of the Chrysler Building and watched the white camp van, thinking it would pull into the Greyhound station, but it just kept driving.

'Where's Argus taking them?' I muttered.

Oh, Argus ain't driving, boss, Blackjack told me. *That girl is.*

'Which girl?'

The Hunter girl. With the silver crown thing in her hair.

'Zoë?'

That's the one. Hey, look! There's a doughnut shop. Can we hit the drive-thru?

I tried explaining to Blackjack that taking a flying horse through the drive-thru would give every cop in the doughnut shop a heart attack, but he didn't seem to get it. Meanwhile, the van kept snaking its way towards the Lincoln Tunnel. It had never even occurred to me that Zoë could drive. I mean, she didn't look sixteen. Then again, she was immortal. I wondered if she had a New York licence and, if so, what her birth date said.

'Well,' I said. 'Let's get after them.'

We were about to leap off the Chrysler Building when Blackjack whinnied in alarm and almost threw me. Something was curling around my leg like a snake. I reached for my sword, but when I looked down, there was no snake. Vines – grapevines – had sprouted from the cracks between the stones of the building. They were wrapping round Blackjack's legs, lashing down my ankles so we couldn't move.

'Going somewhere?' Mr D asked.

He was leaning against the building with his feet levitating in the air, his leopard-skin warm-up suit and black hair whipping around in the wind.

God alert! Blackjack yelled. *It's the wine dude!*

Mr D sighed in exasperation. 'The next person, *or horse,* who calls me "the wine dude" will end up in a bottle of Merlot!'

'Mr D.' I tried to keep my voice calm as the grapevines continued to wrap round my legs. 'What do you want?'

'Oh, what do *I* want? You thought, perhaps, that the immortal, all-powerful director of camp would not notice you leaving without permission?'

'Well . . . maybe.'

'I should throw you off this building, minus the flying horse, and see how heroic you sound on the way down.'

I balled my fists. I knew I should keep my mouth shut, but Mr D was about to kill me or haul me back to camp in shame, and I couldn't stand either idea. 'Why do you hate me so much? What did I ever do to you?'

Purple flames flickered in his eyes. 'You're a hero, boy. I need no other reason.'

'I *have* to go on this quest! I've got to help my friends. That's something you wouldn't understand!'

Um, boss, Blackjack said nervously. *Seeing as how we're wrapped in vines three hundred metres in the air, you might want to talk nice.*

The grapevines coiled tighter round me. Below us, the white van was getting further and further away. Soon it would be out of sight.

'Did I ever tell you about Ariadne?' Mr D asked. 'Beautiful young princess of Crete? She liked helping her friends, too. In fact, she helped a young hero named Theseus, also a son of Poseidon. She gave him a ball of magical thread that let him find his way out of the Labyrinth. And do you know how Theseus rewarded her?'

The answer I wanted to give was *I don't care!* But I didn't figure that would make Mr D finish his story any faster.

'They got married,' I said. 'Happily ever after. The end.'

Mr D sneered. 'Not quite. Theseus *said* he would marry her. He took her aboard his ship and sailed for Athens.

Halfway back, on a little island called Naxos, he – what's the word you mortals use today? – he *dumped* her. I found her there, you know. Alone. Heartbroken. Crying her eyes out. She had given up everything, left everything she knew behind, to help a dashing young hero who tossed her away like a broken sandal.'

'That's wrong,' I said. 'But that was thousands of years ago. What's that got to do with me?'

Mr D regarded me coldly. 'I fell in love with Ariadne, boy. I healed her broken heart. And, when she died, I made her my immortal wife in Olympus. She waits for me even now. I shall go back to her when I am done with this infernal century of punishment at your ridiculous camp.'

I stared at him. 'You're . . . you're married? But I thought you got in trouble for chasing a wood nymph –'

'My *point* is you heroes never change. You accuse us gods of being vain. You should look at yourselves. You take what you want, use whoever you have to, and then you betray everyone around you. So you'll excuse me if I have no love for heroes. They are a selfish, ungrateful lot. Ask Ariadne. Or Medea. For that matter, ask Zoë Nightshade.'

'What do you mean, ask Zoë?'

He waved his hand dismissively. 'Go. Follow your silly friends.'

The vines uncurled from round my legs.

I blinked in disbelief. 'You're . . . you're letting me go? Just like that?'

'The prophecy says at least two of you will die. Perhaps I'll get lucky and you'll be one of them. But mark my words, Son of Poseidon, live or die, you will prove no better than the other heroes.'

With that, Dionysus snapped his fingers. His image folded up like a paper display. There was a *pop* and he was gone, leaving a faint scent of grapes that was quickly blown away by the wind.

Too close, Blackjack said.

I nodded, though I almost would have been less worried if Mr D had hauled me back to camp. The fact that he'd let me go meant he really believed we stood a fair chance of crashing and burning on this quest.

'Come on, Blackjack,' I said, trying to sound upbeat. 'I'll buy you some doughnuts in New Jersey.'

As it turned out, I didn't buy Blackjack doughnuts in New Jersey. Zoë drove south like a crazy person, and we were into Maryland before she finally pulled over at a service station. Blackjack nearly tumbled out of the sky, he was so tired.

I'll be okay, boss, he panted. *Just . . . just catching my breath.*

'Stay here,' I told him. 'I'm going to scout.'

'Stay here' I can handle. I can do that.

I put on my cap of invisibility and walked over to the convenience store. It was difficult not to sneak. I had to keep reminding myself that nobody could see me. It was hard, too, because I had to remember to get out of people's way so they wouldn't slam into me.

I thought I'd go inside and warm up, maybe get a cup of hot chocolate or something. I had a little change in my pocket. I could leave it on the counter. I was wondering if the cup would turn invisible when I picked it up, or if I'd have to deal with a floating hot chocolate problem, when my whole plan was ruined by Zoë, Thalia,

Bianca and Grover all coming out of the store.

'Grover, are you sure?' Thalia was saying.

'Well . . . pretty sure. Ninety-nine per cent. Okay, eighty-five per cent.'

'And you did this with acorns?' Bianca asked, like she couldn't believe it.

Grover looked offended. 'It's a time-honoured tracking spell. I mean, I'm pretty sure I did it right.'

'D.C. is about sixty miles from here,' Bianca said. 'Nico and I . . .' She frowned. 'We used to lived there. That's . . . that's strange. I'd forgotten.'

'I dislike this,' Zoë said. 'We should go straight west. The prophecy said west.'

'Oh, like your tracking skills are better?' Thalia growled.

Zoë stepped towards her. 'You challenge my skills, you scullion? You know *nothing* of being a Hunter!'

'Oh, *scullion*? You're calling *me* a scullion? What the heck is a scullion?'

'Whoa, you two,' Grover said nervously. 'Come on. Not again!'

'Grover's right,' Bianca said. 'D.C. is our best bet.'

Zoë didn't look convinced, but she nodded reluctantly. 'Very well. Let us keep moving.'

'You're going to get us arrested, driving,' Thalia grumbled. 'I look closer to sixteen than you do.'

'Perhaps,' Zoë snapped. 'But I have been driving since automobiles were invented. Let us go.'

As Blackjack and I continued south, following the van, I wondered whether Zoë had been kidding. I didn't know exactly when cars were invented, but I figured that was like prehistoric times – back when people watched black-and-white TV and hunted dinosaurs.

How old *was* Zoë? And what had Mr D been talking about? What bad experience had she had with heroes?

As we got closer to Washington, Blackjack started slowing down and dropping altitude. He was breathing heavily.

'You okay?' I asked him.

Fine, boss. I could . . . I could take on an army.

'You don't sound so good.' And suddenly I felt guilty, because I'd been running the pegasus for half a day, nonstop, trying to keep up with highway traffic. Even for a flying horse, that had to be rough.

Don't worry about me, boss! I'm a tough one.

I figured he was right, but I also figured Blackjack would run himself into the ground before he complained, and I didn't want that.

Fortunately, the van started to slow down. It crossed the Potomac River into central Washington. I started thinking about air patrols and missiles and stuff like that. I didn't know exactly how all those defences worked, and wasn't sure if pegasi even showed up on your typical military radar, but I didn't want to find out by getting shot out of the sky.

'Set me down there,' I told Blackjack. 'That's close enough.'

Blackjack was so tired he didn't complain. He dropped towards the Washington Monument and set me on the grass.

The van was only a few blocks away. Zoë had parked at the kerb.

I looked at Blackjack. 'I want you to go back to camp. Get some rest. Graze. I'll be fine.'

Blackjack cocked his head sceptically. *You sure, boss?*

'You've done enough already,' I said. 'I'll be fine. And thanks a ton.'

A ton of hay, maybe, Blackjack mused. *That sounds good. All right, but be careful, boss. I got a feeling they didn't come here to meet anything friendly and handsome like me.*

I promised to be careful. Then Blackjack took off, circling twice round the monument before disappearing into the clouds.

I looked over at the white van. Everybody was getting out. Grover pointed towards one of the big buildings lining the mall. Thalia nodded, and the four of them trudged off into the cold wind.

I started to follow. But then I froze.

A block away, the door of a black sedan opened. A man with a grey military haircut got out. He was wearing dark shades and a black overcoat. Now, maybe in Washington, you'd expected guys like that to be everywhere. But it dawned on me that I'd seen this same car a couple of times on the highway, going south. It had been following the van.

The guy took out his cell phone and said something into it. Then he looked around, like he was making sure the coast was clear, and started walking down the mall in the direction of my friends.

The worst of it was: when he turned towards me, I recognized his face. It was Dr Thorn, the manticore from Westover Hall.

* * *

Invisibility cap on, I followed Thorn from a distance. My heart was pounding. If *he* had survived that fall from the cliff, then Annabeth must have too. My dreams had been right. She was alive and being held prisoner.

Thorn kept well back from my friends, careful not to be seen.

Finally, Grover stopped in front of a big building that said AIR AND SPACE MUSEUM. The Smithsonian! I'd been here a million years ago with my mom, but everything had looked so much bigger then.

Thalia checked the door. It was open, but there weren't many people going in. Too cold, and it was school holidays. They slipped inside.

Dr Thorn hesitated. I wasn't sure why, but he didn't go into the museum. He turned and headed across the mall. I made a split-second decision and followed him.

Thorn crossed the street and climbed the steps of the Museum of Natural History. There was a big sign on the door. At first I thought it said CLOSED FOR PIRATE EVENT. Then I realized PIRATE must be PRIVATE.

I followed Dr Thorn inside, through a huge chamber full of mastodons and dinosaur skeletons. There were voices up ahead, coming from behind a set of closed doors. Two guards stood outside. They opened the doors for Thorn, and I had to sprint to get inside before they closed them again.

Inside, what I saw was so terrible I almost gasped out loud, which probably would've got me killed.

I was in a huge round room with a balcony ringing the second level. At least a dozen mortal guards stood on the balcony, plus two monsters – reptilian women with double-snake trunks instead of legs. I'd seen them before. Annabeth had called them *Scythian dracaenae.*

But that wasn't the worse of it. Standing between the snake women – I could swear he was looking straight down at me – was my old enemy Luke. He looked terrible. His skin was pale and his blond hair looked almost grey, as if he'd aged ten years in just a few months. The angry light in his eyes was still there, and so was the scar down the side of his face, where a dragon had once scratched him. But the scar was now ugly red, as though it had recently been reopened.

Next to him, sitting down so that the shadows covered him, was another man. All I could see were his knuckles on the gilded arms of the chair, like a throne.

'Well?' asked the man in the chair. His voice was just like the one I'd heard in my dream – not as creepy as Kronos's, but deeper and stronger, like the earth itself was talking. It filled the whole room even though he wasn't yelling.

Dr Thorn took off his shades. His two-coloured eyes, brown and blue, glittered with excitement. He made a stiff bow, then spoke in his weird French accent: 'They are here, General.'

'I know that, you fool,' boomed the man. 'But where?'

'In the rocket museum.'

'The Air and Space Museum,' Luke corrected irritably.

Dr Thorn glared at Luke. 'As you say, *sir*.'

I got the feeling Thorn would just as soon impale Luke with one of his spikes as call him sir.

'How many?' Luke asked.

Thorn pretended not to hear.

'How many?' the General demanded.

'Four, General,' Thorn said. 'The satyr, Grover Underwood. And the girl with the spiky black hair and the – how do you say – *punk* clothes, and the horrible shield.'

'Thalia,' Luke said.

'And two other girls – Hunters. One wears a silver circlet.'

'*That* one I know,' the General growled.

Everyone in the room shifted uncomfortably.

'Let me take them,' Luke said to the General. 'We have more than enough –'

'Patience,' the General said. 'They'll have their hands full already. I've sent a little playmate to keep them occupied.'

'But –'

'We cannot risk you, my boy.'

'Yes, *boy*,' Dr Thorn said with a cruel smile. 'You are much too fragile to risk. Let *me* finish them off.'

'No.' The General rose from his chair, and I got my first look at him.

He was tall and muscular, with light brown skin and slicked-back dark hair. He wore an expensive brown silk suit like the guys on Wall Street wear, but you'd never mistake this dude for a broker. He had a brutal face, huge shoulders, and hands that could snap a flagpole in half. His eyes were like stone. I felt as if I were looking at a living statue. It was amazing he could even move.

'You have already failed me, Thorn,' he said.

'But, General –'

'No excuses!'

Thorn flinched. I'd thought Thorn was scary when I first saw him in his black uniform at the military academy.

But now, standing before the General, Thorn looked like a silly wannabe soldier. The General was the real deal. He didn't need a uniform. He was a born commander.

'I should throw you into the pits of Tartarus for your incompetence,' the General said. 'I send you to capture a child of the three elder gods, and you bring me a scrawny daughter of Athena.'

'But you promised me revenge!' Thorn protested. 'A command of my own!'

'*I* am Lord Kronos's senior commander,' the General said. 'And I will choose lieutenants who get me results! It was only thanks to Luke that we salvaged our plan at all. Now get out of my sight, Thorn, until I find some other menial task for you.'

Thorn's face turned purple with rage. I thought he was going to start frothing at the mouth or shooting spines, but he just bowed awkwardly and left the room.

'Now, my boy.' The General turned to Luke. 'The first thing we must do is isolate the half-blood Thalia. The monster we seek will then come to her.'

'The Hunters will be difficult to dispose of,' Luke said. 'Zoë Nightshade –'

'Do not speak her name!'

Luke swallowed. 'S-sorry, General. I just –'

The General silenced him with a wave of his hand. 'Let me show you, my boy, how we will bring the Hunters down.'

He pointed to a guard on the ground level. 'Do you have the teeth?'

The guy stumbled forward with a ceramic pot. 'Yes, General!'

'Plant them,' he said.

In the centre of the room was a big circle of dirt, where I guess a dinosaur exhibit was supposed to go. I watched nervously as the guard took sharp white teeth out of the pot and pushed them into the soil. He smoothed them over while the General smiled coldly.

The guard stepped back from the dirt and wiped his hands. 'Ready, General!'

'Excellent! Water them, and we will let them scent their prey.'

The guard picked up a little tin watering can with daisies painted on it, which was kind of bizarre, because what he poured out wasn't water. It was dark red liquid, and I got the feeling it wasn't Hawaiian Punch.

The soil began to bubble.

'Soon,' the General said, 'I will show you, Luke, soldiers that will make your army from that little boat look insignificant.'

Luke clenched his fists. 'I've spent a year training my forces! When the *Princess Andromeda* arrives at the mountain, they'll be the best –'

'Ha!' the General said. 'I don't deny your troops will make a fine honour guard for Lord Kronos. And you, of course, will have a role to play –'

I thought Luke turned paler when the General said that.

'– but under my leadership, the forces of Lord Kronos will increase a hundredfold. We will be unstoppable. Behold, my ultimate killing machines.'

The soil erupted. I stepped back nervously.

In each spot where a tooth had been planted, a creature was struggling out of the dirt. The first of them said:

'Mew?'

It was a kitten. A little orange tabby with stripes like a tiger. Then another appeared, until there were a dozen, rolling around and playing in the dirt.

Everyone stared at them in disbelief. The General roared, '*What is this? Cute cuddly kittens? Where did you find those teeth?*'

The guard who'd brought the teeth cowered in fear. 'From the exhibit, sir! Just like you said. The saber-toothed tiger –'

'No, you idiot! I said the tyrannosaurus! Gather up those . . . those infernal fuzzy little beasts and take them outside. And never let me see your face again.'

The terrified guard dropped his watering can. He gathered up the kittens and scampered out of the room.

'You!' The General pointed to another guard. 'Get me the *right teeth. NOW!*'

The new guard ran off to carry out his orders.

'Imbeciles,' muttered the General.

'This is why I don't use mortals,' Luke said. 'They are unreliable.'

'They are weak-minded, easily bought and violent,' the General said. 'I love them.'

A minute later, the guard hustled into the room with his hands full of large pointy teeth.

'Excellent,' the General said. He climbed onto the balcony railing and jumped down, six metres.

Where he landed, the marble floor cracked under his leather shoes. He stood, wincing, and rubbed his shoulders. 'Curse my stiff neck.'

'Another hot pad, sir?' a guard asked. 'More Tylenol?'

'No! It will pass.' The General brushed off his silk suit, then snatched up the teeth. 'I shall do this myself.'

He held up one of the teeth and smiled. 'Dinosaur teeth – ha! Those foolish mortals don't even know when they have dragon teeth in their possession. And not just *any* dragon teeth. These come from the ancient Sybaris herself! They shall do nicely.'

He planted them in the dirt, twelve in all. Then he scooped up the watering can. He sprinkled the soil with red liquid, tossed the can away, and held his arms out wide. 'Rise!'

The dirt trembled. A single, skeletal hand shot out of the ground, grasping at the air.

The General looked up at the balcony. 'Quickly, do you have the scent?'

'Yesssss, lord,' one of the snake ladies said. She took out a sash of silvery fabric, like the kind the Hunters wore.

'Excellent,' the General said. 'Once my warriors catch its scent, they will pursue its owner relentlessly. Nothing can stop them, no weapons known to half-blood or Hunter. They will tear the Hunters and their allies to shreds. Toss it here!'

As he said that, skeletons erupted from the ground. There were twelve of them, one for each tooth the General had planted. They were nothing like Halloween skeletons, or the kind you might see in cheesy movies. These were growing flesh as I watched, turning into men, but men with dull grey skin, yellow eyes and modern clothes – skin-tight grey vests, camo trousers and combat boots. If you didn't look too closely, you could almost believe they were human, but their flesh was transparent and their bones shimmered underneath, like X-ray images.

One of them looked straight at me, regarding me coldly, and I knew that no cap of invisibility would fool it.

The snake lady released the scarf and it fluttered down towards the General's hand. As soon as he gave it to the warriors, they would hunt Zoë and the other Hunters until they were extinct.

I didn't have time to think. I ran and jumped with all my might, ploughing into the warriors and snatching the scarf out of the air.

'What's this?' bellowed the General.

I landed at the feet of a skeleton warrior, who hissed.

'An intruder,' the General growled. 'One cloaked in darkness. Seal the doors!'

'It's Percy Jackson!' Luke yelled. 'It has to be.'

I sprinted for the exit, but heard a ripping sound and realized the skeleton warrior had taken a chunk out of my sleeve. When I glanced back, he was holding the fabric up to his nose, sniffing the scent, handing it around to his friends. I wanted to scream but I couldn't. I squeezed through the door just as the guards slammed it shut behind me.

And then I ran.

10 I BREAK A FEW ROCKET SHIPS

I tore across the mall, not daring to look behind me. I burst into the Air and Space Museum and took off my invisibility cap once I was through the admissions area.

The main part of the museum was one huge room with rockets and aeroplanes hanging from the ceiling. Three levels of balconies curled round, so you could look at the exhibits from all different heights. The place wasn't crowded, just a few families and a couple of tour groups of kids, probably doing one of those holiday school trips. I wanted to yell at them all to leave, but I figured that would only get me arrested. I had to find Thalia and Grover and the Hunters. Any minute, the skeleton dudes were going to invade the museum, and I didn't think they would settle for an audio tour.

I ran into Thalia – literally. I was barrelling up the ramp to the top-floor balcony and slammed into her, knocking her into an Apollo space capsule.

Grover yelped in surprise.

Before I could regain my balance, Zoë and Bianca had arrows notched, aimed at my chest. Their bows had just appeared out of nowhere.

When Zoë realized who I was, she didn't seem anxious to lower her bow. 'You! How dare you show thy face here?'

'Percy!' Grover said. 'Thank goodness.'

Zoë glared at him, and he blushed. 'I mean, um, gosh. You're not supposed to be here!'

'Luke,' I said, trying to catch my breath. 'He's here.'

The anger in Thalia's eyes immediately melted. She put her hand on her silver bracelet. 'Where?'

I told them about the Natural History Museum, Dr Thorn, Luke and the General.

'The General is *here*?' Zoë looked stunned. 'That is impossible! You lie.'

'Why would I lie? Look, there's no time. Skeleton warriors –'

'*What?*' Thalia demanded. 'How many?'

'Twelve,' I said. 'And that's not all. That guy, the General, he said he was sending something, a "playmate", to distract you over here. A monster.'

Thalia and Grover exchanged looks.

'We were following Artemis's trail,' Grover said. 'I was pretty sure it led here. Some powerful monster scent . . . She must've stopped here looking for the mystery monster. But we haven't found anything yet.'

'Zoë,' Bianca said nervously, 'if it *is* the General –'

'It *cannot* be!' Zoë snapped. 'Percy must have seen an Iris-message or some other illusion.'

'Illusions don't crack marble floors,' I told her.

Zoë took a deep breath, trying to calm herself. I didn't know why she was taking it so personally, or how she knew this General guy, but I figured now wasn't the time to ask.

'If Percy is telling the truth about the skeleton warriors,' she said, 'we have no time to argue. They are the worst, the most horrible . . . We must leave now.'

'Good idea,' I said.

'I was *not* including thee, boy,' Zoë said. 'You are not part of this quest.'

'Hey, I'm trying to save your lives!'

'You shouldn't have come, Percy,' Thalia said grimly. 'But you're here now. Come on. Let's get back to the van.'

'That is not thy decision!' Zoë snapped.

Thalia scowled at her. 'You're not the boss here, Zoë. I don't care how old you are! You're still a conceited little brat!'

'You never had any wisdom when it came to boys,' Zoë growled. 'You never could leave them behind!'

Thalia looked like she was about to hit Zoë. Then everyone froze. I heard a growl so loud I thought one of the rocket engines was starting up.

Below us, a few adults screamed. A little kid's voice screeched with delight: 'Kitty!'

Something enormous bounded up the ramp. It was the size of a pick-up truck, with silver claws and golden glittering fur. I'd seen this monster once before. Two years ago, I'd glimpsed it briefly from a train. Now, up close and personal, it looked even bigger.

'The Nemean Lion,' Thalia said. 'Don't move.'

The lion roared so loudly he parted my hair. His fangs gleamed like stainless steel.

'Separate on my mark,' Zoë said. 'Try to keep it distracted.'

'Until when?' Grover asked.

'Until I think of a way to kill it. Go!'

I uncapped Riptide and rolled to the left. Arrows whistled past me, and Grover played a sharp *tweet-tweet* cadence on his reed pipes. I turned and saw Zoë and Bianca climbing the Apollo capsule. They were firing arrows, one after another, all shattering harmlessly against the lion's metallic fur. The lion swiped the capsule and tipped it on its side, spilling the Hunters off the back. Grover played a frantic, horrible tune, and the lion turned towards him, but Thalia stepped into its path, holding up Aegis, and the lion recoiled. '*ROOOAAAR!*'

'Hi-yah!' Thalia said. 'Back!'

The lion growled and clawed the air, but it retreated as if the shield were a blazing fire.

For a second, I thought Thalia had it under control. Then I saw the lion crouching, its leg muscles tensing. I'd seen enough cat fights in the alleys around my apartment in New York. I knew the lion was going to pounce.

'Hey!' I yelled. I don't know what I was thinking, but I charged the beast. I just wanted to get it away from my friends. I slashed with Riptide, a good strike to the flank that should've cut the monster into Meow Mix, but the blade just clanged against its fur in a burst of sparks.

The lion raked me with its claws, ripping off a chunk of my coat. I backed against the railing. It sprang at me, half a ton of monster, and I had no choice but to turn and jump.

I landed on the wing of an old-fashioned silver aeroplane, which pitched and almost spilled me to the floor, three stories below.

An arrow whizzed past my head. The lion jumped onto the aeroplane, and the cords holding it began to groan.

The lion swiped at me, and I dropped onto the next exhibit, a weird-looking spacecraft with blades like a helicopter. I looked up and saw the lion roar – inside its maw, a pink tongue and throat.

Its mouth, I thought. Its fur was completely invulnerable, but if I could strike it in the mouth . . . The only problem was the monster moved too quickly. Between its claws and fangs, I couldn't get close without getting sliced to pieces.

'Zoë!' I shouted. 'Target the mouth!'

The monster lunged. An arrow zipped past it, missing completely, and I dropped from the spaceship onto the top of a floor exhibit, a huge model of the earth. I slid down Russia and dropped off the equator.

The Nemean Lion growled and steadied itself on the spacecraft, but its weight was too much. One of the cords snapped. As the display swung down like a pendulum, the lion leaped off onto the model earth's North Pole.

'Grover!' I yelled. 'Clear the area!'

Groups of kids were running around screaming. Grover tried to corral them away from the monster just as the other cord on the spaceship snapped and the exhibit crashed to the floor. Thalia dropped off the second-floor railing and landed across from me, on the other side of the globe. The lion regarded us both, trying to decide which of us to kill first.

Zoë and Bianca were above us, bows ready, but they kept having to move around to get a good angle.

'No clear shot!' Zoë yelled. 'Get it to open its mouth more!'

The lion snarled from the top of the globe.

I looked around. *Options.* I needed . . .

The gift shop. I had a vague memory from my trip

here as a little kid. Something I'd made my mom buy me, and I'd regretted it. If they still sold that stuff . . .

'Thalia,' I said, 'keep it occupied.'

She nodded grimly.

'Hi-yah!' She pointed her spear and a spidery arc of blue electricity shot out, zapping the lion in the tail.

'*ROOOOOOOAR!*' The lion turned and pounced. Thalia rolled out of its way, holding up Aegis to keep the monster at bay, and I ran for the gift shop.

'This is no time for souvenirs, boy!' Zoë yelled.

I dashed into the shop, knocking over rows of T-shirts, jumping over tables full of glow-in-the-dark planets and space ooze. The sales lady didn't protest. She was too busy cowering behind her cash register.

There! On the far wall – glittery silver packets. Whole racks of them. I scooped up every kind I could find and ran out of the shop with an armful.

Zoë and Bianca were still showering arrows on the monster, but it was no good. The lion seemed to know better than to open its mouth too much. It snapped at Thalia, slashing with its claws. It even kept its eyes narrowed to tiny slits.

Thalia jabbed at the monster and backed up. The lion pressed her.

'Percy,' she called, 'whatever you're going to do –'

The lion roared and swatted her like a cat toy, sending her flying into the side of a Titan rocket. Her head hit the metal and she slid to the floor.

'Hey!' I yelled at the lion. I was too far away to strike, so I took a risk: I hurled Riptide like a throwing knife. It bounced off the lion's side, but that was enough to get the monster's attention. It turned towards me and snarled.

There was only one way to get close enough. I charged and, as the lion leaped to intercept me, I chucked a space-food pouch into its maw – a chunk of cellophane-wrapped freeze-dried strawberry parfait.

The lion's eyes got wide and it gagged like a cat with a hairball.

I couldn't blame it. I remembered feeling the same way when I'd tried to eat space food as a kid. The stuff was just plain nasty.

'Zoë, get ready!' I yelled.

Behind me, I could hear people screaming. Grover was playing another horrible song on his pipes.

I scrambled away from the lion. It managed to choke down the space-food packet and looked at me with pure hate.

'Snack time!' I yelled.

It made the mistake of roaring at me, and I got an ice-cream sandwich in its throat. Fortunately, I had always been a pretty good pitcher, even though baseball wasn't my game. Before the lion could stop gagging, I shot in two more flavours of ice cream and a freeze-dried spaghetti dinner.

The lion's eyes bugged. It opened its mouth wide and reared up on its back paws, trying to get away from me.

'Now!' I yelled.

Immediately, arrows sprouted from the lion's maw – two, four, six. The lion thrashed wildly, turned and fell backwards. And then it was still.

Alarms wailed throughout the museum. People were flocking to the exits. Security guards were running around in a panic with no idea what was going on.

Grover knelt at Thalia's side and helped her up. She seemed okay, just a little dazed. Zoë and Bianca dropped from the balcony and landed next to me.

Zoë eyed me cautiously. 'That was . . . an interesting strategy.'

'Hey, it worked.'

She didn't argue.

The lion seemed to be melting, the way dead monsters do sometimes, until there was nothing left but its glittering fur coat, and even that seemed to be shrinking to the size of a normal lion's pelt.

'Take it,' Zoë told me.

I stared at her. 'What, the lion's fur? Isn't that, like, an animal-rights violation or something?'

'It is a spoil of war,' she told me. 'It is rightly thine.'

'You killed it,' I said.

She shook her head, almost smiling. 'I think thy ice-cream sandwich did that. Fair is fair, Percy Jackson. Take the fur.'

I lifted it up; it was surprisingly light. The fur was smooth and soft. It didn't feel at all like something that could stop a blade. As I watched, the pelt shifted and changed into a full-length golden-brown coat.

'Not exactly my style,' I murmured.

'We have to get out of here,' Grover said. 'The security guards won't stay confused for long.'

I noticed for the first time how strange it was that the guards hadn't rushed forward to arrest us. They were scrambling in all directions except ours, like they were madly searching for something. A few were running into the walls or each other.

'You did that?' I asked Grover.

He nodded, looking a little embarrassed. 'A minor confusion song. I played some Barry Manilow. It works every time. But it'll only last a few seconds.'

'The security guards are not our biggest worry,' Zoë said. 'Look.'

Through the glass walls of the museum, I could see a group of men walking across the lawn. Grey men in grey camouflage outfits. They were too far away for us to see their eyes, but I could feel their gaze aimed straight at me.

'Go,' I said. 'They'll be hunting me. I'll distract them.'

'No,' Zoë said. 'We go together.'

I stared at her. 'But you said –'

'You are part of this quest now,' Zoë said grudgingly. 'I do not like it, but there is no changing fate. *You* are the fifth quest member. And we are not leaving anyone behind.'

11 GROVER GETS A LAMBORGHINI

We were crossing the Potomac when we spotted the helicopter. It was a sleek black military model just like the one we'd seen at Westover Hall. And it was coming straight towards us.

'They know the van,' I said. 'We have to ditch it.'

Zoë swerved into the fast lane. The helicopter was gaining.

'Maybe the military will shoot it down,' Grover said hopefully.

'The military probably thinks it's one of theirs,' I said. 'How can the General use mortals, anyway?'

'Mercenaries,' Zoë said bitterly. 'It is distasteful, but many mortals will fight for any cause as long as they are paid.'

'But don't these mortals see who they're working for?' I asked. 'Don't they notice all the monsters around them?'

Zoë shook her head. 'I do not know how much they see through the Mist. I doubt it would matter to them if they knew the truth. Sometimes mortals can be more horrible than monsters.'

The helicopter kept coming, making a lot better time than we were through D.C. traffic.

Thalia closed her eyes and prayed hard. 'Hey, Dad. A lightning bolt would be nice about now. Please?'

But the sky stayed grey and snowy. No sign of a helpful thunderstorm.

'There!' Bianca said. 'That parking lot!'

'We'll be trapped,' Zoë said.

'Trust me,' Bianca said.

Zoë shot across two lanes of traffic and into a mall parking lot on the south bank of the river. We left the van and followed Bianca down some steps.

'Subway entrance,' Bianca said. 'Let's go south. Alexandria.'

'Anything,' Thalia agreed.

We bought tickets and got through the turnstiles, looking behind us for any signs of pursuit. A few minutes later we were safely aboard a southbound train, riding away from D.C. As our train came above ground, we could see the helicopter circling the parking lot, but it didn't come after us.

Grover let out a sigh. 'Nice job, Bianca, thinking of the subway.'

Bianca looked pleased. 'Yeah, well. I remembered that station from when Nico and I came through last summer. I was really surprised to see it, because it wasn't here when we used to live in D.C.'

Grover frowned. 'New? But that station looked really old.'

'I guess,' Bianca said. 'But trust me, when we lived here as little kids, there was no subway.'

Thalia sat forward. 'Wait a minute. No subway at all?'

Bianca nodded.

Now, I knew nothing about D.C., but I didn't see how their whole subway system could be less than twelve years old. I guess everyone else was thinking the same thing, because they looked pretty confused.

'Bianca,' Zoë said. 'How long ago . . .' Her voice faltered. The sound of the helicopter was getting louder again.

'We need to change trains,' I said. 'Next station.'

Over the next half hour, all we thought about was getting away safely. We changed trains twice. I had no idea where we were going, but after a while we lost the helicopter.

Unfortunately, when we finally got off the train we found ourselves at the end of the line, in an industrial area with nothing but warehouses and railway tracks. And snow. Lots of snow. It seemed much colder here. I was glad of my new lion-fur coat.

We wandered through the railway yard, thinking there might be another passenger train somewhere, but there were just rows and rows of freight cars, most of which were covered in snow, like they hadn't moved in years.

A homeless guy was standing at a trashcan fire. We must've looked pretty pathetic, because he gave us a toothless grin and said, 'Y'all need to get warmed up? Come on over!'

We huddled round his fire. Thalia's teeth were chattering. She said, 'Well this is g-g-g-great.'

'My hooves are frozen,' Grover complained.

'*Feet*,' I corrected, for the sake of the homeless guy.

'Maybe we should contact camp,' Bianca said. 'Chiron –'

'No,' Zoë said. 'They cannot help us any more. We must finish this quest ourselves.'

I gazed miserably around the railway yard. Somewhere, far to the west, Annabeth was in danger. Artemis was in chains. A doomsday monster was on the loose. And we were stuck on the outskirts of D.C. sharing a homeless person's fire.

'You know,' the homeless man said, 'you're never completely without friends.' His face was grimy and his beard tangled, but his expression seemed kindly. 'You kids need a train going west?'

'Yes, sir,' I said. 'You know of any?'

He pointed one greasy hand.

Suddenly I noticed a freight train, gleaming and free of snow. It was one of those automobile-carrier trains, with steel mesh curtains and a triple-deck of cars inside. The side of the freight train said SUN WEST LINE.

'That's . . . convenient,' Thalia said. 'Thanks, uh . . .'

She turned to the homeless guy, but he was gone. The trashcan in front of us was cold and empty, as if he'd taken the flames with him.

An hour later we were rumbling west. There was no problem about who would drive now, because we all got our own luxury car. Zoë and Bianca were crashed out in a Lexus on the top deck. Grover was playing race-car driver behind the wheel of a Lamborghini. And Thalia had hot-wired the radio in a black Mercedes SLK so she could pick up the alt rock stations from D.C.

'Join you?' I asked her.

She shrugged, so I climbed into the shotgun seat.

The radio was playing the White Stripes. I knew the song because it was one of the only CDs I owned that my mom liked. She said it reminded her of Led Zeppelin. Thinking about my mom made me sad, because it didn't seem likely I'd be home for Christmas. I might not live that long.

'Nice coat,' Thalia told me.

I pulled it round me, thankful for the warmth. 'Yeah,

but the Nemean Lion wasn't the monster we're looking for.'

'Not even close. We've got a long way to go.'

'Whatever this mystery monster is, the General said it would come for you. They wanted to isolate you from the group, so the monster will appear and battle you one on one.'

'He said that?'

'Well, something like that. Yeah.'

'That's great. I love being used as bait.'

'No idea what the monster might be?'

She shook her head morosely. 'But you know where we're going, don't you? San Francisco. That's where Artemis was heading.'

I remembered something Annabeth had said at the dance: how her dad was moving to San Francisco, and there was no way she could go. Half-bloods couldn't live there.

'Why?' I asked. 'What's so bad about San Francisco?'

'The Mist is really thick there because the Mountain of Despair is so near. Titan magic – what's left of it – still lingers. Monsters are attracted to that area like you wouldn't believe.'

'What's the Mountain of Despair?'

Thalia raised an eyebrow. 'You really don't know? Ask stupid Zoë. She's the expert.'

She glared out the windshield. I wanted to ask her what she was talking about, but I also didn't want to sound like an idiot. I hated feeling like Thalia knew more than I did, so I kept my mouth shut.

The afternoon sun shone through the steel-mesh side of the freight car, casting a shadow across Thalia's face. I thought about how different she was from Zoë – Zoë all formal and aloof like a princess, Thalia with her ratty clothes and her rebel attitude. But there was something similar about them, too. The same kind of toughness. Right now, sitting in the shadows with a gloomy expression, Thalia looked a lot like one of the Hunters.

Then suddenly it hit me: 'That's why you don't get along with Zoë.'

Thalia frowned. 'What?'

'The Hunters tried to recruit you,' I guessed.

Her eyes got dangerously bright. I thought she was going to zap me out of the Mercedes, but she just sighed.

'I almost joined them,' she admitted. 'Luke, Annabeth and I ran into them once, and Zoë tried to convince me. She almost did, but . . .'

'But?'

Thalia's fingers gripped the wheel. 'I would've had to leave Luke.'

'Oh.'

'Zoë and I got into a fight. She told me I was being stupid. She said I'd regret my choice. She said Luke would let me down some day.'

I watched the sun through the metal curtain. We seemed to be travelling faster each second – shadows flickering like an old movie projector.

'That's harsh,' I said. 'Hard to admit Zoë was right.'

'She *wasn't* right! Luke *never* let me down. Never.'

'We'll have to fight him,' I said. 'There's no way around it.'

Thalia didn't answer.

'You haven't seen him lately,' I warned. 'I know it's hard to believe, but –'

'I'll do what I have to.'

'Even if that means killing him?'

'Do me a favour,' she said. 'Get out of my car.'

I felt so bad for her I didn't argue.

As I was about to leave, she said, 'Percy.'

When I looked back, her eyes were red, but I couldn't tell if it was from anger or sadness. 'Annabeth wanted to join the Hunters, too. Maybe you should think about why.'

Before I could respond, she raised the power windows and shut me out.

I sat in the driver's seat of Grover's Lamborghini. Grover was asleep in the back. He'd finally given up trying to impress Zoë and Bianca with his pipe music after he played 'Poison Ivy' and caused that very stuff to sprout from their Lexus' air conditioner.

As I watched the sun go down, I thought of Annabeth. I was afraid to go to sleep. I was worried what I might dream.

'Oh, don't be afraid of dreams,' a voice said right next me.

I looked over. Somehow, I wasn't surprised to find the homeless guy from the railway yard sitting in the shotgun seat. His jeans were so worn out they were almost white. His coat was ripped, with stuffing coming out. He looked kind of like a teddy bear that had been run over by a truck.

'If it weren't for dreams,' he said, 'I wouldn't know half the things I know about the future. They're better than Olympus tabloids.' He cleared his throat, then held up his hands dramatically:

'Dreams like a podcast,
Downloading truth in my ears.
They tell me cool stuff.'

'Apollo?' I guessed, because I figured nobody else could make a haiku that bad.

He put his finger to his lips. 'I'm incognito. Call me Fred.'

'A god named Fred?'

'Eh, well . . . Zeus insists on certain rules. Hands off, when there's a human quest. Even when something really major is wrong. But nobody messes with my baby sister. *Nobody.*'

'Can you help us, then?'

'Shhh. I already have. Haven't you been looking outside?'

'The train. How fast are we moving?'

Apollo chuckled. 'Fast enough. Unfortunately, we're running out of time. It's almost sunset. But I imagine we'll get you across a good chunk of America, at least.'

'But where is Artemis?'

His face darkened. 'I know a lot, and I see a lot. But even I don't know that. She's . . . clouded from me. I don't like it.'

'And Annabeth?'

He frowned. 'Oh, you mean that girl you lost? Hmm. I don't know.'

I tried not to feel mad. I knew the gods had a hard time taking mortals seriously, even half-bloods. We lived such short lives, compared to the gods.

'What about the monster Artemis was seeking?' I asked. 'Do you know what it is?'

'No,' Apollo said. 'But there is one who might. If you haven't yet found the monster when you reach San Francisco, seek out Nereus, the old man of the sea. He has a long memory and a sharp eye. He has the gift of knowledge sometimes kept obscure from my Oracle.'

'But it's *your* Oracle,' I protested. 'Can't you tell us what the prophecy means?'

Apollo sighed. 'You might as well ask an artist to explain his art, or ask a poet to explain his poem. It defeats the purpose. The meaning is only clear through the search.'

'In other words, you don't know.'

Apollo checked his watch. 'Ah, look at the time! I have to run. I doubt I can risk helping you again, Percy, but remember what I said! Get some sleep! And when you return, I expect a good haiku about your journey!'

I wanted to protest that I wasn't tired and I'd never made up a haiku in my life, but Apollo snapped his fingers, and the next thing I knew I was closing my eyes.

In my dream, I was somebody else. I was wearing an old-fashioned Greek tunic, which was a little too breezy downstairs, and laced leather sandals. The Nemean Lion's skin was wrapped round my back like a cape, and I was running somewhere, being pulled along by a girl who was gripping my hand tightly.

'Hurry!' she said. It was too dark to see her face clearly, but I could hear the fear in her voice. 'He will find us!'

It was night-time. A million stars blazed above. We were running through tall grass, and the scent of a thousand different flowers made the air intoxicating. It was a beautiful garden, and yet the girl was leading me through it as if we were about to die.

'I'm not afraid,' I tried to tell her.

'You should be!' she said, pulling me along. She had long dark hair braided down her back. Her silk robes glowed faintly in the starlight.

We raced up the side of the hill. She pulled me behind a thorn bush and we collapsed, both breathing heavily. I didn't know why the girl was scared. The garden seemed so peaceful. And I felt strong. Stronger than I'd ever felt before.

'There is no need to run,' I told her. My voice sounded deeper, much more confident. 'I have bested a thousand monsters with my bare hands.'

'Not this one,' the girl said. 'Ladon is too strong. You must go round, up the mountain to my father. It is the only way.'

The hurt in her voice surprised me. She was really concerned, almost like she cared about me.

'I don't trust your father,' I said.

'You should not,' the girl agreed. 'You will have to trick him. But you cannot take the prize directly. You will die!'

I chuckled. 'Then why don't you help me, pretty one?'

'I . . . I am afraid. Ladon will stop me. My sisters, if they found out . . . they would disown me.'

'Then there's nothing for it.' I stood up, rubbing my hands together.

'Wait!' the girl said.

She seemed to be agonizing over a decision. Then, her fingers trembling, she reached up and plucked a long white brooch from her hair. 'If you must fight, take this. My mother, Pleoine, gave it to me. She was a daughter of the ocean, and the ocean's power is within it. *My* immortal power.'

The girl breathed on the pin and it glowed faintly. It gleamed in the starlight like polished abalone.

'Take it,' she told me. 'And make of it a weapon.'

I laughed. 'A hairpin? How will this slay Ladon, pretty one?'

'It may not,' she admitted. 'But it is all I can offer, if you insist on being stubborn.'

The girl's voice softened my heart. I reached down and took the hairpin, and, as I did, it grew longer and heavier in my hand, until I held a familiar bronze sword.

'Well balanced,' I said. 'Though, I usually prefer to use my bare hands. What shall I name this blade?'

'Anaklusmos,' the girl said sadly. 'The current that takes one by surprise. And before you know it you have been swept out to sea.'

Before I could thank her, there was a trampling sound in the grass, a hiss like air escaping a tyre, and the girl said, 'Too late! He is here!'

I sat bolt upright in the Lamborghini's driver seat. Grover was shaking my arm.

'Percy,' he said. 'It's morning. The train's stopped. Come on!'

I tried to shake off my drowsiness. Thalia, Zoë and Bianca had already rolled up the metal curtains. Outside were snowy mountains dotted with pine trees, the sun rising red between two peaks.

I fished my pen out of my pocket and stared at it.

Anaklusmos, the Ancient Greek name for Riptide. A different form, but I was sure it was the same blade I'd seen in my dream.

And I was sure of something else, too. The girl I had seen was Zoë Nightshade.

12 I GO SNOWBOARDING WITH A PIG

We'd arrived on the outskirts of a little ski town nestled in the mountains. The sign said WELCOME TO CLOUDCROFT, NEW MEXICO. The air was cold and thin. The roofs of the cabins were heaped with snow, and dirty mounds of it were piled up on the sides of the streets. Tall pine trees loomed over the valley, casting pitch-black shadows, though the morning was sunny.

Even with my lion-skin coat, I was freezing by the time we got to Main Street, which was about half a mile from the train tracks. As we walked, I told Grover about my conversation with Apollo the night before – how he'd told me to seek out Nereus in San Francisco.

Grover looked uneasy. 'That's good, I guess. But we've got to get there first.'

I tried not to get too depressed about our chances. I didn't want to send Grover into a panic, but I knew we had another huge deadline looming, aside from saving Artemis in time for her council of the gods. The General had said Annabeth would only be kept alive until the winter solstice. That was Friday, only four days away. And he'd said something about a sacrifice. I didn't like the sound of that at all.

We stopped in the middle of town. You could pretty much see everything from there: a school, a bunch of tourist stores and cafés, some ski cabins, and a grocery store.

'Great,' Thalia said, looking around. 'No bus station. No taxis. No car rental. No way out.'

'There's a coffee shop!' said Grover.

'Yes,' Zoë said. 'Coffee is good.'

'And pastries,' Grover said dreamily. 'And wax paper.'

Thalia sighed. 'Fine. How about you two go get us some food. Percy, Bianca and I will check in the grocery store. Maybe they can give us directions.'

We agreed to meet back in front of the grocery store in fifteen minutes. Bianca looked a little uncomfortable coming with us, but she did.

Inside the store, we found out a few valuable things about Cloudcroft: there wasn't enough snow for skiing, the grocery store sold rubber rats for a dollar each, and there was no easy way in or out of town unless you had your own car.

'You could call for a taxi from Alamogordo,' the clerk said doubtfully. 'That's down at the bottom of the mountains, but it would take at least an hour to get here. Cost several hundred dollars.'

The clerk looked so lonely, I bought a rubber rat. Then we headed back outside and stood on the porch.

'Wonderful,' Thalia grumped. 'I'm going to walk down the street, see if anybody in the other shops has a suggestion.'

'But the clerk said –'

'I know,' she told me. 'I'm checking anyway.'

I let her go. I knew how it felt to be restless. All half-bloods had attention deficit problems because of our inborn battlefield reflexes. We couldn't stand just waiting around. Also, I had a feeling Thalia was still upset over our conversation last night about Luke.

Bianca and I stood together awkwardly. I mean . . . I was never very comfortable talking one on one with girls anyway, and I'd never been alone with Bianca before. I wasn't sure what to say, especially now that she was a Hunter and everything.

'Nice rat,' she said at last.

I set it on the porch railing. Maybe it would attract more business for the store.

'So . . . how do you like being a Hunter so far?' I asked.

She pursed her lips. 'You're not still mad at me for joining, are you?'

'Nah. Long as, you know . . . you're happy.'

'I'm not sure "happy" is the right word, with Lady Artemis gone. But being a Hunter is definitely cool. I feel calmer somehow. Everything seems to have slowed down around me. I guess that's the immortality.'

I stared at her, trying to see the difference. She did seem more confident than before, more at peace. She didn't hide her face under a green cap any more. She kept her hair tied back, and she looked me right in the eyes when she spoke. With a shiver, I realized that five hundred or a thousand years from now Bianca di Angelo would look exactly the same as she did today. She might be having a conversation like this with some other half-blood, long after I was dead, but Bianca would still look twelve years old.

'Nico didn't understand my decision,' Bianca murmured. She looked at me like she wanted assurance it was okay.

'He'll be all right,' I said. 'Camp Half-Blood takes in a lot of young kids. They did that for Annabeth.'

Bianca nodded. 'I hope we find her. Annabeth, I mean. She's lucky to have a friend like you.'

'Lot of good it did her.'

'Don't blame yourself, Percy. You risked your life to save my brother and me. I mean, that was seriously brave. If I hadn't met you, I wouldn't have felt okay about leaving Nico at the camp. I figured if there were people like you there, Nico would be fine. You're a good guy.'

The compliment took me by surprise. 'Even though I knocked you down in capture the flag?'

She laughed. 'Okay. Except for that, you're a good guy.'

Two hundred metres away, Grover and Zoë came out of the coffee shop loaded down with pastry bags and drinks. I kind of didn't want them to come back yet. It was weird, but I realized I liked talking to Bianca. She wasn't so bad. A lot easier to hang out with than Zoë Nightshade, anyway.

'So what's the story with you and Nico?' I asked her. 'Where did you go to school before Westover?'

She frowned. 'I think it was a boarding school in D.C. It seems like so long ago.'

'You never lived with your parents? I mean, your mortal parent?'

'We were told our parents were dead. There was a bank trust for us. A lot of money, I think. A lawyer would come by once in a while to check on us. Then Nico and I had to leave that school.'

'Why?'

She knitted her eyebrows. 'We had to go somewhere. I remember it was important. We travelled a long way. And we stayed in this hotel for a few weeks. And then . . . I don't know. One day a different lawyer came to get us out. He said it was time for us to leave. He drove us back east, through D.C. Then up into Maine. And we started going to Westover.'

It was a strange story. Then again, Bianca and Nico were half-bloods. Nothing would be normal for them.

'So you've been raising Nico pretty much all your life?' I asked. 'Just the two of you?'

She nodded. 'That's why I wanted to join the Hunters so badly. I mean, I know it's selfish, but I wanted my own life and friends. I love Nico – don't get me wrong – I just needed to find out what it would be like not to be a big sister twenty-four hours a day.'

I thought about last summer, the way I'd felt when I found out I had a Cyclops for a baby brother. I could relate to what Bianca was saying.

'Zoë seems to trust you,' I said. 'What were you guys talking about, anyway – something dangerous about the quest?'

'When?'

'Yesterday morning on the pavilion,' I said, before I could stop myself. 'Something about the General.'

Her face darkened. 'How did you . . . The invisibility hat. Were you eavesdropping?'

'No! I mean, not really. I just –'

I was saved from trying to explain when Zoë and Grover arrived with the drinks and pastries. Hot chocolate for Bianca and me. Coffee for them. I got a blueberry muffin, and it was so good I could almost ignore the outraged look Bianca was giving me.

'We should do the tracking spell,' Zoë said. 'Grover, do you have any acorns left?'

'Umm,' Grover mumbled. He was chewing on a bran muffin, wrapper and all. 'I think so. I just need to –'

He froze.

I was about to ask what was wrong when a warm breeze rustled past, like a gust of springtime had got lost in the middle of winter. Fresh air seasoned with wildflowers and sunshine. And something else – almost like a voice, trying to say something. A warning.

Zoë gasped. 'Grover, thy cup.'

Grover dropped his coffee cup, which was decorated with pictures of birds. Suddenly the birds peeled off the cup and flew away – a tiny flock of doves. My rubber rat squeaked. It scampered off the railing and into the trees – real fur, real whiskers.

Grover collapsed next to his coffee, which steamed against the snow. We gathered round him and tried to wake him up. He groaned, his eyes fluttering.

'Hey!' Thalia said, running up from the street. 'I just . . . What's wrong with Grover?'

'I don't know,' I said. 'He collapsed.'

'Uuuuuhhhh,' Grover groaned.

'Well, get him up!' Thalia said. She had her spear in her hand. She looked behind her as if she were being followed. 'We have to get out of here.'

We made it to the edge of the town before the first two skeleton warriors appeared. They stepped from the trees on either side of the road. Instead of grey camouflage, they were now wearing blue New Mexico State Police uniforms, but they had the same transparent grey skin and yellow eyes.

They drew their handguns. I'll admit I used to think it would be kind of cool to learn how to shoot a gun, but I changed my mind as soon as the skeleton warriors pointed theirs at me.

Thalia tapped her bracelet. Aegis spiralled to life on her arm, but the warriors didn't flinch. Their glowing yellow eyes bored right into me.

I drew Riptide, though I wasn't sure what good it would do against guns.

Zoë and Bianca drew their bows, but Bianca was having trouble because Grover kept swooning and leaning against her.

'Back up,' Thalia said.

We started to – but then I heard a rustling of branches. Two more skeletons appeared on the road behind us. We were surrounded.

I wondered where the other skeletons were. I'd seen a dozen at the Smithsonian. Then one of the warriors raised a cell phone to his mouth and spoke into it.

Except he wasn't speaking. He made a clattering, clicking sound, like dry teeth on bone. Suddenly I understood what was going on. The skeletons had split up to look for us. These skeletons were now calling their brethren. Soon we'd have a full party on our hands.

'It's near,' Grover moaned.

'It's here,' I said.

'No,' he insisted. 'The gift. The gift from the Wild.'

I didn't know what he was talking about, but I was worried about his condition. He was in no shape to walk, much less fight.

'We'll have to go one on one,' Thalia said. 'Four of them. Four of us. Maybe they'll ignore Grover that way.'

'Agreed,' said Zoë.

'The Wild!' Grover moaned.

A warm wind blew through the canyon, rustling the trees, but I kept my eyes on the skeletons. I remembered the General gloating over Annabeth's fate. I remembered the way Luke had betrayed her.

And I charged.

The first skeleton fired. Time slowed down. I won't say I could see the bullet, but I could feel its path, the same way I felt water currents in the ocean. I deflected it off the edge of my blade and kept charging.

The skeleton drew a baton and I sliced off his arms at the elbows. Then I swung Riptide through his waist and cut him in half.

His bones unknitted and clattered to the tarmac in a heap. Almost immediately, they began to move, reassembling themselves. The second skeleton clattered his teeth at me and tried to fire, but I knocked his gun into the snow.

I thought I was doing pretty well, until the other two skeletons shot me in the back.

'Percy!' Thalia screamed.

I landed facedown in the street. Then I realized something . . . I wasn't dead. The impact of the bullets had been dull, like a push from behind, but they hadn't hurt me.

The Nemean Lion's fur! My coat was bulletproof.

Thalia charged the second skeleton. Zoë and Bianca started firing arrows at the third and fourth. Grover stood there and held his hands out to the trees, looking like he wanted to hug them.

There was a crashing sound in the forest to our left, like a bulldozer. Maybe the skeletons' reinforcements were arriving. I got to my feet and ducked a police baton. The skeleton I'd cut in half was already fully re-formed, coming after me.

There was no way to stop them. Zoë and Bianca fired at their heads point-blank, but the arrows just whistled straight through their empty skulls. One lunged at Bianca, and I thought she was a goner, but she whipped out her hunting knife and stabbed the warrior in the chest. The whole skeleton erupted into flames, leaving a little pile of ashes and a police badge.

'How did you do that?' Zoë asked.

'I don't know,' Bianca said nervously. 'Lucky shot?'

'Well, do it again!'

Bianca tried, but the remaining three skeletons were wary of her now. They pressed us back, keeping us at baton's length.

'Plan?' I said as we retreated.

Nobody answered. The trees behind the skeletons were shivering. Branches were cracking.

'A gift,' Grover muttered.

And then, with a mighty roar, the largest pig I'd ever seen came crashing into the road. It was a wild boar, ten metres high, with a snotty pink snout and tusks the size of canoes. Its back bristled with brown hair, and its eyes were wild and angry.

'*REEEEEEEEET!*' it squealed, and raked the three skeletons aside with its tusks. The force was so great they went flying over the trees and into the side of the mountain, where they smashed to pieces, thigh bones and arm bones twirling everywhere.

Then the pig turned on us.

Thalia raised her spear, but Grover yelled, 'Don't kill it!'

The boar grunted and pawed the ground, ready to charge.

'That's the Erymanthian Boar,' Zoë said, trying to stay calm. 'I don't think we *can* kill it.'

'It's a gift,' Grover said. 'A blessing from the Wild!'

The boar said *'REEEEEET!'* and swung its tusk. Zoë and Bianca dived out of the way. I had to push Grover so he wouldn't get launched into the mountain on the Boar Tusk Express.

'Yeah, I feel blessed!' I said. 'Scatter!'

We ran in different directions, and for a moment the boar was confused.

'It wants to kill us!' Thalia said.

'Of course,' Grover said. 'It's wild!'

'So how is that a blessing?' Bianca asked.

It seemed a fair question to me, but the pig was offended and charged her. She was faster than I'd realized. She rolled out of the way of its hooves and came up behind the beast. It lashed out with its tusks and pulverized the WELCOME TO CLOUDCROFT sign.

I racked my brain, trying to remember the myth of the boar. I was pretty sure Hercules had fought this thing once, but I couldn't remember how he'd beaten it. I had a vague memory of the boar ploughing down several Greek cities before Hercules managed to subdue it. I hoped Cloudcroft was insured against giant wild boar attacks.

'Keep moving!' Zoë yelled. She and Bianca ran in opposite directions. Grover danced around the boar, playing his pipes while the boar snorted and tried to gouge him. But Thalia and I won the prize for bad luck. When the boar turned on us, Thalia made the mistake of raising Aegis in defence. The sight of the Medusa head made the boar squeal in outrage. Maybe it looked too much like one of his relatives. The boar charged us.

We only managed to keep ahead of it because we ran uphill, and we could dodge in and out of trees while the boar had to plough through them.

On the other side of the hill, I found an old stretch of train tracks, half buried in the snow.

'This way!' I grabbed Thalia's arm and we ran along the rails while the boar roared behind us, slipping and sliding as it tried to navigate the steep hillside. Its hooves were just not made for this, thank the gods.

Ahead of us, I saw a covered tunnel. Past that, an old trestle bridge spanning a gorge. I had a crazy idea.

'Follow me!'

Thalia slowed down – I didn't have time to ask why – but I pulled her along and she reluctantly followed. Behind us, a ten-ton pig tank was knocking down pine trees and crushing boulders under its hooves as it chased us.

Thalia and I ran into the tunnel and came out on the other side.

'No!' Thalia screamed.

She'd turned as white as ice. We were at the edge of the bridge. Below, the mountain dropped away into a snow-filled gorge about twenty metres below.

The boar was right behind us.

'Come on!' I said. 'It'll hold our weight, probably.'

'I can't!' Thalia yelled. Her eyes were wild with fear.

The boar smashed into the covered tunnel, tearing through at full speed.

'Now!' I yelled at Thalia.

She looked down and swallowed. I swear she was turning green.

I didn't have time to process why. The boar was charging through the tunnel, straight towards us. Plan B. I tackled Thalia and sent us both sideways off the edge of the bridge, into the side of the mountain. We slid on Aegis like a snowboard, over rocks and mud and snow, racing downhill. The boar was less fortunate; it couldn't turn that fast, so all ten tons of the monster charged out onto the tiny trestle, which buckled under its weight. The boar free-fell into the gorge with a mighty squeal and landed in a snowdrift with a huge *POOOOOF!*

Thalia and I skidded to a stop. We were both breathing hard. I was cut up and bleeding. Thalia had pine needles in her hair. Next to us, the wild boar was squealing and struggling. All I could see was the bristly tip of its back. It was wedged completely in the snow like Styrofoam packing. It didn't seem to be hurt, but it wasn't going anywhere, either.

I looked at Thalia. 'You're afraid of heights.'

Now that we were safely down the mountain, her eyes had their usual angry look. 'Don't be stupid.'

'That explains why you freaked out on Apollo's bus. Why you didn't want to talk about it.'

She took a deep breath. Then she brushed the pine needles out of her hair. 'If you tell anyone, I swear –'

'No, no,' I said. 'That's cool. It's just . . . the daughter of Zeus, the lord of the sky, afraid of heights?'

She was about to knock me into the snow when, above us, Grover's voice called, 'Helloooooo?'

'Down here!' I called.

A few minutes later, Zoë, Bianca and Grover joined us. We stood watching the wild boar struggle in the snow.

'A blessing of the Wild,' Grover said, though he now looked agitated.

'I agree,' Zoë said. 'We must use it.'

'Hold up,' Thalia said irritably. She still looked like she'd just lost a fight with a Christmas tree. 'Explain to me why you're so sure this pig is a blessing.'

Grover looked over, distracted. 'It's our ride west. Do you have any idea how fast this boar can travel?'

'Fun,' I said. 'Like . . . pig cowboys.'

Grover nodded. 'We need to get aboard. I wish . . . I wish I had more time to look around. But it's gone now.'

'What's gone?'

Grover didn't seem to hear me. He walked over to the boar and jumped onto its back. Already the boar was starting to make some headway through the drift. Once it broke free, there'd be no stopping it. Grover took out his pipes. He started playing a snappy tune and tossed an apple in front of the boar. The apple floated and spun right above the boar's nose, and the boar went nuts, straining to get it.

'Automatic steering,' Thalia murmured. 'Great.'

She trudged over and jumped on behind Grover, which still left plenty of room for the rest of us.

Zoë and Bianca walked towards the boar.

'Wait a second,' I said. 'Do you two know what Grover is talking about – this wild blessing?'

'Of course,' Zoë said. 'Did you not feel it in the wind? It was so strong . . . I never thought I would sense that presence again.'

'What presence?'

She stared at me like I was an idiot. 'The Lord of the Wild, of course. Just for a moment, in the arrival of the boar, I felt the presence of Pan.'

13 WE VISIT THE JUNKYARD OF THE GODS

We rode the boar until sunset, which was about as much as my backside could take. Imagine riding a giant steel brush over a bed of gravel all day. That's about how comfortable boar-riding was.

I have no idea how many miles we covered, but the mountains faded into the distance and were replaced by miles of flat dry land. The grass and scrub brush got sparser until we were galloping (do boars gallop?) across the desert.

As night fell, the boar came to a stop at a creek bed and snorted. He started drinking the muddy water, then ripped a saguaro cactus out of the ground and chewed it, needles and all.

'This is as far as he'll go,' Grover said. 'We need to get off while he's eating.'

Nobody needed convincing. We slipped off the boar's back while he was busy ripping up cacti. Then we waddled away as best we could with our saddle sores.

After its third saguaro and another drink of muddy water, the boar squealed and belched, then whirled round and galloped back towards the east.

'It likes the mountains better,' I guessed.

'I can't blame it,' Thalia said. 'Look.'

Ahead of us was a two-lane road half blown over with sand. On the other side of the road was a cluster of buildings too small to be a town: a boarded-up house, a taco shop that looked like it hadn't been open since before Zoë Nightshade was born, and a white stucco post office with a sign that said GILA CLAW, ARIZONA hanging crooked above the door. Beyond that was a range of hills . . . but then I noticed they weren't regular hills. The countryside was way too flat for that. The hills were enormous mounds of old cars, appliances, and other scrap metal. It was a junkyard that seemed to go on forever.

'Whoa,' I said.

'Something tells me we're not going to find a car rental here,' Thalia said. She looked at Grover. 'I don't suppose you got another wild boar up your sleeve?'

Grover was sniffing the wind, looking nervous. He fished out his acorns and threw them into the sand, then played his pipes. They rearranged themselves in a pattern that made no sense to me, but Grover looked concerned.

'That's us,' he said. 'Those five nuts right there.'

'Which one is me?' I asked.

'The little deformed one,' Zoë suggested.

'Oh, shut up.'

'That cluster right there,' Grover said, pointing to the left, 'that's trouble.'

'A monster?' Thalia asked.

Grover looked uneasy. 'I don't smell anything, which doesn't make sense. But the acorns don't lie. Our next challenge . . .'

He pointed straight towards the junkyard. With the sunlight almost gone now, the hills of metal looked like something on an alien planet.

* * *

We decided to camp for the night and try the junkyard in the morning. None of us wanted to go dump-diving in the dark.

Zoë and Bianca produced five sleeping bags and foam mattresses out of their backpacks. I don't know how they did it, because the packs were tiny, but they must've been enchanted to hold more stuff. I'd noticed their bows and quivers were also magic. I never really thought about it, but when the Hunters needed them, they just appeared slung over their backs. And when they didn't, they were gone.

The night got chilly fast, so Grover and I collected old boards from the ruined house, and Thalia zapped them with an electric shock to start a campfire. Pretty soon we were about as comfy as you can get in a rundown ghost town in the middle of nowhere.

'The stars are out,' Zoë said.

She was right. There were millions of them, with no city lights to turn the sky orange.

'Amazing,' Bianca said. 'I've never actually seen the Milky Way.'

'This is nothing,' Zoë said. 'In the old days, there were more. Whole constellations have disappeared because of human light pollution.'

'You talk like you're not human,' I said.

Zoë raised an eyebrow. 'I am a Hunter. I care what happens to the wild places of the world. Can the same be said for thee?'

'For *you*,' Thalia corrected. 'Not *thee*.'

'But you use *you* for the beginning of a sentence.'

'And for the end,' Thalia said. 'No *thou*. No *thee*. Just *you*.'

Zoë threw up her hands in exasperation. 'I *hate* this language. It changes too often!'

Grover sighed. He was still looking up at the stars like he was thinking about the light pollution problem. 'If only Pan were here, he would set things right.'

Zoë nodded sadly.

'Maybe it was the coffee,' Grover said. 'I was drinking coffee, and the wind came. Maybe if I drank more coffee . . .'

I was pretty sure coffee had nothing to do with what had happened in Cloudcroft, but I didn't have the heart to tell Grover. I thought about the rubber rat and the paper birds that had suddenly come alive when the wind blew. 'Grover, do you really think that was Pan? I mean, I know you *want* it to be.'

'He sent us help,' Grover insisted. 'I don't know how or why. But it was his presence. After this quest is done, I'm going back to New Mexico and drinking a lot of coffee. It's the best lead we've got in two thousand years. I was *so close*.'

I didn't answer. I didn't want to squash Grover's hopes.

'What I want to know,' Thalia said, looking at Bianca, 'is how you destroyed one of the zombies. There are a lot more out there somewhere. We need to figure out how to fight them.'

Bianca shook her head. 'I don't know. I just stabbed it and it went up in flames.'

'Maybe there's something special about your knife,' I said.

'It is the same as mine,' Zoë said. 'Celestial bronze, yes. But mine did not affect the warriors that way.'

'Maybe you have to hit the skeleton in a certain spot,' I said.

Bianca looked uncomfortable with everybody paying attention to her.

'Never mind,' Zoë told her. 'We will find the answer. In the meantime, we should plan our next move. When we get through this junkyard, we must continue west. If we can find a road, we can hitchhike to the nearest city. I think that would be Las Vegas.'

I was about to protest that Grover and I had had bad experiences in that town, but Bianca beat us to it.

'No!' she said. 'Not there!'

She looked really freaked out, like she'd just been dropped off the steep end of a roller coaster.

Zoë frowned. 'Why?'

Bianca took a shaky breath. 'I . . . I think we stayed there for a while. Nico and I. When we were travelling. And then, I can't remember . . .'

Suddenly I had a really bad thought. I remembered what Bianca had told me about Nico and her staying in a hotel for a while. I met Grover's eyes, and I got the feeling he was thinking the same thing.

'Bianca,' I said. 'That hotel you stayed at. Was it possibly called the Lotus Hotel and Casino?'

Her eyes widened. 'How could you know that?'

'Oh, great,' I said.

'Wait,' Thalia said. 'What is the Lotus Casino?'

'A couple of years ago,' I said, 'Grover, Annabeth and I got trapped there. It's designed so you never want to leave. We stayed for about an hour. When we came out, five days had passed. It makes time speed up.'

'No,' Bianca said. 'No, that's not possible.'

'You said somebody came and got you out,' I remembered.

'Yes.'

'What did he look like? What did he say?'

'I . . . I don't remember. Please, I really don't want to talk about this.'

Zoë sat forward, her eyebrows knitted with concern. 'You said that Washington, D.C. had changed when you went back last summer. You didn't remember the subway being there.'

'Yes, but –'

'Bianca,' Zoë said, 'can you tell me the name of the president of the United States right now?'

'Don't be silly,' Bianca said. She told us the correct name of the president.

'And who was the president before that?' Zoë asked.

Bianca thought for a while. 'Roosevelt.'

Zoë swallowed. 'Theodore or Franklin?'

'Franklin,' Bianca said. 'F.D.R.'

'Like F.D.R. Drive?' I asked. Because, seriously, that's about all I knew about F.D.R.

'Bianca,' Zoë said. 'F.D.R. was not the last president. That was about seventy years ago.'

'That's impossible,' Bianca said. 'I . . . I'm not that old.'

She stared at her hands as if to make sure they weren't wrinkled.

Thalia's eyes turned sad. I guess she knew what it was like to get pulled out of time for a while. 'It's okay, Bianca. The important thing is you and Nico are safe. You made it out.'

'But how?' I said. 'We were only in there for an hour and we barely escaped. How could you have escaped after being there for so long?'

'I told you.' Bianca looked about ready to cry. 'A man came and said it was time to leave. And –'

'But who? Why did he do it?'

Before she could answer, we were hit with a blazing light from down the road. The headlights of a car appeared out of nowhere. I was half hoping it was Apollo, come to give us a ride again, but the engine was way too silent for the sun chariot, and, besides, it was night-time. We grabbed our sleeping bags and got out of the way as a deathly white limousine slid to a stop in front of us.

The back door of the limo opened right next to me. Before I could step away, the point of a sword touched my throat.

I heard the sound of Zoë and Bianca drawing their bows. As the owner of the sword got out of the car, I moved back very slowly. I had to, because he was pushing the point under my chin.

He smiled cruelly. 'Not so fast now, are you, punk?'

He was a big man with a crew cut, a black leather biker's jacket, black jeans, a skin-tight white vest and combat boots. Wraparound shades hid his eyes, but I knew what was behind those glasses – hollow sockets filled with flames.

'Ares,' I growled.

The war god glanced at my friends. 'At ease, people.'

He snapped his fingers, and their weapons fell to the ground.

'This is a friendly meeting.' He dug the point of his

blade a little further under my chin. 'Of course I'd *like* to take your head for a trophy, but someone wants to see you. And I never behead my enemies in front of a lady.'

'What lady?' Thalia asked.

Ares looked over at her. 'Well, well. I heard you were back.'

He lowered his sword and pushed me away.

'Thalia, daughter of Zeus,' Ares mused. 'You're not hanging out with very good company.'

'What's your business, Ares?' she said. 'Who's in the car?'

Ares smiled, enjoying the attention. 'Oh, I doubt she wants to meet the rest of you. Particularly not *them*.' He jutted his chin towards Zoë and Bianca. 'Why don't you all go get some tacos while you wait? Only take Percy a few minutes.'

'We will not leave him alone with thee, Lord Ares,' Zoë said.

'Besides,' Grover managed, 'the taco place is closed.'

Ares snapped his fingers again. The lights inside the taqueria suddenly blazed to life. The boards flew off the door and the CLOSED sign flipped to OPEN. 'You were saying, goat boy?'

'Go on,' I told my friends. 'I'll handle this.'

I tried to sound more confident than I felt. I don't think Ares was fooled.

'You heard the boy,' Ares said. 'He's big and strong. He's got things under control.'

My friends reluctantly headed over to the taco restaurant. Ares regarded me with loathing then opened the limousine door like a chauffeur.

'Get inside, punk,' he said. 'And mind your manners. She's not as forgiving of rudeness as I am.'

When I saw her, my jaw dropped.

I forgot my name. I forgot where I was. I forgot how to speak in complete sentences.

She was wearing a red satin dress and her hair was curled in a cascade of ringlets. Her face was the most beautiful I'd ever seen: perfect makeup, dazzling eyes, a smile that would've lit up the dark side of the moon.

Thinking back on it, I can't tell you who she looked like. Or even what colour her hair or her eyes were. Pick the most beautiful actress you can think of. The goddess was ten times more beautiful than that. Pick your favourite hair colour, eye colour, whatever. The goddess had that.

When she smiled at me, just for a moment she looked a little like Annabeth. Then like this television actress I used to have a crush on in fifth grade. Then . . . well, you get the idea.

'Ah, there you are, Percy,' the goddess said. 'I am Aphrodite.'

I slipped into the seat across from her and said something like, 'Um uh gah.'

She smiled. 'Aren't you sweet. Hold this, please.'

She handed me a polished mirror the size of a dinner plate and had me hold it up for her. She leaned forward and dabbed at her lipstick, though I couldn't see anything wrong with it.

'Do you know why you're here?' she asked.

I wanted to respond. Why couldn't I form a complete

sentence? She was only a lady. A seriously beautiful lady. With eyes like pools of spring water . . . Whoa.

I pinched my own arm, hard.

'I . . . I don't know,' I managed.

'Oh, dear,' Aphrodite said. 'Still in denial?'

Outside the car, I could hear Ares chuckling. I had a feeling he could hear every word we said. The idea of him being out there made me angry, and that helped clear my mind.

'I don't know what you're talking about,' I said.

'Well then, why are you on this quest?'

'Artemis has been captured!'

Aphrodite rolled her eyes. 'Oh, Artemis. *Please.* Talk about a hopeless case. I mean, if they were going to kidnap a goddess, she should be breathtakingly beautiful, don't you think? I pity the poor dears who have to imprison Artemis. Bo-ring!'

'But she was chasing a monster,' I protested. 'A really, really bad monster. We have to find it!'

Aphrodite made me hold the mirror a little higher. She seemed to have found a microscopic problem at the corner of her eye and dabbed at her mascara. 'Always some monster. But, my dear Percy, that is why the *others* are on this quest. I'm more interested in *you*.'

My heart pounded. I didn't want to answer, but her eyes drew an answer right out of my mouth. 'Annabeth is in trouble.'

Aphrodite beamed. 'Exactly!'

'I have to help her,' I said. 'I've been having these dreams.'

'Ah, you even dream about her! That's *so cute!*'

'No! I mean . . . that's not what I meant.'

She made a *tsk tsk* sound. 'Percy, I'm on your side. I'm the reason you're here, after all.'

I stared at her. 'What?'

'The poisoned T-shirt the Stoll brothers gave Phoebe,' she said. 'Did you think that was an accident? Sending Blackjack to find you? Helping you sneak out of the camp?'

'*You* did that?'

'Of course! Because, really, how boring these Hunters are! A quest for some monster, blah blah blah. Saving Artemis. Let her stay lost, I say. But a quest for true love –'

'Wait a second, I never said –'

'Oh, my dear. You don't need to say it. You *do* know Annabeth was close to joining the Hunters, don't you?'

I blushed. 'I wasn't sure –'

'She was about to throw her life away! And you, my dear, you can save her from that. It's so romantic!'

'Uh . . .'

'Oh, put the mirror down,' Aphrodite ordered. 'I look fine.'

I hadn't realized I was still holding it, but as soon as I put it down, I noticed my arms were sore.

'Now listen, Percy,' Aphrodite said. 'The Hunters are your enemies. Forget them and Artemis and the monster. That's not important. You just concentrate on finding and saving Annabeth.'

'Do you know where she is?'

Aphrodite waved her hand irritably. 'No, no. I leave the details to you. But it's been ages since we've had a good tragic love story.'

'Whoa, first of all, I never said anything about love. And second, what's up with *tragic*?'

'Love conquers all,' Aphrodite promised. 'Look at Helen and Paris. Did they let anything come between them?'

'Didn't they start the Trojan War and get thousands of people killed?'

'Pfft. That's not the point. Follow your heart.'

'But . . . I don't know where it's going. My heart, I mean.'

She smiled sympathetically. She really was beautiful. And not just because she had a pretty face or anything. She believed in love so much, it was impossible not to feel giddy when she talked about it.

'Not knowing is half the fun,' Aphrodite said. 'Exquisitely painful, isn't it? Not being sure who you love and who loves you? Oh, you kids! It's so cute I'm going to cry.'

'No, no,' I said. 'Don't do that.'

'And don't worry,' she said. 'I'm not going let this be easy and boring for you. No, I have some wonderful surprises in store. Anguish. Indecision. Oh, you just wait.'

'That's really okay,' I told her. 'Don't go to any trouble.'

'You're *so* cute. I wish all my daughters could break the heart of a boy as nice as you.' Aphrodite's eyes were tearing up. 'Now, you'd better go. And do be careful in my husband's territory, Percy. Don't take anything. He is awfully fussy about his trinkets and trash.'

'What?' I asked. 'You mean Hephaestus?'

But the car door opened and Ares grabbed my shoulder, pulling me out of the car and back into the desert night.

My audience with the goddess of love was over.

'You're lucky, punk.' Ares pushed me away from the limo. 'Be grateful.'

'For what?'

'That we're being so nice. If it was up to me –'

'So why haven't you killed me?' I shot back. It was a stupid thing to say to the god of war, but being around him always made me feel angry and reckless.

Ares nodded, like I'd finally said something intelligent. 'I'd love to kill you, seriously,' he said. 'But, see, I got a situation. Word on Olympus is that you might start the biggest war in history. I can't risk messing that up. Besides, Aphrodite thinks you're some kinda soap-opera star or something. I kill you, that makes me look bad with her. But don't worry. I haven't forgotten my promise. Some day soon, kid – *real* soon – you're going to raise your sword to fight, and you're going to remember the wrath of Ares.'

I balled my fists. 'Why wait? I beat you once. How's that ankle healing up?'

He grinned crookedly. 'Not bad, punk. But you got nothing on the master of taunts. I'll start the fight when I'm good and ready. Until then . . . Get lost.'

He snapped his fingers and the world did a three-sixty, spinning in a cloud of red dust. I fell to the ground.

When I stood up again, the limousine was gone. The road, the taco restaurant, the whole town of Gila Claw was gone. My friends and I were standing in the middle of the junkyard, mountains of scrap metal stretched out in every direction.

'What did she *want* with you?' Bianca asked, once I'd told them about Aphrodite.

'Oh, uh, not sure,' I lied. 'She said to be careful in her husband's junkyard. She said not to pick anything up.'

Zoë narrowed her eyes. 'The goddess of love would not make a special trip to tell thee that. Be careful, Percy. Aphrodite has led many heroes astray.'

'For once, I agree with Zoë,' Thalia said. 'You can't trust Aphrodite.'

Grover was looking at me funny. Being empathic and all, he could usually read my emotions, and I got the feeling he knew exactly what Aphrodite had talked to me about.

'So,' I said, anxious to change the subject, 'how do we get out of here?'

'That way,' Zoë said. 'That is west.'

'How can you tell?'

In the light of the full moon, I was surprised how well I could see her roll her eyes at me. 'Ursa Major is in the north,' she said, 'which means *that* must be west.'

She pointed west, then at the northern constellation, which was hard to make out because there were so many other stars.

'Oh, yeah,' I said. 'The bear thing.'

Zoë looked offended. 'Show some respect. It was a fine bear. A worthy opponent.'

'You act like it was real.'

'Guys,' Grover broke in. 'Look!'

We'd reached the crest of a junk mountain. Piles of metal objects glinted in the moonlight: broken heads of bronze horses, metal legs from human statues, smashed chariots, tons of shields and swords and other weapons, along with more modern stuff, like cars that gleamed gold and silver, refrigerators, washing machines and computer monitors.

'Whoa,' Bianca said. 'That stuff . . . some of it looks like real gold.'

'It is,' Thalia said grimly. 'Like Percy said, don't touch anything. This is the junkyard of the gods.'

'Junk?' Grover picked up a beautiful crown made of gold, silver and jewels. It was broken on one side, as if it had been split by an axe. 'You call this junk?'

He bit off a point and began to chew. 'It's delicious!'

Thalia swatted the crown out of his hands. 'I'm serious!'

'Look!' Bianca said. She raced down the hill, tripping over bronze coils and golden plates. She picked up a bow that glowed silver in moonlight. 'A Hunter's bow!'

She yelped in surprise as the bow began to shrink, and became a hair clip shaped like a crescent moon. 'It's just like Percy's sword!'

Zoë's face was grim. 'Leave it, Bianca.'

'But –'

'It is here for a reason. Anything thrown away in this junkyard must stay in this yard. It is defective. Or cursed.'

Bianca reluctantly set the hair clip down.

'I don't like this place,' Thalia said. She gripped the shaft of her spear.

'You think we're going to get attacked by killer refrigerators?' I asked.

She gave me a hard look. 'Zoë is right, Percy. Things get thrown away here for a reason. Now come on, let's get across the yard.'

'That's the second time you've agreed with Zoë,' I muttered, but Thalia ignored me.

We started picking our way through the hills and valleys of junk. The stuff seemed to go on forever, and if it hadn't been for Ursa Major, we would've got lost. All the hills pretty much looked the same.

I'd like to say we left the stuff alone, but there was too much cool junk not to check out some of it. I found an electric guitar shaped like Apollo's lyre that was so sweet I had to pick it up. Grover found a broken tree made out of metal. It had been chopped to pieces, but some of the branches still had golden birds in them, and they whirred around when Grover picked them up, trying to flap their wings.

Finally, we saw the edge of the junkyard about half a mile ahead of us, the lights of a highway stretching through the desert. But between us and the road . . .

'What is that?' Bianca gasped.

Ahead of us was a hill much bigger and longer than the others. It was like a metal mesa, the length of a football field and as tall as goalposts. At one end of the mesa was a row of ten thick metal columns, wedged tightly together.

Bianca frowned. 'They look like –'

'Toes,' Grover said.

Bianca nodded. 'Really, really large toes.'

Zoë and Thalia exchanged nervous looks.

'Let's go around,' Thalia said. '*Far* around.'

'But the road is right over there,' I protested. 'Quicker to climb over.'

Ping.

Thalia hefted her spear and Zoë drew her bow, but then I realized it was only Grover. He had thrown a piece of scrap metal at the toes and hit one, making a deep echo, as if the column were hollow.

'Why did you do that?' Zoë demanded.

Grover cringed. 'I don't know. I, uh, don't like fake feet?'

'Come on.' Thalia looked at me. *'Around.'*

I didn't argue. The toes were starting to freak me out, too. I mean, who sculpts three-metre-tall metal toes and sticks them in a junkyard?

After several minutes of walking, we finally stepped onto the highway, an abandoned but well-lit stretch of black tarmac.

'We made it out,' Zoë said. 'Thank the gods.'

But apparently the gods didn't want to be thanked. At that moment I heard a sound like a thousand trash compactors crushing metal.

I whirled round. Behind us, the scrap mountain was boiling, rising up. The ten toes tilted over, and I realized why they looked like toes. They *were* toes. The thing that rose up from the metal was a bronze giant in full Greek battle armour. He was impossibly tall – a skyscraper with legs and arms. He gleamed wickedly in the moonlight. He looked down at us, and his face was deformed. The left side was partially melted off. His joints creaked with rust, and across his armoured chest, written in thick dust by some giant finger, were the words WASH ME.

'Talos!' Zoë gasped.

'Who . . . who's Talos?' I stuttered.

'One of Hephaestus's creations,' Thalia said. 'But that can't be the original. It's too small. A prototype, maybe. A defective model.'

The metal giant didn't like the word *defective*.

He moved one hand to his sword belt and drew his weapon. The sound of it coming out of its sheath was horrible, metal screeching against metal. The blade was thirty metres long, easy. It looked rusty and dull, but I didn't figure that mattered. Getting hit with that thing would be like getting hit with a battleship.

'Someone took something,' Zoë said. 'Who took something?'

She stared accusingly at me.

I shook my head. 'I'm a lot of things, but I'm not a thief.'

Bianca didn't say anything. I could swear she looked guilty, but I didn't have much time to think about it, because the giant defective Talos took one step towards us, closing half the distance and making the ground shake.

'Run!' Grover yelped.

Great advice, except that it was hopeless. At a leisurely stroll, this thing could outdistance us easily.

We split up, the way we'd done with the Nemean Lion. Thalia drew her shield and held it up as she ran down the highway. The giant swung his sword and took out a row of power lines, which exploded in sparks and scattered across Thalia's path.

Zoë's arrows whistled towards the creature's face but shattered harmlessly against the metal. Grover brayed like a baby goat and went climbing up a mountain of metal.

Bianca and I ended up next to each other, hiding behind a broken chariot.

'You took something,' I said. 'That bow.'

'No!' she said, but her voice was quivering.

'Give it back!' I said. 'Throw it down!'

'I . . . I didn't take the bow! Besides, it's too late.'

'What did you take?'

Before she could answer, I heard a massive creaking noise, and a shadow blotted out the sky.

'Move!' I tore down the hill, Bianca right behind me, as the giant's foot smashed a crater in the ground where we'd been hiding.

'Hey, Talos!' Grover yelled, but the monster raised his sword, looking down at Bianca and me.

Grover played a quick melody on his pipes. Over at the highway, the downed power lines began to dance. I understood what Grover was going to do a split second before it happened. One of the poles with power lines still attached flew towards Talos's back leg and wrapped around his calf. The lines sparked and sent a jolt of electricity up the giant's backside.

Talos whirled around, creaking and sparking. Grover had bought us a few seconds.

'Come on!' I told Bianca. But she stayed frozen. From her pocket, she brought out a small metal figurine, a statue of a god. 'It . . . it was for Nico. It was the only statue he didn't have.'

'How can you think of Mythomagic at a time like this?' I said.

There were tears in her eyes.

'Throw it down,' I said. 'Maybe the giant will leave us alone.'

She dropped it reluctantly, but nothing happened.

The giant kept coming after Grover. It stabbed its sword into a junk hill, missing Grover by a metre or so, but scrap metal made an avalanche over him, and then I couldn't see him any more.

'No!' Thalia yelled. She pointed her spear, and a blue arc of lightning shot out, hitting the monster in his rusty knee, which buckled. The giant collapsed, but immediately started to rise again. It was hard to tell if it could feel anything. There weren't any emotions in its half-melted face, but I got the sense that it was about as ticked off as a twenty-storey-tall metal warrior could be.

He raised his foot to stomp and I saw that his sole was treaded like the bottom of a trainer. There was a hole in his heel, like a large manhole, and there were red words painted around it, which I deciphered only after the foot came down: FOR MAINTENANCE ONLY.

'Crazy-idea time,' I said.

Bianca looked at me nervously. 'Anything.'

I told her about the maintenance hatch. 'There may be a way to control the thing. Switches or something. I'm going to get inside.'

'How? You'll have to stand under its foot! You'll be crushed.'

'Distract it,' I said. 'I'll just have to time it right.'

Bianca's jaw tightened. 'No. I'll go.'

'You can't. You're new at this! You'll die.'

'It's my fault the monster came after us,' she said. 'It's my responsibility. Here.' She picked up the little god statue and pressed it into my hand. 'If anything happens, give that to Nico. Tell him . . . tell him I'm sorry.'

'Bianca, no!'

But she wasn't waiting for me. She charged at the monster's left foot.

Thalia had its attention for the moment. She'd learned that the giant was big but slow. If you could stay close to it and not get smashed, you could run around it and stay alive. At least, it was working so far.

Bianca got right next to the giant's foot, trying to

balance herself on the metal scraps that swayed and shifted with his weight.

Zoë yelled, 'What are you doing?'

'Get it to raise its foot!' she said.

Zoë shot an arrow towards the monster's face and it flew straight into one nostril. The giant straightened and shook its head.

'Hey, Junk Boy!' I yelled. 'Down here.'

I ran up to its big toe and stabbed it with Riptide. The magic blade cut a gash in the bronze.

Unfortunately, my plan worked. Talos looked down at me and raised his foot to squash me like a bug. I didn't see what Bianca was doing. I had to turn and run. The foot came down right behind me and I was knocked into the air. I hit something hard and sat up, dazed. I'd been thrown into an Olympus-Air refrigerator.

The monster was about to finish me off, but Grover somehow dug himself out of the junk pile. He played his pipes frantically, and his music sent another power line pole whacking against Talos's thigh. The monster turned. Grover should've run, but he must've been too exhausted from the effort of so much magic. He took two steps, fell and didn't get back up.

'Grover!' Thalia and I both ran towards him, but I knew we'd be too late.

The monster raised his sword to smash Grover. Then he froze.

Talos cocked his head to one side, like he was hearing strange new music. He started moving his arms and legs in weird ways, doing the Funky Chicken. Then he made a fist and punched himself in the face.

'Go, Bianca!' I yelled.

Zoë looked horrified. 'She is *inside*?'

The monster staggered around, and I realized we were still in danger. Thalia and I grabbed Grover and ran with him towards the highway. Zoë was already ahead of us. She yelled, 'How will Bianca get out?'

The giant hit itself in the head again and dropped his sword. A shudder ran through his whole body and he staggered towards the power lines.

'Look out!' I yelled, but it was too late.

The giant's ankle snared the lines, and blue flickers of electricity shot up his body. I hoped the inside was insulated. I had no idea what was going on in there. The giant careened back into the junkyard, and his right hand fell off, landing in the scrap metal with a horrible *CLANG!*

His left arm came loose, too. He was falling apart at the joints.

Talos began to run.

'Wait!' Zoë yelled. We ran after him, but there was no way we could keep up. Pieces of the robot kept falling off, getting in our way.

The giant crumbled from the top down: his head, pieces of his chest, and finally his torso and legs collapsed. When we reached the wreckage we searched frantically, yelling Bianca's name. We crawled around in the vast hollow chest pieces and the legs and the torso. We searched until the sun started to rise, but no luck.

Zoë sat down and wept. I was stunned to see her cry.

Thalia yelled in rage and impaled her sword in the giant's smashed face.

'We can keep searching,' I said. 'It's light now. We'll find her.'

'No we won't,' Grover said miserably. 'It happened just as it was supposed to.'

'What are you talking about?' I demanded.

He looked up at me with big watery eyes. 'The prophecy. *One shall be lost in the land without rain.*'

Why hadn't I seen it? Why had I let her go instead of me?

Here we were in the desert. And Bianca di Angelo was gone.

14 I HAVE A DAM PROBLEM

At the edge of the dump, we found a tow truck so old it might've been thrown away itself. But the engine started, and it had a full tank of fuel, so we decided to borrow it.

Thalia drove. She didn't seem as stunned as Zoë or Grover or me.

'The skeletons are still out there,' she reminded us. 'We need to keep moving.'

She navigated us through the desert, under clear blue skies, the sand so bright it hurt to look at it. Zoë sat up front with Thalia. Grover and I sat in the back, leaning against the tow winch. The air was cool and dry, but the nice weather just seemed like an insult after losing Bianca.

My hand closed around the little figurine that had cost Bianca her life. I still couldn't even tell what god it was supposed to be. Nico would know.

Oh, gods . . . what was I going to tell Nico?

I wanted to believe that Bianca was still alive somewhere. But I had a bad feeling that she was gone for good.

'It should've been me,' I said. 'I should've gone into the giant.'

'Don't say that!' Grover panicked. 'It's bad enough Annabeth is gone, and now Bianca. Do you think I could stand it if . . .' He sniffled. 'Do you think anybody *else* would be my best friend?'

'Ah, Grover . . .'

He wiped under his eyes with an oily cloth that left his face grimy like he had war paint on. 'I'm . . . I'm okay.'

But he wasn't okay. Ever since the encounter in New Mexico – whatever had happened when that wild wind blew through – he seemed really fragile, even more emotional than usual. I was afraid to talk to him about it, because he might start bawling.

At least there's one good thing about having a friend who gets freaked out more than you do. I realized I couldn't stay depressed. I had to set aside thinking about Bianca and keep us going forward, the way Thalia was doing. I wondered what she and Zoë were talking about in the front of the truck.

The tow truck ran out of fuel at the edge of a river canyon. That was just as well, because the road dead-ended.

Thalia got out and slammed the door. Immediately, one of the tyres blew. 'Great. What now?'

I scanned the horizon. There wasn't much to see. Desert in all directions, occasional clumps of barren mountains plopped here and there. The canyon was the only thing interesting. The river itself wasn't very big, maybe fifty metres across, green water with a few rapids, but it carved a huge scar out of the desert. The rock cliffs dropped away below us.

'There's a path,' Grover said. 'We could get to the river.'

I tried to see what he was talking about, and finally noticed a tiny ledge winding down the cliff face. 'That's a goat path,' I said.

'So?' he asked.

'The rest of us aren't goats.'

'We can make it,' Grover said. 'I think.'

I thought about that. I'd done cliffs before, but I didn't like them. Then I looked over at Thalia and saw how pale she'd got. Her problem with heights . . . she'd never be able to do it.

'No,' I said. 'I, uh, think we should go further upstream.'

Grover said, 'But –'

'Come on,' I said. 'A walk won't hurt us.'

I glanced at Thalia. Her eyes said a quick *Thank you.*

We followed the river for about half a mile before coming to an easier slope that led down to the water. On the shore was a canoe rental operation that was closed for the season, but I left a stack of golden drachma on the counter and a note saying *I.O.U. two canoes.*

'We need to go upstream,' Zoë said. It was the first time I'd heard her speak since the junkyard, and I was worried about how bad she sounded, like somebody with the flu.

'The rapids are too swift.'

'Leave that to me,' I said. We put the canoes in the water.

Thalia pulled me aside as we were getting the oars. 'Thanks for back there.'

'Don't mention it.'

'Can you really . . .' She nodded to the rapids. 'You know.'

'I think so. Usually I'm good with water.'

'Would you take Zoë?' she asked. 'I think, ah, maybe you can talk to her.'

'She's not going to like that.'

'Please? I don't know if I can stand being in the same boat with her. She's . . . she's starting to worry me.'

It was about the last thing I wanted to do, but I nodded.

Thalia's shoulders relaxed. 'I owe you one.'

'Two.'

'One and a half,' Thalia said.

She smiled and, for a second, I remembered that I actually liked her when she wasn't yelling at me. She turned and helped Grover get their canoe into the water.

As it turned out, I didn't even need to control the currents. As soon as we got in the river, I looked over the edge of the boat and found a couple of naiads staring at me.

They looked like regular teenage girls, the kind you'd see in any mall, except for the fact that they were underwater.

Hey, I said.

They made a bubbling sound that may have been giggling. I wasn't sure. I had a hard time understanding naiads.

We're heading upstream, I told them. *Do you think you could –*

Before I could even finish, the naiads each chose a canoe and began pushing us up the river. We started so fast Grover fell into his canoe with his hooves sticking up in the air.

'I hate naiads,' Zoë grumbled.

A stream of water squirted up from the back of the boat and hit Zoë in the face.

'She-devils!' Zoë went for her bow.

'Whoa,' I said. 'They're just playing.'

'Cursed water spirits. They've never forgiven me.'

'Forgiven you for what?'

She slung her bow back over her shoulder. 'It was a long time ago. Never mind.'

We sped up the river, the cliffs looming up on either side of us.

'What happened to Bianca wasn't your fault,' I told her. 'It was my fault. I let her go.'

I figured this would give Zoë an excuse to start yelling at me. At least that might shake her out of feeling depressed.

Instead, her shoulders slumped. 'No, Percy. I pushed her into going on the quest. I was too anxious. She was a powerful half-blood. She had a kind heart, as well. I . . . I thought she would be the next lieutenant.'

'But you're the lieutenant.'

She gripped the strap of her quiver. She looked more tired than I'd ever seen her. 'Nothing can last forever, Percy. Over two thousand years I have led the Hunt, and my wisdom has not improved. Now Artemis herself is in danger.'

'Look, you can't blame yourself for that.'

'If I had insisted on going with her –'

'You think you could've fought something powerful enough to kidnap Artemis? There's nothing you could have done.'

Zoë didn't answer.

The cliffs along the river were getting taller. Long shadows fell across the water, making it a lot colder, even though the day was bright.

Without thinking about it, I took Riptide out of my pocket. Zoë looked at the pen, and her expression was pained.

'You made this,' I said.

'Who told thee?'

'I had a dream about it.'

She studied me. I was sure she was going to call me crazy, but she just sighed. 'It was a gift. And a mistake.'

'Who was the hero?' I asked.

Zoë shook her head. 'Do not make me say his name. I swore never to speak it again.'

'You act like I should know him.'

'I am sure you do, hero. Don't all you boys want to be just like him?'

Her voice was so bitter, I decided not to ask what she meant. I looked down at Riptide and, for the first time, I wondered if it was cursed.

'Your mother was a water goddess?' I asked.

'Yes, Pleoine. She had five daughters. My sisters and I. The Hesperides.'

'Those were the girls who lived in a garden at the edge of the West. With the golden apple tree, and a dragon guarding it.'

'Yes,' Zoë said wistfully. 'Ladon.'

'But weren't there only four sisters?'

'There are now. I was exiled. Forgotten. Blotted out as if I never existed.'

'Why?'

Zoë pointed to my pen. 'Because I betrayed my family and helped a hero. You won't find that in the legend either. He never spoke of me. After his direct assault on Ladon failed, I gave him the idea of how to steal the apples, how to trick my father, but *he* took all the credit.'

'But –'

Gurgle, gurgle, the naiad spoke in my mind. The canoe was slowing down.

I looked ahead, and I saw why.

This was as far as they could take us. The river was blocked. A dam the size of a football stadium stood in our path.

'Hoover Dam,' Thalia said. 'It's huge.'

We stood at the river's edge, looking up at a curve of concrete that loomed between the cliffs. People were walking along the top of the dam. They were so tiny they looked like fleas.

The naiads had left with a lot of grumbling – not in words I could understand, but it was obvious they hated this dam blocking up their nice river. Our canoes floated back downstream, swirling in the wake from the dam's discharge vents.

'Over two hundred metres tall,' I said. 'Built in the 1930s.'

'Five million cubic acres of water,' Thalia said.

Grover sighed. 'Largest construction project in the United States.'

Zoë stared at us. 'How do you know all that?'

'Annabeth,' I said. 'She liked architecture.'

'She was nuts about monuments,' Thalia said.

'Spouted facts all the time.' Grover sniffled. 'So annoying.'

'I wish she were here,' I said.

The others nodded. Zoë was still looking at us strangely, but I didn't care. It seemed like cruel fate that we'd come to Hoover Dam, one of Annabeth's personal favourites, and she wasn't here to see it.

'We should go up there,' I said. 'For her sake. Just to say we've been.'

'You are mad,' Zoë decided. 'But that's where the road

is.' She pointed to a huge parking garage next to the top of the dam. 'And so sightseeing it is.'

We had to walk for almost an hour before we found a path that led up to the road. It came up on the east side of the river. Then we straggled back towards the dam. It was cold and windy on top. On one side, a big lake spread out, ringed by barren desert mountains. On the other side, the dam dropped away like the world's most dangerous skateboard ramp, down to the river more than two hundred metres below, and water that churned from the dam's vents.

Thalia walked in the middle of the road, far away from the edges. Grover kept sniffing the wind and looking nervous. He didn't say anything, but I knew he smelled monsters.

'How close are they?' I asked him.

He shook his head. 'Maybe not close. The wind on the dam, the desert all around us . . . the scent can probably carry for miles. But it's coming from several directions. I don't like that.'

I didn't either. It was already Wednesday, only two days until winter solstice, and we still had a long way to go. We didn't need any more monsters.

'There's a snack bar in the visitor centre,' Thalia said.

'You've been here before?' I asked.

'Once. To see the guardians.' She pointed to the far end of the dam. Carved into the side of the cliff was a little plaza with two big bronze statues. They looked kind of like Oscar statues with wings.

'They were dedicated to Zeus when the dam was built,' Thalia said. 'A gift from Athena.'

Tourists were clustered all around them. They seemed to be looking at the statues' feet.

'What are they doing?' I asked.

'Rubbing the toes,' Thalia said. 'They think it's good luck.'

'Why?'

She shook her head. 'Mortals get crazy ideas. They don't know the statues are sacred to Zeus, but they know there's something special about them.'

'When you were here last, did they talk to you or anything?'

Thalia's expression darkened. I could tell that she'd come here before hoping for exactly that – some kind of sign from her dad. Some connection. 'No. They don't do anything. They're just big metal statues.'

I thought about the last big metal statue we'd run into. That hadn't gone so well. But I decided not to bring it up.

'Let us find the dam snack bar,' Zoë said. 'We should eat while we can.'

Grover cracked a smile. 'The dam snack bar?'

Zoë blinked. 'Yes. What is funny?'

'Nothing,' Grover said, trying to keep a straight face. 'I could use some dam French fries.'

Even Thalia smiled at that. 'And I need to use the dam restroom.'

Maybe it was the fact that we were so tired and strung out emotionally, but I started cracking up, and Thalia and Grover joined in, while Zoë just looked at us. 'I do not understand.'

'I want to use the dam water fountain,' Grover said.

'And . . .' Thalia tried to catch her breath. 'I want to buy a dam T-shirt.'

I cracked up, and I probably would've kept laughing all day, but then I heard a noise:

'Moooo.'

The smile melted off my face. I wondered if the noise was just in my head, but Grover had stopped laughing, too. He was looking around, confused. 'Did I just hear a cow?'

'A dam cow?' Thalia laughed.

'No,' Grover said. 'I'm serious.'

Zoë listened. 'I hear nothing.'

Thalia was looking at me. 'Percy, are you okay?'

'Yeah,' I said. 'You guys go ahead. I'll be right in.'

'What's wrong?' Grover asked.

'Nothing,' I said. 'I . . . I just need a minute. To think.'

They hesitated, but I guess I must've looked upset, because they finally went into the visitor centre without me. As soon as they were gone, I jogged to the north edge of the dam and looked over.

'Moo.'

She was about ten metres below in the lake, but I could see her clearly: my friend from Long Island Sound, Bessie the cow serpent.

I looked around. There were groups of kids running along the dam. A lot of senior citizens. Some families. But nobody seemed to be paying Bessie any attention yet.

'What are you doing here?' I asked her.

'Moo!'

Her voice was urgent, like she was trying to warn me of something.

'How did you get here?' I asked. We were thousands of

miles from Long Island, hundreds of miles inland. There was no way she could've swum all the way here. And yet, here she was.

Bessie swam in a circle and butted her head against the side of the dam. 'Moo!'

She wanted me to come with her. She was telling me to hurry.

'I can't,' I told her. 'My friends are inside.'

She looked at me with her sad brown eyes. Then she gave one more urgent 'Moo!,' did a flip and disappeared into the water.

I hesitated. Something was wrong. She was trying to tell me that. I considered jumping over the side and following her, but then I tensed. The hairs on my arms bristled. I looked down the dam road to the east and I saw two men walking slowly towards me. They wore grey camouflage outfits that flickered over skeletal bodies.

They passed through a group of kids and pushed them aside. A kid yelled, 'Hey!' One of the warriors turned, his face changing momentarily into a skull.

'Ah!' the kid yelled, and his whole group backed away.

I ran for the visitor centre.

I was almost at the stairs when I heard tyres squeal. On the west side of the dam, a black van swerved to a stop in the middle of the road, nearly ploughing into some old people.

The van doors opened and more skeleton warriors piled out. I was surrounded.

I bolted down the stairs and through the museum entrance. The security guard at the metal-detector yelled, 'Hey, kid!' But I didn't stop.

I ran through the exhibits and ducked behind a tour group. I looked for my friends, but I couldn't see them anywhere. Where was the dam snack bar?

'Stop!' The metal detector guy yelled.

There was no place to go but into an elevator with the tour group. I ducked inside just as the door closed.

'We'll be going down two hundred and twenty-two metres,' our tour guide said cheerfully. She was a park ranger, with long black hair pulled back in a ponytail and tinted glasses. I guess she hadn't noticed that I was being chased. 'Don't worry, ladies and gentlemen, the elevator hardly ever breaks.'

'Does this go to the snack bar?' I asked her.

A few people behind me chuckled. The tour guide looked at me. Something about her gaze made my skin tingle.

'To the turbines, young man,' the lady said. 'Weren't you listening to my fascinating presentation upstairs?'

'Oh, uh, sure. Is there another way out of the dam?'

'It's a dead end,' a tourist behind me said. 'For heaven's sake. The only way out is the other elevator.'

The doors opened.

'Go right ahead, folks,' the tour guide told us. 'Another ranger is waiting for you at the end of the corridor.'

I didn't have much choice but to go out with the group.

'And, young man,' the tour guide called. I looked back. She'd taken off her glasses. Her eyes were startlingly grey, like storm clouds. 'There is always a way out for those clever enough to find it.'

The doors closed with the tour guide still inside, leaving me alone.

Before I could think too much about the woman in the

elevator, a *ding* came from round the corner. The second elevator was opening, and I heard an unmistakable sound – the clattering of skeleton teeth.

I ran after the tour group, through a tunnel carved out of solid rock. It seemed to run forever. The walls were moist, and the air hummed with electricity and the roar of water. I came out on a U-shaped balcony that overlooked this huge warehouse area. Fifteen metres below, enormous turbines were running. It was a big room, but I didn't see any other exit, unless I wanted to jump into the turbines and get churned up to make electricity. I didn't.

Another tour guide was talking over the microphone, telling the tourists about water supplies in Nevada. I prayed that Thalia, Zoë and Grover were okay. They might already be captured, or eating at the snack bar, completely unaware that we were being surrounded. And stupid me: I had trapped myself in a hole a couple of hundred metres below the surface.

I worked my way around the crowd, trying not to be too obvious about it. There was a hallway at the other side of the balcony – maybe some place I could hide. I kept my hand on Riptide, ready to strike.

By the time I got to the opposite side of the balcony, my nerves were shot. I backed into the little hallway and watched the tunnel I'd come from.

Then right behind me I heard a sharp *Chhh!* like the voice of a skeleton.

Without thinking, I uncapped Riptide and spun, slashing with my sword.

The girl I'd just tried to slice in half yelped and dropped her Kleenex.

'Oh my god!' she shouted. 'Do you always kill people when they blow their nose?'

The first thing that went through my head was that the sword hadn't hurt her. It had passed clean through her body, harmlessly. 'You're mortal!'

She looked at me in disbelief. 'What's *that* supposed to mean? Of course I'm mortal! How did you get that sword past security?'

'I didn't – Wait, you can see it's a sword?'

The girl rolled her eyes, which were green like mine. She had frizzy reddish-brown hair. Her nose was also red, like she had a cold. She wore a big maroon Harvard sweatshirt and jeans that were covered with marker stains and little holes, like she spent her free time poking them with a fork.

'Well, it's either a sword or the biggest toothpick in the world,' she said. 'And why didn't it hurt me? I mean, not that I'm complaining. Who are you? And, whoa, what is that you're wearing? Is that made of lion fur?'

She asked so many questions so fast, it was like she was throwing rocks at me. I couldn't think of what to say. I looked at my sleeves to see if the Nemean Lion pelt had somehow changed back to fur, but it still looked like a brown winter coat to me.

I knew the skeleton warriors were still chasing me. I had no time to waste. But I just stared at the redheaded girl. Then I remembered what Thalia had done at Westover Hall to fool the teachers. Maybe I could manipulate the Mist.

I concentrated hard and snapped my fingers. 'You don't see a sword,' I told the girl. 'It's just a ballpoint pen.'

She blinked. 'Um . . . no. It's a sword, weirdo.'

'Who *are* you?' I demanded.

She huffed indignantly. 'Rachel Elizabeth Dare. Now, are you going to answer *my* questions or should I scream for security?'

'No!' I said. 'I mean, I'm kind of in a hurry. I'm in trouble.'

'In a hurry or in trouble?'

'Um, sort of both.'

She looked over my shoulder and her eyes widened. 'Bathroom!'

'What?'

'Bathroom! Behind me! Now!'

I don't know why, but I listened to her. I slipped inside the boy's bathroom and left Rachel Elizabeth Dare standing outside. Later, that seemed cowardly to me. I'm also pretty sure it saved my life.

I heard the clattering, hissing sounds of skeletons as they came closer.

My grip tightened on Riptide. What was I thinking? I'd left a mortal girl out there to die. I was preparing to burst out and fight when Rachel Elizabeth Dare started talking in that rapid-fire machine gun way of hers.

'Oh my god! Did you *see* that kid? It's about time you got here. He tried to kill me! He had a sword, for god's sake. You security guys let a sword-swinging lunatic inside a national landmark? I mean, jeez! He ran that way towards those turbine thingies. I think he went over the side or something. Maybe he fell.'

The skeletons clattered excitedly. I heard them moving off.

Rachel opened the door. 'All clear. But you'd better hurry.'

She looked shaken. Her face was grey and sweaty.

I peeked round the corner. Three skeleton warriors were running towards the other end of the balcony. The way to the elevator was clear for a few seconds.

'I owe you one, Rachel Elizabeth Dare.'

'What are those things?' she asked. 'They looked like –'

'Skeletons?'

She nodded uneasily.

'Do yourself a favour,' I said. 'Forget it. Forget you ever saw me.'

'Forget you tried to kill me?'

'Yeah. That, too.'

'But who are you?'

'Percy –' I started to say. Then the skeletons turned round. 'Gotta go!'

'What kind of name is Percy Gotta-go?'

I bolted for the exit.

The café was packed with kids enjoying the best part of the tour – the dam lunch. Thalia, Zoë and Grover were just sitting down with their food.

'We need to leave,' I gasped. 'Now!'

'But we just got our burritos!' Thalia said.

Zoë stood up, muttering an Ancient Greek curse. 'He's right! Look.'

The café windows wrapped all the way round the observation floor, which gave us a beautiful panoramic view of the skeletal army that had come to kill us.

I counted two on the east side of the dam road, blocking

the way to Arizona. Three more on the west side, guarding Nevada. All of them were armed with batons and pistols.

But our immediate problem was a lot closer. The three skeleton warriors who'd been chasing me in the turbine room now appeared on the stairs. They saw me from across the cafeteria and clattered their teeth.

'Elevator!' Grover said. We bolted in that direction, but the doors opened with a pleasant *ding,* and three more warriors stepped out. Every warrior was accounted for, minus the one Bianca had blasted to flames in New Mexico. We were completely surrounded.

Then Grover had a brilliant, totally Grover-like idea.

'Burrito fight!' he yelled, and flung his Guacamole Grande at the nearest skeleton.

Now, if you have never been hit by a flying burrito, count yourself lucky. In terms of deadly projectiles, it's right up there with grenades and cannonballs. Grover's lunch hit the skeleton and knocked his skull clean off his shoulders. I'm not sure what the other kids in the café saw, but they went crazy and started throwing their burritos and baskets of chips and sodas at each other, shrieking and screaming.

The skeletons tried to aim their guns, but it was hopeless. Bodies and food and drinks were flying everywhere.

In the chaos, Thalia and I tackled the other two skeletons on the stairs and sent them flying into the condiment table. Then we all raced downstairs, Guacamole Grandes whizzing past our heads.

'What now?' Grover asked as we burst outside.

I didn't have an answer. The warriors on the road were

closing in from either direction. We ran across the street to the plaza with the winged bronze statues, but that just put our backs to the mountain.

The skeletons moved forward, forming a crescent round us. Their brethren from the café were running up to join them. One was still putting its skull back on its shoulders. Another was covered in ketchup and mustard. Two more had burritos lodged in their ribcages. They didn't look happy about it. They drew batons and advanced.

'Four against eleven,' Zoë muttered. 'And *they* cannot die.'

'It's been nice adventuring with you guys,' Grover said, his voice trembling.

Something shiny caught the corner of my eye. I glanced behind me at the statues' feet. 'Whoa,' I said. 'Their toes really are bright.'

'Percy!' Thalia said. 'This isn't the time.'

But I couldn't help staring at the two giant bronze guys with tall bladed wings like letter openers. They were weathered brown except for their toes, which shone like new pennies from all the times people had rubbed them for good luck.

Good luck. The blessing of Zeus.

I thought about the tour guide in the elevator. Her grey eyes and her smile. What had she said? *There is always a way for those clever enough to find it.*

'Thalia,' I said. 'Pray to your dad.'

She glared at me. 'He never answers.'

'Just this once,' I pleaded. 'Ask for help. I think . . . I think the statues can give us some luck.'

Six skeletons raised their guns. The other five came forward with batons. Fifteen metres away. Ten metres.

'Do it!' I yelled.

'No!' Thalia said. 'He won't answer me.'

'This time is different!'

'Who says?'

I hesitated. 'Athena, I think.'

Thalia scowled like she was sure I'd gone crazy.

'Try it,' Grover pleaded.

Thalia closed her eyes. Her lips moved in a silent prayer. I put in my own prayer to Annabeth's mom, hoping I was right that it had been her in that elevator – that she was trying to help us save her daughter.

And nothing happened.

The skeletons closed in. I raised Riptide to defend myself. Thalia held up her shield. Zoë pushed Grover behind her and aimed an arrow at a skeleton's head.

A shadow fell over me. I thought maybe it was the shadow of death. Then I realized it was the shadow of an enormous wing. The skeletons looked up too late. A flash of bronze, and all five of the baton-wielders were swept aside.

The other skeletons opened fire. I raised my lion coat for protection, but I didn't need it. The bronze angels stepped in front of us and folded their wings like shields. Bullets pinged off them like rain off a corrugated roof. Both angels slashed outwards, and the skeletons went flying across the road.

'Man, it feels good to stand up!' the first angel said. His voice sounded tinny and rusty, like he hadn't had a drink since he'd been built.

'Will ya look at my toes?' the other said. 'Holy Zeus, what were those tourists thinking?'

As stunned as I was by the angels, I was more concerned with the skeletons. A few of them were getting up again, reassembling, bony hands groping for their weapons.

'Trouble!' I said.

'Get us out of here!' Thalia yelled.

Both angels looked down at her. 'Zeus's kid?'

'Yes!'

'Could I get a *please,* Miss Zeus's Kid?' an angel asked.

'Please!'

The angels looked at each other and shrugged.

'Could use a stretch,' one decided.

And the next thing I knew, one of them grabbed Thalia and me, the other grabbed Zoë and Grover, and we flew straight up, over the dam and the river, the skeleton warriors shrinking to tiny specks below us and the sound of gunfire echoing off the sides of the mountains.

15 I WRESTLE SANTA'S EVIL TWIN

'Tell me when it's over,' Thalia said. Her eyes were shut tight. The statue was holding onto us so we couldn't fall, but still Thalia clutched his arm like it was the most important thing in the world.

'Everything's fine,' I promised.

'Are . . . are we very high?'

I looked down. Below us, a range of snowy mountains zipped by. I stretched out my foot and kicked snow off one of the peaks.

'Nah,' I said. 'Not that high.'

'We are in the Sierras!' Zoë yelled. She and Grover were hanging from the arms of the other statue. 'I have hunted here before. At this speed, we should be in San Francisco in a few hours.'

'Hey, hey, Frisco!' our angel said. 'Yo, Chuck! We could visit those guys at the Mechanics Monument again! They know how to party!'

'Oh, man,' the other angel said. 'I am *so* there!'

'You guys have visited San Francisco?' I asked.

'We automatons gotta have some fun once in a while, right?' our statue said. 'Those mechanics took us over to the de Young Museum and introduced us to these marble lady statues, see. And –'

'Hank!' the other statue Chuck cut in. 'They're kids, man.'

'Oh, right.' If bronze statues could blush, I swear Hank did. 'Back to flying.'

We sped up, so I could tell the angels were excited. The mountains fell away into hills, and then we were zipping along over farmland and towns and highways.

Grover played his pipes to pass the time. Zoë got bored and started shooting arrows at random billboards as we flew by. Every time she saw a Target department store – and we passed dozens of them – she would peg the store's sign with a few bullseyes at a hundred miles an hour.

Thalia kept her eyes closed the whole way. She muttered to herself a lot, like she was praying.

'You did good back there,' I told her. 'Zeus listened.'

It was hard to tell what she was thinking with her eyes closed.

'Maybe,' she said. 'How did you get away from the skeletons in the generator room, anyway? You said they cornered you.'

I told her about the weird mortal girl, Rachel Elizabeth Dare, who seemed to be able to see right through the Mist. I thought Thalia was going to call me crazy, but she just nodded.

'Some mortals are like that,' she said. 'Nobody knows why.'

Suddenly I flashed on something I'd never considered. My *mom* was like that. She had seen the Minotaur on Half-Blood Hill and known exactly what it was. She hadn't been surprised at all last year when I'd told her my friend Tyson was really a Cyclops. Maybe she'd known all along. No wonder she'd been so scared for me as I was growing up. She saw through the Mist even better than I did.

'Well, the girl was annoying,' I said. 'But I'm glad I didn't vaporize her. That would've been bad.'

Thalia nodded. 'Must be nice to be a regular mortal.'

She said that as if she'd given it a lot of thought.

'Where you guys want to land?' Hank asked, waking me from a night of fitful sleep.

I looked down and said, 'Whoa.'

I'd seen San Francisco in pictures before, but never in real life. It was probably the most beautiful city I'd ever seen: kind of like a smaller, cleaner Manhattan, if Manhattan had been surrounded by green hills and fog. There was a huge bay and ships, islands and sailboats, and the Golden Gate Bridge sticking up out of the fog. I felt like I should take a picture or something. *Greetings from Frisco. Haven't Died Yet. Wish You Were Here.*

'There,' Zoë suggested. 'By the Embarcadero Building.'

'Good thinking,' Chuck said. 'Me and Hank can blend in with the pigeons.'

We all looked at him.

'Kidding,' he said. 'Sheesh, can't statues have a sense of humour?'

As it turned out, there wasn't much need to blend in. It was early morning and not many people were around. We freaked out a homeless guy on the ferry dock when we landed. He screamed when he saw Hank and Chuck and ran off yelling something about metal angels from Mars.

We said our goodbyes to the angels, who flew off to party with their statue friends. That's when I realized I had no idea what we were going to do next.

We'd made it to the West Coast. Artemis was here

somewhere. Annabeth, too, I hoped. But I had no idea how to find them, and tomorrow was the winter solstice. Nor did I have any clue what monster Artemis had been hunting. It was supposed to find *us* on the quest. It was supposed to 'show the trail', but it never had. Now we were stuck on the ferry dock with not much money, no friends and no luck.

After a brief discussion, we agreed that we needed to figure out just what this mystery monster was.

'But how?' I asked.

'Nereus,' Grover said.

I looked at him. 'What?'

'Isn't that what Apollo told you to do? Find Nereus?'

I nodded. I'd completely forgotten my last conversation with the sun god.

'The old man of the sea,' I remembered. 'I'm supposed to find him and force him to tell us what he knows. But how do I find him?'

Zoë made a face. 'Old Nereus, eh?'

'You know him?' Thalia asked.

'My mother was a sea goddess. Yes, I know him. Unfortunately, he is never very hard to find. Just follow the smell.'

'What do you mean?' I asked.

'Come,' she said, without enthusiasm. 'I will show thee.'

I knew I was in trouble when we stopped at the Goodwill drop box. Five minutes later, Zoë had me outfitted in a ragged flannel shirt and jeans three sizes too big, bright red trainers and a floppy rainbow hat.

'Oh, yeah,' Grover said, trying not to burst out laughing, 'you look completely inconspicuous now.'

Zoë nodded with satisfaction. 'A typical male vagrant.'

'Thanks a lot,' I grumbled. 'Why am I doing this again?'

'I told thee. To blend in.'

She led the way back down to the waterfront. After a long time spent searching the docks, Zoë finally stopped in her tracks. She pointed down a pier where a bunch of homeless guys were huddled together in blankets, waiting for the soup kitchen to open for lunch.

'He will be down there somewhere,' Zoë said. 'He never travels very far from the water. He likes to sun himself during the day.'

'How do I know which one is him?'

'Sneak up,' she said. 'Act homeless. You will know him. He will smell . . . different.'

'Great.' I didn't want to ask for particulars. 'And once I find him?'

'Grab him,' she said. 'And hold on. He will try anything to get rid of thee. Whatever he does, do not let go. Force him to tell thee about the monster.'

'We've got your back,' Thalia said. She picked something off the back of my shirt – a big clump of fuzz that came from who knows where. 'Eww. On second thought . . . I don't want your back. But we'll be rooting for you.'

Grover gave me a big thumbs-up.

I grumbled how nice it was to have super-powerful friends. Then I headed towards the dock.

I pulled my cap down and stumbled like I was about to pass out, which wasn't hard considering how tired I was. I passed our homeless friend from the Embarcadero, who was still trying to warn the other guys about the metal angels from Mars.

He didn't smell good, but he didn't smell . . . different. I kept walking.

A couple of grimy dudes with plastic grocery bags for hats checked me out as I came close.

'Beat it, kid!' one of them muttered.

I moved away. They smelled pretty bad, but just regular old bad. Nothing unusual.

There was a lady with a bunch of plastic flamingos sticking out of a shopping cart. She glared at me like I was going to steal her birds.

At the end of the pier, a guy who looked about a million years old was passed out in a patch of sunlight. He wore pyjamas and a fuzzy bathrobe that probably used to be white. He was fat, with a white beard that had turned yellow, kind of like Santa Claus, if Santa had been rolled out of bed and dragged through a landfill.

And his smell?

As I got closer, I froze. He smelled bad, all right – but *ocean* bad. Like hot seaweed and dead fish and brine. If the ocean had an ugly side . . . this guy was it.

I tried not to gag. I sat down near him like I was tired. Santa opened one eye suspiciously. I could feel him staring at me, but I didn't look. I muttered something about stupid school and stupid parents, figuring that might sound reasonable.

Santa Claus went back to sleep.

I tensed. I knew this was going to look strange. I didn't know how the other homeless people would react. But I jumped Santa Claus.

'Ahhhhh!' he screamed. I meant to grab him, but he seemed to grab me instead. It was as if he'd never been asleep at all. He certainly didn't act like a weak old man. He had a grip like steel. 'Help me!' he screamed as he squeezed me to death.

'That's a crime!' one of the other homeless guys yelled. 'Kid rolling an old man like that!'

I rolled, all right – straight down the pier until my head slammed into a post. I was dazed for a second, and Nereus's grip slackened. He was making a break for it. Before he could, I regained my senses and tackled him from behind.

'I don't have any money!' He tried to get up and run, but I locked my arms round his chest. His rotten fish smell was awful, but I held on.

'I don't want money,' I said as he fought. 'I'm a half-blood! I want information!'

That just made him struggle harder. 'Heroes! Why do you always pick on me?'

'Because you know everything!'

He growled and tried to shake me off his back. It was like holding on to a roller coaster. He thrashed around, making it impossible for me to keep on my feet, but I gritted my teeth and squeezed tighter. We staggered towards the edge of the pier and I got an idea.

'Oh, no!' I said. 'Not the water!'

The plan worked. Immediately, Nereus yelled in triumph and jumped off the edge. Together, we plunged into San Francisco Bay.

He must've been surprised when I tightened my grip, the ocean filling me with extra strength. But Nereus had a few tricks left, too. He changed shape until I was holding a sleek black seal.

I've heard people make jokes about trying to hold a greased pig but, I'm telling you, holding onto a seal in the water is harder. Nereus plunged straight down, wriggling and thrashing and spiralling through the dark water. If I hadn't been Poseidon's son, there's no way I could've stayed with him.

Nereus spun and expanded, turning into a killer whale, but I grabbed his dorsal fin as he burst out of the water.

A whole bunch of tourists went, 'Whoa!'

I managed to wave at the crowd. *Yeah, we do this every day here in San Francisco.*

Nereus plunged into the water and turned into a slimy eel. I started to tie him into a knot until he realized what was going on and changed back to human form. 'Why won't you drown?' he wailed, pummelling me with his fists.

'I'm Poseidon's son,' I said.

'Curse that upstart! I was here first!'

Finally he collapsed on the edge of the boat dock. Above us was one of those tourist piers lined with shops, like a mall on water. Nereus was heaving and gasping. I was feeling great. I could've gone on all day, but I didn't tell him that. I wanted him to feel like he'd put up a good fight.

My friends ran down the steps from the pier.

'You got him!' Zoë said.

'You don't have to sound so amazed,' I said.

Nereus moaned. 'Oh, wonderful. An audience for my humiliation! The normal deal, I suppose? You'll let me go if I answer your question?'

'I've got more than one question,' I said.

'Only one question per capture! That's the rule.'

I looked at my friends.

This wasn't good. I needed to find Artemis, and I needed to figure out what the doomsday creature was. I also needed to know if Annabeth was still alive, and how to rescue her. How could I ask all that in one question?

A voice inside me was screaming *Ask about Annabeth!* That's what I cared about most.

But then I imagined what Annabeth might say. She would never forgive me if I saved her and didn't save Olympus. Zoë would want me to ask about Artemis, but Chiron had told us the monster was even more important.

I sighed. 'All right, Nereus. Tell me where to find this terrible monster that could bring an end to the gods. The one Artemis was hunting.'

The Old Man of the Sea smiled, showing off his mossy green teeth.

'Oh, that's too easy,' he said evilly. 'He's right there.'

Nereus pointed to the water at my feet.

'Where?' I said.

'The deal is complete!' Nereus gloated. With a pop, he turned into a goldfish and did a backflip into the sea.

'You tricked me!' I yelled.

'Wait.' Thalia's eyes widened. 'What is *that*?'

'*MOOOOOOOO!*'

I looked down, and there was my friend the cow serpent, swimming next to the dock. She nudged my shoe and gave me the sad brown eyes.

'Ah, Bessie,' I said. 'Not now.'

'*Mooo!*'

Grover gasped. 'He says his name isn't Bessie.'

'You can understand her . . . er, him?'

Grover nodded. 'It's a very old form of animal speech. But he says his name is the Ophiotaurus.'

'The Ophi-what?'

'It means serpent bull in Greek,' Thalia said. 'But what's it doing here?'

'*Moooooooo!*'

'He says Percy is his protector,' Grover announced. 'And he's running from the bad people. He says they are close.'

I was wondering how you got all that out of a single *moooooo*.

'Wait,' Zoë said, looking at me. 'You know this cow?'

I was feeling impatient, but I told them the story.

Thalia shook her head in disbelief. 'And you just forgot to mention this before?'

'Well . . . yeah.' It seemed silly, now that she said it, but things had been happening so fast. Bessie the Ophiotaurus seemed like a minor detail.

'I am a fool,' Zoë said suddenly. 'I know this story!'

'What story?'

'From the War of the Titans,' she said. 'My . . . my father told me this tale, thousands of years ago. This is the beast we are looking for.'

'Bessie?' I looked down at the bull serpent. 'But . . . he's too cute. He couldn't destroy the world.'

'That is how we were wrong,' Zoë said. 'We've been anticipating a huge dangerous monster, but the Ophiotaurus does not bring down the gods that way. He must be sacrificed.'

'*MMMM*,' Bessie lowed.

'I don't think he likes the S-word,' Grover said.

I patted Bessie on the head, trying to calm him down. He let me scratch his ear, but he was trembling.

'How could anyone hurt him?' I said. 'He's harmless.'

Zoë nodded. 'But there is power in killing innocence. Terrible power. The Fates ordained a prophecy aeons ago, when this creature was born. They said that whoever killed the Ophiotaurus and sacrificed its entrails to fire would have the power to destroy the gods.'

'*MMMMMM!*'

'Um,' Grover said. 'Maybe we could avoid talking about *entrails*, too.'

Thalia stared at the cow serpent with wonder. 'The power to destroy the gods . . . how? I mean, what would happen?'

'No one knows,' Zoë said. 'The first time, during the Titan war, the Ophiotaurus was in fact slain by a giant ally of the Titans, but thy father Zeus sent an eagle to snatch the entrails away before they could be tossed into the fire. It was a close call. Now, after three thousand years, the Ophiotaurus is reborn.'

Thalia sat down on the dock. She stretched out her hand. Bessie went right to her. Thalia placed her hand on his head. Bessie shivered.

Thalia's expression bothered me. She almost looked . . . hungry.

'We have to protect him,' I told her. 'If Luke gets hold of him –'

'Luke wouldn't hesitate,' Thalia muttered. 'The power to overthrow Olympus. That's . . . that's huge.'

'Yes, it is, my dear,' said a man's voice in a heavy French accent. 'And it is a power *you* shall unleash.'

The Ophiotaurus made a whimpering sound and submerged.

I looked up. We'd been so busy talking, we'd allowed ourselves to be ambushed.

Standing behind us, his two-colour eyes gleaming wickedly, was Dr Thorn, the manticore himself.

'This is just pairrr-fect,' the manticore gloated.

He was wearing a ratty black trench coat over his Westover Hall uniform, which was torn and stained. His military haircut had grown out spiky and greasy. He hadn't shaved recently, so his face was covered in silver stubble. Basically, he didn't look much better than the guys down at the soup kitchen.

'Long ago, the gods banished me to Persia,' the manticore said. 'I was forced to scrounge for food on the edges of the world, hiding in forests, devouring insignificant human farmers for my meals. I never got to fight any great heroes. I was not feared and admired in the old stories! But now that will change. The Titans shall honour me, and I shall feast on the flesh of half-bloods!'

On either side of him stood two armed security guys, some of the mortal mercenaries I'd seen in D.C. Two more stood on the next boat dock over, just in case we tried to escape that way. There were tourists all around – walking down the waterfront, shopping at the pier above us – but I knew that wouldn't stop the manticore from acting.

'Where . . . where are the skeletons?' I asked the manticore.

He sneered. 'I do not need those foolish undead! The General thinks I am worthless? He will change his mind when I defeat you myself!'

I needed time to think. I had to save Bessie. I could dive into the sea, but how could I make a quick getaway with a two-hundred-kilogram cow serpent? And what about my friends?

'We beat you once before,' I said.

'Ha! You could barely fight me with a goddess on your side. And, alas . . . that goddess is preoccupied at the moment. There will be no help for you now.'

Zoë notched an arrow and aimed it straight at the manticore's head. The guards on either side of us raised their guns.

'Wait!' I said. 'Zoë, don't!'

The manticore smiled. 'The boy is right, Zoë Nightshade. Put away your bow. It would be a shame to kill you before you witnessed Thalia's great victory.'

'What are you talking about?' Thalia growled. She had her shield and spear ready.

'Surely it is clear,' the manticore said. 'This is your moment. This is why Lord Kronos brought you back to life. You will sacrifice the Ophiotaurus. You will bring its entrails to the sacred fire on the mountain. You will gain unlimited power. And for your sixteenth birthday, you will overthrow Olympus.'

No one spoke. It made terrible sense. Thalia was only two days away from turning sixteen. She was a child of the Big Three. And here was a choice, a terrible choice that could mean the end of the gods. It was just like the prophecy said. I wasn't sure if I felt relieved, horrified or disappointed. I wasn't the prophecy kid after all. Doomsday was happening right now.

I waited for Thalia to tell the manticore off, but she

hesitated. She looked completely stunned.

'You know it is the right choice,' the manticore told her. 'Your friend Luke recognized it. You shall be reunited with him. You shall rule this world together under the auspices of the Titans. Your father abandoned you, Thalia. He cares nothing for you. And now you shall gain power over him. Crush the Olympians underfoot, as they deserve. Call the beast! It will come to you. Use your spear.'

'Thalia,' I said, 'snap out of it!'

She looked at me the same way she had the morning she woke up on Half-Blood Hill, dazed and uncertain. It was almost like she didn't know me. 'I . . . I don't –'

'Your father helped you,' I said. 'He sent the metal angels. He turned you into a tree to preserve you.'

Her hand tightened on the shaft of her spear.

I looked at Grover desperately. Thank the gods, he understood what I needed. He raised his pipes to his mouth and played a quick riff.

The manticore yelled, 'Stop him!'

The guards had been targeting Zoë, and before they could figure out that the kid with the pipes was the bigger problem, the wooden planks at their feet sprouted new branches and tangled their legs. Zoë let loose two quick arrows that exploded at their feet in clouds of sulphurous yellow smoke. Fart arrows!

The guards started coughing. The manticore shot spines in our direction but they ricocheted off my lion's coat.

'Grover,' I said, 'tell Bessie to dive deep and stay down!'

'*Moooooo!*' Grover translated. I could only hope that Bessie got the message.

'The cow . . .' Thalia muttered, still in a daze.

'Come on!' I pulled her along as we ran up the stairs to the shopping centre on the pier. We dashed round the corner of the nearest store. I heard the manticore shouting at his minions, 'Get them!' Tourists screamed as the guards shot blindly into the air.

We scrambled to the end of the pier. We hid behind a little kiosk filled with souvenir crystals – wind chimes and dream catchers and stuff like that, glittering in the sunlight. There was a water fountain next to us. Down below, a bunch of sea lions were sunning themselves on the rocks. The whole of San Francisco Bay spread out before us: the Golden Gate Bridge, Alcatraz Island and the green hills and fog beyond that to the north. A picture-perfect moment, except for the fact that we were about to die and the world was going to end.

'Go over the side!' Zoë told me. 'You can escape in the sea, Percy. Call on thy father for help. Maybe you can save the Ophiotaurus.'

She was right, but I couldn't do it.

'I won't leave you guys,' I said. 'We fight together.'

'You have to get word to camp!' Grover said. 'At least let them know what's going on!'

Then I noticed the crystals making rainbows in the sunlight. There was a drinking fountain next to me . . .

'Get word to camp,' I muttered. 'Good idea.'

I uncapped Riptide and slashed off the top of the water fountain. Water burst out of the busted pipe and sprayed all over us.

Thalia gasped as the water hit her. The fog seemed to clear from her eyes. 'Are you crazy?' she asked.

But Grover understood. He was already fishing around

in his pockets for a coin. He threw a golden drachma into the rainbows created by the mist and yelled, 'O goddess, accept my offering!'

The mist rippled.

'Camp Half-Blood!' I said.

And there, shimmering in the Mist right next to us, was the last person I wanted to see: Mr D, wearing his leopard-skin jogging suit and rummaging through the refrigerator.

He looked up lazily. 'Do you mind?'

'Where's Chiron!' I shouted.

'How rude.' Mr D took a swig from a jug of grape juice. 'Is that how you say hello?'

'Hello,' I amended. 'We're about to die! Where's Chiron?'

Mr D considered that. I wanted to scream at him to hurry up, but I knew that wouldn't work. Behind us, footsteps and shouting – the manticore's troops were closing in.

'About to die,' Mr D mused. 'How exciting. I'm afraid Chiron isn't here. Would you like me to take a message?'

I looked at my friends. 'We're dead.'

Thalia gripped her spear. She looked like her old angry self again. 'Then we'll die fighting.'

'How noble,' Mr D said, stifling a yawn. 'So what is the problem, exactly?'

I didn't see that it would make any difference, but I told him about the Ophiotaurus.

'Mmm.' He studied the contents of the fridge. 'So that's it. I see.'

'You don't even care!' I screamed. 'You'd just as soon watch us die!'

'Let's see. I think I'm in the mood for pizza tonight.'

I wanted to slash through the rainbow and disconnect, but I didn't have time. The manticore screamed, 'There!' And we were surrounded. Two of the guards stood behind him. The other two appeared on the roofs of the pier shops above us. The manticore threw off his coat and transformed into his true self, his lion claws extended and his spiky tail bristling with poison barbs.

'Excellent,' he said. He glanced at the apparition in the mist and snorted. 'Alone, without any *real* help. Wonderful.'

'You could *ask* for help,' Mr D murmured to me, as if this were an amusing thought. 'You could say please.'

When wild boars fly, I thought. There was no way I was going to die begging a slob like Mr D, just so he could laugh as we all got gunned down.

Zoë readied her arrows. Grover lifted his pipes. Thalia raised her shield, and I noticed a tear running down her cheek. Suddenly it occurred to me: this had happened to her before. She had been cornered on Half-Blood Hill. She'd willingly given her life for her friends. But, this time, she couldn't save us.

How could I let that happen to her?

'Please, Mr D,' I muttered. 'Help.'

Of course, nothing happened.

The manticore grinned. 'Spare the daughter of Zeus. She will join us soon enough. Kill the others.'

The men raised their guns, and something strange happened. You know how you feel when all the blood rushes to your head, like if you hang upside down and turn right-side up too quickly? There was a rush like that all around me, and a sound like a huge sigh. The sunlight tinged with purple. I smelled grapes and something more sour – wine.

SNAP!

It was the sound of many minds breaking at the same time. The sound of madness. One guard put his pistol between his teeth like it was a bone and ran around on all fours. Two others dropped their guns and started waltzing with each other. The fourth began doing what looked like an Irish clogging dance. It would have been funny if it hadn't been so terrifying.

'No!' screamed the manticore. 'I will deal with you myself!'

His tail bristled, but the planks under his paws erupted into grapevines that immediately began wrapping round the monster's body, sprouting new leaves and clusters of green baby grapes that ripened in seconds as the manticore shrieked, until he was engulfed in a huge mass of vines, leaves and full clusters of purple grapes. Finally the grapes stopped shivering, and I had a feeling that somewhere inside there, the manticore was no more.

'Well,' said Dionysus, closing his refrigerator. 'That was fun.'

I stared at him, horrified. 'How could you . . . How did you –'

'Such gratitude,' he muttered. 'The mortals will come out of it. Too much explaining to do if I made their condition permanent. I hate writing reports to Father.'

He stared resentfully at Thalia. 'I hope you learned your lesson, girl. It isn't easy to resist power, is it?'

Thalia blushed as if she were ashamed.

'Mr D,' Grover said in amazement. 'You . . . you saved us.'

'Mmm. Don't make me regret it, satyr. Now get going,

Percy Jackson. I've bought you a few hours at most.'

'The Ophiotaurus,' I said. 'Can you get it to camp?'

Mr D sniffed. 'I do not transport livestock. That's your problem.'

'But where do we go?'

Dionysus looked at Zoë. 'Oh, I think the huntress knows. You must enter at sunset today, you know, or all is lost. Now goodbye. My pizza is waiting.'

'Mr D,' I said.

He raised his eyebrow.

'You called me by my right name,' I said. 'You called me Percy Jackson.'

'I most certainly did not, Peter Johnson. Now off with you!'

He waved his hand, and his image disappeared in the mist.

All around us, the manticore's minions were still acting completely nuts. One of them had found our friend the homeless guy, and they were having a serious conversation about metal angels from Mars. Several other guards were harassing the tourists, making animal noises and trying to steal their shoes.

I looked at Zoë. 'What did he mean . . . "the huntress knows"?'

Her face was the colour of the fog. She pointed across the bay, past the Golden Gate Bridge. In the distance, a single mountain rose up above the cloud layer.

'The garden of my sisters,' she said. 'I must go home.'

16 WE MEET THE DRAGON OF ETERNAL BAD BREATH

'We will never make it,' Zoë said. 'We are moving too slowly. But we cannot leave the Ophiotaurus.'

'Mooo,' Bessie said. He swam next to me as we jogged along the waterfront. We'd left the shopping-centre pier far behind. We were heading towards the Golden Gate Bridge, but it was a lot further than I'd realized. The sun was already dipping in the west.

'I don't get it,' I said. 'Why do we have to get there at sunset?'

'The Hesperides are the nymphs of the sunset,' Zoë said. 'We can only enter their garden as day changes to night.'

'What happens if we miss it?'

'Tomorrow is winter solstice. If we miss sunset tonight, we would have to wait until tomorrow evening. And by then, the Olympian Council will be over. We must free Lady Artemis tonight.'

Or Annabeth will be dead, I thought, but I didn't say that.

'We need a car,' Thalia said.

'But what about Bessie?' I asked.

Grover stopped in his tracks. 'I've got an idea! The Ophiotaurus can appear in different bodies of water, right?'

'Well, yeah,' I said. 'I mean, he was in Long Island Sound.

Then he just popped into the water at Hoover Dam. And now he's here.'

'So maybe we could coax him back to Long Island Sound,' Grover said. 'Then Chiron could help us get him to Olympus.'

'But he was following *me*,' I said. 'If I'm not there, would he know where he's going?'

'Moo,' Bessie said forlornly.

'I . . . I can show him,' Grover said. 'I'll go with him.'

I stared at him. Grover was no fan of the water. He'd almost drowned last summer in the Sea of Monsters, and he couldn't swim very well with his goat hooves.

'I'm the only one who can talk to him,' Grover said. 'It makes sense.'

He bent down and said something in Bessie's ear. Bessie shivered, then made a contented, lowing sound.

'The blessing of the Wild,' Grover said. 'That should help with safe passage. Percy, pray to your dad, too. See if he will grant us safe passage through the seas.'

I didn't understand how they could possibly swim back to Long Island from California. Then again, monsters didn't travel the same way as humans. I'd seen plenty of evidence of that.

I tried to concentrate on the waves, the smell of the ocean, the sound of the tide.

'Dad,' I said. 'Help us. Get the Ophiotaurus and Grover safely to camp. Protect them at sea.'

'A prayer like that needs a sacrifice,' Thalia said. 'Something big.'

I thought for a second. Then I took off my coat.

'Percy,' Grover said. 'Are you sure? That lion skin . . . that's really helpful. Hercules used it!'

As soon as he said that, I realized something.

I glanced at Zoë, who was watching me carefully. I realized I *did* know who Zoë's hero had been; the one who'd ruined her life, got her kicked out of her family and never even mentioned how she'd helped him. Hercules, a hero I'd admired all my life.

'If I'm going to survive,' I said, 'it won't be because I've got a lion-skin cloak. I'm not Hercules.'

I threw the coat into the bay. It turned back into a golden lion skin, flashing in the light. Then, as it began to sink beneath the waves, it seemed to dissolve into sunlight on the water.

The sea breeze picked up.

Grover took a deep breath. 'Well, no time to lose.'

He jumped in the water and immediately began to sink. Bessie glided next to him and let Grover take hold of his neck.

'Be careful,' I told them.

'We will,' Grover said. 'Okay, um . . . Bessie? We're going to Long Island. It's east. Over that way.'

'*Moooo?*' Bessie said.

'Yes,' Grover answered. 'Long Island. It's this island. And . . . it's long. Oh, let's just start.'

'*Mooo!*'

Bessie lurched forward. He started to submerge and Grover said, 'I can't breathe underwater! Just thought I'd mention –' *Glub!*

Under they went, and I hoped my father's protection would extend to little things, like breathing.

'Well, that is one problem addressed,' Zoë said. 'But how can we get to my sisters' garden?'

'Thalia's right,' I said. 'We need a car. But there's nobody to help us here. Unless we, uh, borrowed one.'

I didn't like that option. I mean, sure this was a life-or-death situation, but still it was stealing, and it was bound to get us noticed.

'Wait,' Thalia said. She started rifling through her backpack. 'There *is* somebody in San Francisco who can help us. I've got the address here somewhere.'

'Who?' I asked.

Thalia pulled out a crumpled piece of notebook paper and held it up. 'Professor Chase. Annabeth's dad.'

After hearing Annabeth gripe about her dad for two years, I was expecting him to have devil horns and fangs. I was *not* expecting him to be wearing an old-fashioned aviator's cap and goggles. He looked so weird, with his eyes bugging out through the glasses, that we all took a step back on the front porch.

'Hello,' he said in a friendly voice. 'Are you delivering my aeroplanes?'

Thalia, Zoë and I looked at each other warily.

'Um, no, sir,' I said.

'Drat,' he said. 'I need three more Sopwith Camels.'

'Right,' I said, though I had no clue what he was talking about. 'We're friends of Annabeth.'

'Annabeth?' He straightened as if I'd just given him an electric shock. 'Is she all right? Has something happened?'

None of us answered, but our faces must've told him that something was very wrong. He took off his cap and goggles. He had sandy-coloured hair like Annabeth and intense brown eyes. He was handsome, I guess, for an older guy, but it looked like he hadn't shaved in a couple of days, and his shirt was buttoned wrong, so one side of his collar stuck up higher than the other side.

'You'd better come in,' he said.

It didn't look like a house they'd just moved into. There were LEGO robots on the stairs and two cats sleeping on the sofa in the living room. The coffee table was stacked with magazines, and a little kid's winter coat was spread on the floor. The whole house smelled like fresh-baked chocolate-chip cookies. There was jazz music coming from the kitchen. It seemed like a messy, happy kind of home – the kind of place that had been lived in forever.

'Dad!' a little boy screamed. 'He's taking apart my robots!'

'Bobby,' Dr Chase called absently, 'don't take apart your brother's robots.'

'*I'm* Bobby,' the little boy protested. 'He's Matthew!'

'Matthew,' Dr Chase called, 'don't take apart your brother's robots!'

'Okay, Dad!'

Dr Chase turned to us. 'We'll go upstairs to my study. This way.'

'Honey?' a woman called. Annabeth's stepmom appeared in the living room, wiping her hands on a dish towel. She was a pretty Asian woman with red highlighted hair tied in a bun.

'Who are our guests?' she asked.

'Oh,' Dr Chase said. 'This is . . .'

He stared at us blankly.

'Frederick,' she chided. 'You forgot to ask them their names?'

We introduced ourselves a little uneasily, but Mrs Chase seemed really nice. She asked if we were hungry. We admitted we were, and she told us she'd bring us some cookies and sandwiches and sodas.

'Dear,' Dr Chase said. 'They came about Annabeth.'

I half expected Mrs Chase to turn into a raving lunatic at the mention of her stepdaughter, but she just pursed her lips and looked concerned. 'All right. Go on up to the study and I'll bring you some food.' She smiled at me. 'Nice meeting you, Percy. I've heard a lot about you.'

Upstairs, we walked into Dr Chase's study and I said, 'Whoa!'

The room was wall-to-wall books, but what really caught my attention were the war toys. There was a huge table with miniature tanks and soldiers fighting along a blue painted river, with hills and fake trees and stuff. Old-fashioned biplanes hung on strings from the ceiling, tilted at crazy angles like they were in the middle of a dogfight.

Dr Chase smiled. 'Yes. The Third Battle of Ypres. I'm writing a paper, you see, on the use of Sopwith Camels to strafe enemy lines. I believe they played a much greater role than they've been given credit for.'

He plucked a biplane from its string and swept it across the battlefield, making aeroplane engine noises as he knocked down little German soldiers.

'Oh, right,' I said. I knew Annabeth's dad was a professor of military history. She'd never mentioned he played with toy soldiers.

Zoë came over and studied the battlefield. 'The German lines were further from the river.'

Dr Chase stared at her. 'How do you know that?'

'I was there,' she said matter-of-factly. 'Artemis wanted to show us how horrible war was, the way mortal men fight each other. And how foolish, too. The battle was a complete waste.'

Dr Chase opened his mouth in shock. 'You –'

'She's a Hunter, sir,' Thalia said. 'But that's not why we're here. We need –'

'You saw the Sopwith Camels?' Dr Chase said. 'How many were there? What formations did they fly?'

'Sir,' Thalia broke in again. 'Annabeth is in danger.'

That got his attention. He set the biplane down.

'Of course,' he said. 'Tell me everything.'

It wasn't easy, but we tried. Meanwhile, the afternoon light was fading outside. We were running out of time.

When we'd finished, Dr Chase collapsed in his leather recliner. He laced his hands. 'My poor brave Annabeth. We must hurry.'

'Sir, we need transportation to Mount Tamalpais,' Zoë said. 'And we need it immediately.'

'I'll drive you. Hmm, it would be faster to fly in my Camel, but it only seats two.'

'Whoa, you have an actual biplane?' I said.

'Down at Crissy Field,' Dr Chase said proudly. 'That's the reason I had to move here. My sponsor is a private collector with some of the finest World War I relics in the world. He let me restore the Sopwith Camel –'

'Sir,' Thalia said. 'Just a car would be great. And it might be better if we went without you. It's too dangerous.'

Dr Chase frowned uncomfortably. 'Now wait a minute, young lady. Annabeth is my daughter. Dangerous or not, I . . . I can't just –'

'Snacks,' Mrs Chase announced. She pushed through the door with a tray full of peanut-butter-and-jam sandwiches and Cokes and cookies fresh out of the oven, the chocolate chips still gooey. Thalia and I inhaled a few cookies while Zoë said, 'I can drive, sir. I'm not as young as I look. I promise not to destroy your car.'

Mrs Chase knitted her eyebrows. 'What's this about?'

'Annabeth is in danger,' Dr Chase said. 'On Mount Tam. I would drive them, but . . . apparently it's no place for mortals.'

It sounded like it was really hard for him to get that last part out.

I waited for Mrs Chase to say no. I mean, what mortal parent would allow three underage teenagers to borrow their car? To my surprise, Mrs Chase nodded. 'Then they'd better get going.'

'Right!' Dr Chase jumped up and started patting his pockets. 'My keys . . .'

His wife sighed. 'Frederick, honestly. You'd lose your head if it weren't wrapped inside your aviator hat. The keys are hanging on the peg by the front door.'

'Right!' Dr Chase said.

Zoë grabbed a sandwich. 'Thank you both. We should go. *Now*.'

We hustled out the door and down the stairs, the Chases right behind us.

'Percy,' Mrs Chase called as I was leaving, 'tell Annabeth . . . Tell her she still has a home here, will you? Remind her of that.'

I took one last look at the messy living room, Annabeth's half-brothers spilling LEGOs and arguing, the smell of cookies filling the air. Not a bad place, I thought.

'I'll tell her,' I promised.

We ran out to the yellow VW convertible parked in the driveway. The sun was going down. I figured we had less than an hour to save Annabeth.

'Can't this thing go any faster?' Thalia demanded.

Zoë glared at her. 'I cannot control traffic.'

'You both sound like my mother,' I said.

'Shut up!' they said in unison.

Zoë weaved in and out of traffic on the Golden Gate Bridge. The sun was sinking on the horizon when we finally got into Marin County and exited the highway.

The roads were insanely narrow, winding through forests and up the sides of hills and round the edges of steep ravines. Zoë didn't slow down at all.

'Why does everything smell like cough drops?' I asked.

'Eucalyptus.' Zoë pointed to the huge trees all around us.

'The stuff koala bears eat?'

'And monsters,' she said. 'They love chewing the leaves. Especially dragons.'

'Dragons chew eucalyptus leaves?'

'Believe me,' Zoë said, 'if you had dragon breath, you would chew eucalyptus, too.'

I didn't question her, but I did keep my eyes peeled as we drove. Ahead of us loomed Mount Tamalpais. I guess, in terms of mountains, it was a small one, but it looked plenty huge as we were driving towards it.

'So that's the Mountain of Despair?' I asked.

'Yes,' Zoë said tightly.

'Why do they call it that?'

She was silent for almost a mile before answering. 'After the war between the Titans and the gods, many of the Titans were punished and imprisoned. Kronos was sliced to pieces and thrown into Tartarus. Kronos's right-hand man, the general of his forces, was imprisoned up there, on the summit, just beyond the Garden of the Hesperides.'

'The General,' I said. Clouds seemed to be swirling round its peak, as though the mountain were drawing them in, spinning them like a top. 'What's going on up there? A storm?'

Zoë didn't answer. I got the feeling she knew exactly what the clouds meant, and she didn't like it.

'We have to concentrate,' Thalia said. 'The Mist is really strong here.'

'The magical kind or the natural kind?' I asked.

'Both.'

The grey clouds swirled even thicker over the mountain, and we kept driving straight towards them. We were out of the forest now, into wide open spaces of cliffs and grass and rocks and fog.

I happened to glance down at the ocean as we passed a scenic curve, and I saw something that made me jump out of my seat.

'Look!' But we turned a corner and the ocean disappeared behind the hills.

'What?' Thalia asked.

'A big white ship,' I said. 'Docked near the beach. It looked like a cruise ship.'

Her eyes widened. 'Luke's ship?'

I wanted to say I wasn't sure. It might be a coincidence. But I knew better. The *Princess Andromeda,* Luke's demon cruise ship, was docked at that beach. That's why he'd sent his ship all the way down to the Panama Canal. It was the only way to sail it from the East Coast to California.

'We will have company, then,' Zoë said grimly. 'Kronos's army.'

I was about to answer, when suddenly the hairs on the back of my neck stood up. Thalia shouted, 'Stop the car. NOW!'

Zoë must've sensed something was wrong, because she slammed on the brakes without question. The yellow VW spun twice before coming to a stop at the edge of the cliff.

'Out!' Thalia opened the door and pushed me hard. We both rolled onto the pavement. The next second: *BOOOM!*

Lightning flashed, and Dr Chase's Volkswagen erupted like a canary-yellow grenade. I probably would've been killed by shrapnel except for Thalia's shield, which appeared over me. I heard a sound like metal rain, and when I opened my eyes, we were surrounded by wreckage. One of the VW's doors had impaled itself in the street. The smoking bonnet was spinning in circles. Pieces of yellow metal were strewn across the road.

I swallowed the taste of smoke out of my mouth, and looked at Thalia. 'You saved my life.'

'*One shall perish by a parent's hand,*' she muttered. 'Curse him. He would destroy me? *Me?*'

It took me a second to realize she was talking about her dad. 'Oh, hey, that couldn't have been Zeus's lightning bolt. No way.'

'Whose, then?' Thalia demanded.

'I don't know. Zoë said Kronos's name. Maybe he –'

Thalia shook her head, looking angry and stunned. 'No. That wasn't it.'

'Wait,' I said. 'Where's Zoë? Zoë!'

We both got up and ran round the blasted VW. Nothing inside. Nothing either direction down the road. I looked down the cliff. No sign of her.

'Zoë!' I shouted.

Then she was standing right next to me, pulling me by my arm. 'Silence, fool! Do you want to wake Ladon?'

'You mean we're here?'

'Very close,' she said. 'Follow me.'

Sheets of fog were drifting right across the road. Zoë stepped into one of them, and, when the fog passed, she was no longer there. Thalia and I looked at each other.

'Concentrate on Zoë,' Thalia advised. 'We are following her. Go straight into the fog and keep that in mind.'

'Wait, Thalia. About what happened back on the pier . . . I mean, with the manticore and the sacrifice –'

'I don't want to talk about it.'

'You wouldn't actually have . . . you know?'

She hesitated. 'I was just shocked. That's all.'

'Zeus didn't send that lighting bolt at the car. It was Kronos. He's trying to manipulate you, make you angry at your dad.'

She took a deep breath. 'Percy, I know you're trying to make me feel better. Thanks. But come on. We need to go.'

She stepped into the fog, into the Mist, and I followed.

When the fog cleared, I was still on the side of the mountain, but the road was dirt. The grass was thicker. The sunset made a blood-red slash across the sea. The summit of the mountain seemed closer now, swirling with storm clouds and raw power. There was only one path to the top, directly in front of us. And it led through a lush meadow of shadows and flowers: the garden of twilight, just like I'd seen in my dream.

If it hadn't been for the enormous dragon, the garden would've been the most beautiful place I'd ever seen. The grass shimmered with silvery evening light, and the flowers were such brilliant colours they almost glowed in the dark. Stepping stones of polished black marble led round either side of a five-storey-tall apple tree, every bough glittering with golden apples, and I don't mean *yellow* golden apples like in the grocery store. I mean *real* golden apples. I can't describe why they were so appealing, but, as soon as I smelled their fragrance, I knew that one bite would be the most delicious thing I'd ever tasted.

'The apples of immortality,' Thalia said. 'Hera's wedding gift from Zeus.'

I wanted to step right up and pluck one, except for the dragon coiled round the tree.

Now, I don't know what you think of when I say *dragon*. Whatever it is, it's not scary enough. The serpent's body was as thick as a booster rocket, glinting with coppery scales. It had more heads than I could count, as if a hundred deadly pythons had been fused together. It appeared to be asleep. The heads lay curled in a big spaghetti-like mound on the grass, all the eyes closed.

Then the shadows in front of us began to move. There was a beautiful, eerie singing, like voices from the bottom of a well. I reached for Riptide, but Zoë stopped my hand.

Four figures shimmered into existence, four young women who looked very much like Zoë. They all wore white Greek chitons. Their skin was like caramel. Silky black hair tumbled loose around their shoulders. It was strange, but I'd never realized how beautiful Zoë was until I saw her siblings, the Hesperides. They looked just like Zoë – gorgeous, and probably very dangerous.

'Sisters,' Zoë said.

'We do not see any sister,' one of the girls said coldly. 'We see two half-bloods and a Hunter. All of whom shall soon die.'

'You've got it wrong.' I stepped forward. 'Nobody is going to die.'

The girls studied me. They had eyes like volcanic rock, glassy and completely black.

'Perseus Jackson,' one of them said.

'Yes,' mused another. 'I do not see why he is a threat.'

'Who said I was a threat?'

The first Hesperid glanced behind her, towards the top of the mountain. 'They fear thee. They are unhappy that *this* one has not yet killed thee.'

She pointed at Thalia.

'Tempting sometimes,' Thalia admitted. 'But no thanks. He's my friend.'

'There are no friends here, daughter of Zeus,' the girl said. 'Only enemies. Go back.'

'Not without Annabeth,' Thalia said.

'And Artemis,' Zoë said. 'We must approach the mountain.'

'You know he will kill thee,' the girl said. 'You are no match for him.'

'Artemis must be freed,' Zoë insisted. 'Let us pass.'

The girl shook her head. 'You have no rights here any more. We have only to raise our voices and Ladon will wake.'

'He will not hurt me,' Zoë said.

'No? And what about thy so-called friends?'

Then Zoë did the last thing I expected. She shouted, 'Ladon! Wake!'

The dragon stirred, glittering like a mountain of pennies. The Hesperides yelped and scattered. The lead girl said to Zoë, 'Are you mad?'

'You never had any courage, sister,' Zoë said. 'That is thy problem.'

The dragon Ladon was writhing now, a hundred heads whipping around, tongues flickering and tasting the air. Zoë took a step forward, her arms raised.

'Zoë, don't,' Thalia said. 'You're not a Hesperid any more. He'll kill you.'

'Ladon is trained to protect the tree,' Zoë said. 'Skirt round the edges of the garden. Go up the mountain. As long as I am a bigger threat, he should ignore thee.'

'*Should*,' I said. 'Not exactly reassuring.'

'It is the only way,' she said. 'Even the three of us together cannot fight him.'

Ladon opened his mouths. The sound of a hundred heads hissing at once sent a shiver down my spine, and that was before his breath hit me. The smell was like acid. It made my eyes burn, my skin crawl and my hair stand on end. I remembered the time a rat had died inside our apartment wall in New York in the middle of the summer. This stench was like that, except a hundred times stronger, and mixed with the smell of chewed eucalyptus. I promised myself right then that I would *never* ask a school nurse for another cough drop.

I wanted to draw my sword. But then I remembered my dream of Zoë and Hercules, and how Hercules had failed in a head-on assault. I decided to trust Zoë's judgement.

Thalia went left. I went right. Zoë walked straight towards the monster.

'It's me, my little dragon,' Zoë said. 'Zoë has come back.'

Ladon shifted forward, then back. Some of the mouths closed. Some kept hissing. Dragon confusion. Meanwhile, the Hesperides shimmered and turned into shadows. The voice of the eldest whispered, 'Fool.'

'I used to feed thee by hand,' Zoë continued, speaking in a soothing voice as she stepped towards the golden tree. 'Do you still like lamb's meat?'

The dragon's eyes glinted.

Thalia and I were about halfway round the garden. Ahead, I could see a single rocky trail leading up to the black peak of the mountain. The storm swirled above it, spinning on the summit like it was the axis for the whole world.

We'd almost made it out of the meadow when something went wrong. I felt the dragon's mood shift. Maybe Zoë got too close. Maybe the dragon realized he was hungry. Whatever the reason, he lunged at Zoë.

Two thousand years of training kept her alive. She dodged one set of slashing fangs and tumbled under another, weaving through the dragon's heads as she ran in our direction, gagging from the monster's horrible breath.

I drew Riptide to help.

'No!' Zoë panted. 'Run!'

The dragon snapped at her side, and Zoë cried out. Thalia uncovered Aegis and the dragon hissed in pain. In his moment of indecision, Zoë sprinted past us up the mountain, and we followed.

The dragon didn't try to pursue. He hissed and stomped the ground, but I guess he was well trained to guard that tree. He wasn't going to be lured off, even by the tasty prospect of eating some heroes.

We ran up the mountain as the Hesperides resumed their song in the shadows behind us. The music didn't sound so beautiful to me now – more like the soundtrack for a funeral.

At the top of the mountain were ruins, blocks of black granite and marble as big as houses. Broken columns. Statues of bronze that looked as though they'd been half melted.

'The ruins of Mount Othrys,' Thalia whispered in awe.

'Yes,' Zoë said. 'It was not here before. This is bad.'

'What's Mount Othrys?' I asked, feeling like a fool as usual.

'The mountain fortress of the Titans,' Zoë said. 'In the first war, Olympus and Othrys were the two rival capitals of the world. Othrys was –' She winced and held her side.

'You're hurt,' I said. 'Let me see.'

'No! It is nothing. I was saying . . . in the first war, Othrys was blasted to pieces.'

'But . . . how is it here?'

Thalia looked around cautiously as we picked our way through the rubble, past blocks of marble and broken archways. 'It moves in the same way that Olympus moves.

It always exists on the edges of civilization. But the fact that it is here, on *this* mountain, is not good.'

'Why?'

'This is Atlas's mountain,' Zoë said. 'Where he holds –' She froze. Her voice was ragged with despair. 'Where he used to hold up the sky.'

We had reached the summit. A few metres ahead of us, grey clouds swirled in a heavy vortex, making a funnel cloud that almost touched the mountaintop, but instead rested on the shoulders of a twelve-year-old girl with auburn hair and a tattered silvery dress: Artemis, her legs bound to the rock with celestial bronze chains. This is what I had seen in my dream. It hadn't been a cavern roof that Artemis was forced to hold. It was the roof of the world.

'My lady!' Zoë rushed forward, but Artemis said, 'Stop! It is a trap. You must leave now.'

Her voice was strained. She was drenched in sweat. I had never seen a goddess in pain before, but the weight of the sky was clearly too much for Artemis.

Zoë was crying. She ran forward despite Artemis's protests, and tugged at the chains.

A booming voice spoke behind us: 'Ah, how touching.'

We turned. The General was standing there in his brown silk suit. At his side were Luke and half a dozen *dracaenae* bearing the golden sarcophagus of Kronos. Annabeth stood at Luke's side. She had her hands cuffed behind her back, a gag in her mouth and Luke was holding the point of his sword to her throat.

I met her eyes, trying to ask her a thousand questions. There was just one message she was sending me, though: *RUN!*

'Luke,' Thalia snarled. 'Let her go.'

Luke's smile was weak and pale. He looked even worse than he had three days ago in D.C. 'That is the General's decision, Thalia. But it's good to see you again.'

Thalia spat at him.

The General chuckled. 'So much for old friends. And you, Zoë. It's been a long time. How is my little traitor? I will enjoy killing you.'

'Do not respond,' Artemis groaned. 'Do not challenge him.'

'Wait a second,' I said. 'You're Atlas?'

The General glanced at me. 'So, even the stupidest of heroes can finally figure something out. Yes, I am Atlas, the general of the Titans and terror of the gods. Congratulations. I will kill you presently, as soon as I deal with this wretched girl.'

'You're not going to hurt Zoë,' I said. 'I won't let you.'

The General sneered. 'You have no right to interfere, little hero. This is a family matter.'

I frowned. 'A family matter?'

'Yes,' Zoë said bleakly. 'Atlas is my father.'

17 I PUT ON A FEW MILLION EXTRA KILOGRAMS

The horrible thing was: I could see the family resemblance. Atlas had the same regal expression as Zoë, the same cold, proud look in his eyes that Zoë sometimes got when she was mad, though on him it just looked evil. He was all the things I'd originally disliked about Zoë, with none of the good I'd come to appreciate.

'Let Artemis go,' Zoë demanded.

Atlas walked closer to the chained goddess. 'Perhaps you'd like to take the sky for her, then? Be my guest.'

Zoë opened her mouth to speak, but Artemis said, 'No! Do not offer, Zoë! I forbid you.'

Atlas smirked. He knelt next to Artemis and tried to touch her face, but the goddess bit at him, almost taking off his fingers.

'Hoo-hoo,' Atlas chuckled. 'You see, daughter? Lady Artemis likes her new job. I think I will have all the Olympians take turns carrying my burden, once Lord Kronos rules again, and this is the centre of our palace. It will teach those weaklings some humility.'

I looked at Annabeth. She was desperately trying to tell me something. She motioned her head towards Luke. But all I could do was stare at her. I hadn't noticed before, but something about her had changed. Her blonde hair was now streaked with grey.

'From holding the sky,' Thalia muttered, as if she'd read my mind. 'The weight should've killed her.'

'I don't understand,' I said. 'Why can't Artemis just let go of the sky?'

Atlas laughed. 'How little you understand, young one. This is the point where the sky and the earth first met, where Ouranos and Gaia first brought forth their mighty children, the Titans. The sky still yearns to embrace the earth. Someone must hold it at bay, or else it would crush down upon this place, instantly flattening the mountain and everything within a hundred leagues. Once you have taken the burden, there is no escape.' Atlas smiled. 'Unless someone else takes it from you.'

He approached us, studying Thalia and me. 'So these are the best heroes of the age, eh? Not much of a challenge.'

'Fight us,' I said. 'And let's see.'

'Have the gods taught you nothing? An immortal does not fight a mere mortal directly. It is beneath our dignity. I will have Luke crush you instead.'

'So you're another coward,' I said.

Atlas's eyes glowed with hatred. With difficulty, he turned his attention to Thalia.

'As for you, daughter of Zeus, it seems Luke was wrong about you.'

'I wasn't wrong,' Luke managed. He looked terribly weak, and he spoke every word as if it were painful. If I didn't hate his guts so much, I almost would've felt sorry for him. 'Thalia, you still can join us. Call the Ophiotaurus. It will come to you. Look!'

He waved his hand, and next to us a pool of water appeared: a pond ringed in black marble, big enough for the Ophiotaurus. I could imagine Bessie in that pool. In fact, the more I thought about it, the more I was sure I could hear Bessie mooing.

Don't think about him! Suddenly Grover's voice was inside my mind – the empathy link. I could feel his emotions. He was on the verge of panic. *I'm losing Bessie. Block the thoughts!*

I tried to make my mind go blank. I tried to think about basketball players, skateboards, the different kinds of candy in my mom's shop. Anything but Bessie.

'Thalia, call the Ophiotaurus,' Luke persisted. 'And you will be more powerful than the gods.'

'Luke . . .' Her voice was full of pain. 'What happened to you?'

'Don't you remember all those times we talked? All those times we cursed the gods? Our fathers have done nothing for us. They have no right to rule the world!'

Thalia shook her head. 'Free Annabeth. Let her go.'

'If you join me,' Luke promised, 'it can be like old times. The three of us together. Fighting for a better world. Please, Thalia, if you don't agree . . .'

His voice faltered. 'It's my last chance. He will use the other way if you don't agree. Please.'

I didn't know what he meant, but the fear in his voice sounded real enough. I believed that Luke was in danger. His life depended on Thalia's joining his cause. And I was afraid Thalia might believe it, too.

'Do not, Thalia,' Zoë warned. 'We must fight them.'

Luke waved his hand again, and a fire appeared. A bronze brazier, just like the one at camp. A sacrificial flame.

'Thalia,' I said. 'No.'

Behind Luke, the golden sarcophagus began to glow. As

it did, I saw images in the mist all around us: black marble walls rising, the ruins becoming whole, a terrible and beautiful palace rising around us, made of fear and shadow.

'We will raise Mount Othrys right here,' Luke promised, in a voice so strained it was hardly his. 'Once more, it will be stronger and greater than Olympus. Look, Thalia. We are not weak.'

He pointed towards the ocean, and my heart fell. Marching up the side of the mountain, from the beach where the *Princess Andromeda* was docked, was a great army. *Dracaenae* and Laestrygonians, monsters and half-bloods, hell hounds, harpies and other things I couldn't even name. The whole ship must've been emptied, because there were hundreds, many more than I'd seen on board last summer. And they were marching towards us. In a few minutes, they would be here.

'This is only a taste of what is to come,' Luke said. 'Soon we will be ready to storm Camp Half-Blood. And after that, Olympus itself. All we need is your help.'

For a terrible moment, Thalia hesitated. She gazed at Luke, her eyes full of pain, as if the only thing she wanted in the world was to believe him. Then she levelled her spear. 'You aren't Luke. I don't know you any more.'

'Yes, you do, Thalia,' he pleaded. 'Please. Don't make me . . . Don't make *him* destroy you.'

There was no time. If that army got to the top of the hill, we would be overwhelmed. I met Annabeth's eyes again. She nodded.

I looked at Thalia and Zoë, and I decided it wouldn't be the worst thing in the world to die fighting with friends like this.

'Now,' I said.

Together, we charged.

Thalia went straight for Luke. The power of her shield was so great that his dragon-women bodyguards fled in a panic, dropping the golden coffin and leaving him alone. But despite his sickly appearance, Luke was still quick with his sword. He snarled like a wild animal and counter-attacked. When his sword Backbiter met Thalia's shield, a ball of lightning erupted between them, frying the air with yellow tendrils of power.

As for me, I did the stupidest thing of my life, which is saying a lot. I attacked the Titan Lord Atlas.

He laughed as I approached. A huge javelin appeared in his hands. His silk suit melted into full Greek battle armour. 'Go on, then!'

'Percy!' Zoë said. 'Beware!'

I knew what she was warning me about. Chiron had told me long ago: *Immortals are constrained by ancient rules. But a hero can go anywhere, challenge anyone, as long as he has the nerve.* Once I attacked, Atlas was free to retaliate directly, with all his might.

I swung my sword, and Atlas knocked me aside with the shaft of his javelin. I flew through the air and slammed into a black wall. It wasn't Mist any more. The palace was rising, brick by brick. It was becoming real.

'Fool!' Atlas screamed gleefully, swatting aside one of Zoë's arrows. 'Did you think, simply because you could challenge that petty war god, that you could stand up to *me*?'

The mention of Ares sent a jolt through me. I shook

off my daze and charged again. If I could get to that pool of water I could double my strength.

The javelin's point slashed towards me like a scythe. I raised Riptide, planning to cut off his weapon at the shaft, but my arm felt like lead. My sword suddenly weighed a ton.

And I remembered Ares's warning, spoken on the beach in Los Angeles so long ago: *When you need it most, your sword will fail you.*

Not now! I pleaded. But it was no good. I tried to dodge, but the javelin caught me in the chest and sent me flying like a rag doll. I slammed into the ground, my head spinning. I looked up and found I was at the feet of Artemis, still straining under the weight of the sky.

'Run, boy,' she told me. 'You must run!'

Atlas was taking his time coming towards me. My sword was gone. It had skittered away over the edge of the cliff. It might reappear in my pocket – maybe in a few seconds – but it didn't matter. I'd be dead by then. Luke and Thalia were fighting like demons, lightning crackling around them. Annabeth was on the ground, desperately struggling to free her hands.

'Die, little hero,' Atlas said.

He raised his javelin to impale me.

'No!' Zoë yelled, and a volley of silver arrows sprouted from the armpit chink in Atlas's armour.

'ARGH!' He bellowed and turned towards his daughter.

I reached down and felt Riptide back in my pocket. I couldn't fight Atlas, even with a sword. And then a chill went down my spine. I remembered the words of the prophecy: *The Titan's curse must one withstand.* I couldn't hope to beat Atlas.

But there was someone else who might stand a chance.

'The sky,' I told the goddess. 'Give it to me.'

'No, boy,' Artemis said. Her forehead was beaded with metallic sweat, like quicksilver. 'You don't know what you're asking. It will crush you!'

'Annabeth took it!'

'She barely survived. She had the spirit of a true huntress. You will not last so long.'

'I'll die anyway,' I said. 'Give me the weight of the sky!'

I didn't wait for her answer. I took out Riptide and slashed through her chains. Then I stepped next to her and braced myself on one knee – holding up my hands – and touched the cold, heavy clouds. For a moment, Artemis and I bore the weight together. It was the heaviest thing I'd ever felt, as if I were being crushed under a thousand trucks. I wanted to black out from the pain, but I breathed deeply. *I can do this.*

Then Artemis slipped out from under the burden, and I held it alone.

Afterwards, I tried many times to explain what it felt like. I couldn't.

Every muscle in my body turned to fire. My bones felt like they were melting. I wanted to scream, but I didn't have the strength to open my mouth. I began to sink, lower and lower to the ground, the sky's weight crushing me.

Fight back! Grover's voice said inside my head. *Don't give up.*

I concentrated on breathing. If I could just keep the sky aloft a few more seconds. I thought about Bianca, who had given her life so we could get here. If she could do that, I could hold the sky.

My vision turned fuzzy. Everything was tinged with red. I caught glimpses of the battle, but I wasn't sure if I was seeing clearly. There was Atlas in full battle armour, jabbing with his javelin, laughing insanely as he fought. And Artemis, a blur of silver. She had two wicked hunting knives, each as long as her arm, and she slashed wildly at the Titan, dodging and leaping with unbelievable grace. She seemed to change form as she manoeuvred. She was a tiger, a gazelle, a bear, a falcon. Or perhaps that was just my fevered brain. Zoë shot arrows at her father, aiming for the chinks in his armour. He roared in pain each time one found its mark, but they affected him like bee stings. He just got madder and kept fighting.

Thalia and Luke went spear on sword, lightning still flashing around them. Thalia pressed Luke back with the aura of her shield. Even he was not immune to it. He retreated, wincing and growling in frustration.

'Yield!' Thalia yelled. 'You never could beat me, Luke.'

He bared his teeth. 'We'll see, my old friend.'

Sweat poured down my face. My hands were slippery. My shoulders would've screamed with agony if they could. I felt like the vertebrae in my spine were being welded together by a blowtorch.

Atlas advanced, pressing Artemis. She was fast, but his strength was unstoppable. His javelin slammed into the earth where Artemis had been a split second before, and a fissure opened in the rocks. He leaped over it and kept pursuing her. She was leading him back towards me.

Get ready, she spoke in my mind.

I was losing the ability to think through the pain. My response was something like *Agggghh-owwwwwwww.*

'You fight well for a girl.' Atlas laughed. 'But you are no match for me.'

He feinted with the tip of his javelin and Artemis dodged. I saw the trick coming. Atlas's javelin swept round and knocked Artemis's legs off the ground. She fell, and Atlas brought up his javelin tip for the kill.

'No!' Zoë screamed. She leaped between her father and Artemis and shot an arrow straight into the Titan's forehead, where it lodged like a unicorn's horn. Atlas bellowed in rage. He swept aside his daughter with the back of his hand, sending her flying into the black rocks.

I wanted to shout her name, run to her aid, but I couldn't speak or move. I couldn't even see where Zoë had landed. Then Atlas turned on Artemis with a look of triumph in his face. Artemis seemed to be wounded. She didn't get up.

'The first blood in a new war,' Atlas gloated. And he stabbed downward.

As fast as thought, Artemis grabbed his javelin shaft. It hit the earth right next to her and she pulled backwards, using the javelin like a lever, kicking the Titan Lord and sending him flying over her. I saw him coming down on top of me and I realized what would happen. I loosened my grip on the sky, and as Atlas slammed into me I didn't try to hold on. I let myself be pushed out of the way and rolled for all I was worth.

The weight of the sky dropped onto Atlas's back, almost smashing him flat until he managed to get to his knees, struggling to get out from under the crushing weight of the sky. But it was too late.

'*NOOOOOO!*' He bellowed so hard it shook the mountain. '*NOT AGAIN!*'

Atlas was trapped under his old burden.

I tried to stand and fell back again, dazed from pain. My body felt like it was burning up.

Thalia backed Luke to the edge of a cliff, but still they fought on, next to the golden coffin. Thalia had tears in her eyes. Luke had a bloody slash across his chest and his pale face glistened with sweat.

He lunged at Thalia and she slammed him with her shield. Luke's sword spun out of his hands and clattered to the rocks. Thalia put her spear point to his throat.

For a moment, there was silence.

'Well?' Luke asked. He tried to hide it, but I could hear fear in his voice.

Thalia trembled with fury.

Behind her, Annabeth came scrambling, finally free from her bonds. Her face was bruised and streaked with dirt. 'Don't kill him!'

'He's a traitor,' Thalia said. 'A traitor!'

In my daze, I realized that Artemis was no longer with me. She had run off towards the black rocks where Zoë had fallen.

'We'll bring Luke back,' Annabeth pleaded. 'To Olympus. He . . . he'll be useful.'

'Is that what you want, Thalia?' Luke sneered. 'To go back to Olympus in triumph? To please your dad?'

Thalia hesitated, and Luke made a desperate grab for her spear.

'No!' Annabeth shouted. But it was too late. Without thinking, Thalia kicked Luke away. He lost his balance, terror on his face, and then he fell.

'Luke!' Annabeth screamed.

We rushed to the cliff's edge. Below us, the army from the *Princess Andromeda* had stopped in amazement. They were staring at Luke's broken form on the rocks. Despite how much I hated him, I couldn't stand to see it. I wanted to believe he was still alive, but that was impossible. The fall was fifteen metres at least, and he wasn't moving.

One of the giants looked up and growled, 'Kill them!'

Thalia was stiff with grief, tears streaming down her cheeks. I pulled her back as a wave of javelins sailed over our heads. We ran for the rocks, ignoring the curses and threats of Atlas as we passed.

'Artemis!' I yelled.

The goddess looked up, her face almost as grief-stricken as Thalia's. Zoë lay in the goddess's arms. She was breathing. Her eyes were open. But still . . .

'The wound is poisoned,' Artemis said.

'Atlas poisoned her?' I asked.

'No,' the goddess said. 'Not Atlas.'

She showed us the wound in Zoë's side. I'd almost forgotten her scrape with Ladon the dragon. The bite was much worse than Zoë had let on. I could barely look at the wound. She had charged into battle against her father with a horrible cut already sapping her strength.

'The stars,' Zoë murmured. 'I cannot see them.'

'Nectar and ambrosia,' I said. 'Come on! We have to get her some.'

No one moved. Grief hung in the air. The army of Kronos was just below the rise. Even Artemis was too shocked to stir. We might've met our doom right there, but then I heard a strange buzzing noise.

Just as the army of monsters came over the hill, a

Sopwith Camel swooped down out of the sky.

'Get away from my daughter!' Dr Chase called down, and his machine guns burst into life, peppering the ground with bullet holes and startling the whole group of monsters into scattering.

'Dad?' yelled Annabeth in disbelief.

'Run!' he called back, his voice growing fainter as the biplane swooped by.

This shook Artemis out of her grief. She stared up at the antique plane, which was now banking round for another strafe.

'A brave man,' Artemis said with grudging approval. 'Come. We must get Zoë away from here.'

She raised her hunting horn to her lips, and its clear sound echoed down the valleys of Marin. Zoë's eyes were fluttering.

'Hang in there!' I told her. 'It'll be all right!'

The Sopwith Camel swooped down again. A few giants threw javelins, and one flew straight between the wings of the plane, but the machine guns blazed. I realized with amazement that somehow Dr Chase must've got hold of celestial bronze to fashion his bullets. The first row of snake women wailed as the machine gun's volley blew them into sulphurous yellow powder.

'That's . . . my dad!' Annabeth said in amazement.

We didn't have time to admire his flying. The giants and snake women were already recovering from their surprise. Dr Chase would be in trouble soon.

Just then, the moonlight brightened, and a silver chariot appeared from the sky, drawn by the most beautiful deer I had ever seen. It landed right next to us.

'Get in,' Artemis said.

Annabeth helped me get Thalia on board. Then I helped Artemis with Zoë. We wrapped Zoë in a blanket as Artemis pulled the reins and the chariot sped away from the mountain, straight into the air.

'Like Santa Claus's sleigh,' I murmured, still dazed with pain.

Artemis took time to look back at me. 'Indeed, young half-blood. And where do you think that legend came from?'

Seeing us safely away, Dr Chase turned his biplane and followed us like an honour guard. It must have been one of the strangest sights ever, even for the Bay Area: a silver flying chariot pulled by deer, escorted by a Sopwith Camel.

Behind us, the army of Kronos roared in anger as they gathered on the summit of Mount Tamalpais, but the loudest sound was the voice of Atlas, bellowing curses against the gods as he struggled under the weight of the sky.

18 A FRIEND SAYS GOODBYE

We landed at Crissy Field after nightfall.

As soon as Dr Chase stepped out of his Sopwith Camel, Annabeth ran to him and gave him a huge hug. 'Dad! You flew . . . you shot . . . oh my gods! That was the most amazing thing I've ever seen!'

Her father blushed. 'Well, not bad for a middle-aged mortal, I suppose.'

'But the celestial bronze bullets! How did you *get* those?'

'Ah, well. You did leave quite a few half-blood weapons in your room in Virginia, the last time you . . . left.'

Annabeth looked down, embarrassed. I noticed Dr Chase was very careful not to say *ran away*.

'I decided to try melting some down to make bullet casings,' he continued. 'Just a little experiment.'

He said it like it was no big deal, but he had a gleam in his eye. I could understand all of a sudden why Athena, Goddess of Crafts and Wisdom, had taken a liking to him. He was an excellent mad scientist at heart.

'Dad . . .' Annabeth faltered.

'Annabeth, Percy,' Thalia interrupted. Her voice was urgent. She and Artemis were kneeling at Zoë's side, binding the huntress's wounds.

Annabeth and I ran over to help, but there wasn't much we could do. We had no ambrosia or nectar. No regular medicine would help. It was dark, but I could see that Zoë didn't look good. She was shivering, and the faint glow that usually hung around her was fading.

'Can't you heal her with magic?' I asked Artemis. 'I mean . . . you're a goddess.'

Artemis looked troubled. 'Life is a fragile thing, Percy. If the Fates will the string to be cut, there is little I can do. But I can try.'

She tried to set her hand on Zoë's side, but Zoë gripped her wrist. She looked into the goddess's eyes, and some kind of understanding passed between them.

'Have I . . . served thee well?' Zoë whispered.

'With great honour,' Artemis said softly. 'The finest of my attendants.'

Zoë's face relaxed. 'Rest. At last.'

'I can try to heal the poison, my brave one.'

But in that moment, I knew it wasn't just the poison that was killing her. It was her father's final blow. Zoë had known all along that the Oracle's prophecy was about her: she would die by a parent's hand. And yet she'd taken the quest anyway. She had chosen to save me, and Atlas's fury had broken her inside.

She saw Thalia, and took her hand.

'I am sorry we argued,' Zoë said. 'We could have been sisters.'

'It's my fault,' Thalia said, blinking hard. 'You were right about Luke, about heroes, men – everything.'

'Perhaps not all men,' Zoë murmured. She smiled weakly at me. 'Do you still have the sword, Percy?'

I couldn't speak, but I brought out Riptide and put the pen in her hand. She grasped it contentedly. 'You spoke the truth, Percy Jackson. You are nothing like . . . like Hercules. I am honoured that you carry this sword.'

A shudder ran through her body.

'Zoë –' I said.

'Stars,' she whispered. 'I can see the stars again, my lady.'

A tear trickled down Artemis's cheek. 'Yes, my brave one. They are beautiful tonight.'

'Stars,' Zoë repeated. Her eyes fixed on the night sky. And she did not move again.

Thalia lowered her head. Annabeth gulped down a sob, and her father put his hands on her shoulders. I watched as Artemis cupped her hand above Zoë's mouth and spoke a few words in Ancient Greek. A silvery wisp of smoke exhaled from Zoë's lips and was caught in the hand of the goddess. Zoë's body shimmered and disappeared.

Artemis stood, said a kind of blessing, breathed into her cupped hand and released the silver dust to the sky. It flew up, sparkling, and vanished.

For a moment, I didn't see anything different. Then Annabeth gasped. Looking up in the sky, I saw that the stars were brighter now. They made a pattern I had never noticed before – a gleaming constellation that looked a lot like a girl's figure – a girl with a bow, running across the sky.

'Let the world honour you, my huntress,' Artemis said. 'Live forever in the stars.'

It wasn't easy saying our goodbyes. The thunder and lightning were still boiling over Mount Tamalpais in the north. Artemis was so upset she flickered with silver light. This made me nervous, because if she suddenly lost control and appeared in her fully divine form, we would disintegrate if we looked at her.

'I must go to Olympus immediately.' Artemis said. 'I will not be able to take you, but I will send help.'

The goddess set her hand on Annabeth's shoulder. 'You are brave beyond measure, my girl. You will do what is right.'

Then she looked quizzically at Thalia, as if she weren't sure what to make of this younger daughter of Zeus. Thalia seemed reluctant to look up, but something made her, and she held the goddess's eyes. I wasn't sure what passed between them, but Artemis's gaze softened with sympathy. Then she turned to me.

'You did well,' she said. 'For a man.'

I wanted to protest. But then I realized it was the first time she hadn't called me a boy.

She mounted her chariot, which began to glow. We averted our eyes. There was a flash of silver, and the goddess was gone.

'Well,' Dr Chase sighed. 'She was impressive, though I must say I still prefer Athena.'

Annabeth turned towards him. 'Dad, I . . . I'm sorry that –'

'Shh.' He hugged her. 'Do what you must, my dear. I know this isn't easy for you.'

His voice was a little shaky, but he gave Annabeth a brave smile.

Then I heard the whoosh of large wings. Three pegasi descended through the fog: two white winged horses and one pure black one.

'Blackjack!' I called.

Yo, boss! he called. *You manage to stay alive okay without me?*

'It was rough,' I admitted.

I brought Guido and Porkpie with me.

How ya doin? The other two pegasi spoke in my mind.

Blackjack looked me over with concern, then checked out Dr Chase, Thalia and Annabeth. *Any of these goons you want us to stampede?*

'Nah,' I said aloud. 'These are my friends. We need to get to Olympus pretty fast.'

No problem, Blackjack said. *Except for the mortal over there. Hope he's not going.*

I assured him Dr Chase was not. The professor was staring open-mouthed at the pegasi.

'Fascinating,' he said. 'Such manoeuvrability! How does the wingspan compensate for the weight of the horse's body, I wonder?'

Blackjack cocked his head. *Whaaaat?*

'Why, if the British had had these pegasi in the cavalry charges in the Crimea,' Dr Chase said, 'the charge of the Light Brigade –'

'Dad!' Annabeth interrupted.

Dr Chase blinked. He looked at his daughter and managed a smile. 'I'm sorry, my dear. I know you must go.'

He gave her one last awkward, well-meaning hug. As she turned to climb aboard the pegasus Guido, Dr Chase called, 'Annabeth. I know . . . I know San Francisco is a dangerous place for you. But please remember you always have a home with us. We will keep you safe.'

Annabeth didn't answer, but her eyes were red as she turned away. Dr Chase started to say more, then apparently thought better of it. He raised his hand in sad farewell and trudged away across the dark field.

Thalia and Annabeth and I mounted our pegasi. Together we soared over the bay and flew towards the eastern hills. Soon San Francisco was only a glittering crescent behind us, with an occasional flicker of lightning in the north.

Thalia was so exhausted she fell asleep on Porkpie's back. I knew she had to be really tired to sleep in the air, despite her fear of heights, but she didn't have much to worry about. Her pegasus flew with ease, adjusting himself every once in a while so Thalia stayed safely on his back.

Annabeth and I flew along side by side.

'Your dad seems cool,' I told her.

It was too dark to see her expression. She looked back, even though California was far behind us now.

'I guess so,' she said. 'We've been arguing for so many years.'

'Yeah, you said.'

'You think I was lying about that?' It sounded like a challenge, but a pretty half-hearted one, like she was asking it of herself.

'I didn't say you were lying. It's just . . . he seems okay. Your stepmom, too. Maybe they've, uh, got cooler since you saw them last.'

She hesitated. 'They're still in San Francisco, Percy. I can't live so far from camp.'

I didn't want to ask my next question. I was scared to know the answer. But I asked it anyway. 'So what are you going to do now?'

We flew over a town, an island of lights in the middle of the dark. It whisked by so fast we might've been in an aeroplane.

'I don't know,' she admitted. 'But thank you for rescuing me.'

'Hey, no big deal. We're friends.'

'You didn't believe I was dead?'

'Never.'

She hesitated. 'Neither is Luke, you know. I mean . . . he isn't dead.'

I stared at her. I didn't know if she was cracking under the stress or what. 'Annabeth, that fall was pretty bad. There's no way –'

'He isn't dead,' she insisted. 'I know it. The same way you knew about me.'

That comparison didn't make me too happy.

The towns were zipping by faster now, islands of light thicker together, until the whole landscape below was a glittering carpet. Dawn was close. The eastern sky was turning grey. And, up ahead, a huge white-and-yellow glow spread out before us – the lights of New York.

How's that for speedy, boss? Blackjack bragged. *We get extra hay for breakfast or what?*

'You're the man, Blackjack,' I told him. 'Er, the horse, I mean.'

'You don't believe me about Luke,' Annabeth said, 'but we'll see him again. He's in trouble, Percy. He's under Kronos's spell.'

I didn't feel like arguing, though it made me mad. How could she still have any feelings for that creep? How could she possibly make excuses for him? He deserved that fall. He deserved . . . okay, I'll say it. He deserved to die. Unlike Bianca. Unlike Zoë. Luke couldn't be alive. It wouldn't be fair.

'There it is.' Thalia's voice; she'd woken up. She was pointing towards Manhattan, which was quickly zooming into view. 'It's started.'

'What's started?' I asked.

Then I looked where she was pointing. High above the Empire State Building, Olympus was its own island of light, a floating mountain ablaze with torches and braziers, white marble palaces gleaming in the early morning air.

'The winter solstice,' Thalia said. 'The Council of the Gods.'

19 THE GODS VOTE HOW TO KILL US

Flying was bad enough for a son of Poseidon, but flying straight up to Zeus's palace, with thunder and lightning swirling round it, was even worse.

We circled over midtown Manhattan, making one complete orbit round Mount Olympus. I'd only been there once before, travelling by elevator up to the secret six hundredth floor of the Empire State Building. This time, if it were possible, Olympus amazed me even more.

In the early-morning darkness, torches and fires made the mountainside palaces glow twenty different colours, from blood red to indigo. Apparently no one ever slept on Olympus. The twisting streets were full of demigods and nature spirits and minor godlings bustling about, riding chariots or sedan chairs carried by Cyclopes. Winter didn't seem to exist here. I caught the scent of the gardens in full bloom, jasmine and roses and even sweeter things I couldn't name. Music drifted up from many windows, the soft sounds of lyres and reed pipes.

Towering at the peak of the mountain was the greatest palace of all, the glowing white hall of the gods.

Our pegasi set us down in the outer courtyard, in front of huge silver gates. Before I could even think to knock, the gates opened by themselves.

Good luck, boss, Blackjack said.

'Yeah.' I didn't know why, but I had a sense of doom. I'd never seen all the gods together. I knew any one of them could blast me to dust, and a few of them would like to.

Hey, if ya don't come back, can I have your cabin for my stable?

I looked at the pegasus.

Just a thought, he said. *Sorry.*

Blackjack and his friends flew off, leaving Thalia, Annabeth and me alone. For a minute we stood there regarding the palace, the way we'd stood together in front of Westover Hall, that seemed like a million years ago.

And then, side by side, we walked into the throne room.

Twelve enormous thrones made a U round a central hearth, just like the placement of the cabins at camp. The ceiling above glittered with constellations – even the newest one, Zoë the Huntress, making her way across the heavens with her bow drawn.

All of the seats were occupied. Each god and goddess was about five metres tall, and I'm telling you, if you've ever had a dozen all-powerful super-huge beings turn their eyes on you at once . . . Well, suddenly, facing monsters seemed like a picnic.

'Welcome, heroes,' Artemis said.

'Mooo!'

That's when I noticed Bessie and Grover.

A sphere of water was hovering in the centre of the room, next to the hearth fire. Bessie was swimming happily around, swishing his serpent tail and poking his head out of the sides and the bottom of the sphere. He seemed to be enjoying the novelty of swimming in a magic bubble. Grover was kneeling at Zeus's throne, as if he'd just been giving a report, but, when he saw us, he cried, 'You made it!'

He started to run towards me, then remembered he was turning his back on Zeus, and looked for permission.

'Go on,' Zeus said. But he wasn't really paying attention to Grover. The lord of the sky was staring intently at Thalia.

Grover trotted over. None of the gods spoke. Every clop of Grover's hooves echoed on the marble floor. Bessie splashed in his bubble of water. The hearth fire crackled.

I looked nervously at my father, Poseidon. He was dressed similarly to the last time I'd seen him: beach shorts, a Hawaiian shirt and sandals. He had a weathered, suntanned face with a dark beard and deep green eyes. I wasn't sure how he would feel about seeing me again, but the corners of his eyes crinkled with smile lines. He nodded as if to say *It's okay.*

Grover gave Annabeth and Thalia big hugs. Then he grasped my arms. 'Percy, Bessie and I made it! But you have to convince them! They can't do it!'

'Do what?' I asked.

'Heroes,' Artemis called.

The goddess slid down from her throne and turned to human size, a young auburn-haired girl, perfectly at ease in the midst of the giant Olympians. She walked towards us, her silver robes shimmering. There was no emotion in her face. She seemed to walk in a column of moonlight.

'The Council has been informed of your deeds,' Artemis told us. 'They know that Mount Othrys is rising in the West. They know of Atlas's attempt for freedom, and the gathering armies of Kronos. We have voted to act.'

There was some mumbling and shuffling among the

gods, as if they weren't all happy with this plan, but nobody protested.

'At my Lord Zeus's command,' Artemis said, 'my brother Apollo and I shall hunt the most powerful monsters, seeking to strike them down before they can join the Titans' cause. Lady Athena shall personally check on the other Titans to make sure they do not escape their various prisons. Lord Poseidon has been given permission to unleash his full fury on the cruise ship *Princess Andromeda* and send it to the bottom of the sea. And as for you, my heroes . . .'

She turned to face the other immortals. 'These half-bloods have done Olympus a great service. Would any here deny that?'

She looked around at the assembled gods, meeting their faces individually. Zeus in his dark pinstriped suit, his black beard neatly trimmed, and his eyes sparking with energy. Next to him sat a beautiful woman with silver hair braided over one shoulder and a dress that shimmered with colours like peacock feathers. The Lady Hera.

On Zeus's right, my father Poseidon. Next to him, a huge lump of a man with a leg in a steel brace, a misshapen head and a wild brown beard, fire flickering through his whiskers. The Lord of the Forges, Hephaestus.

Hermes winked at me. He was wearing a business suit today, checking messages on his caduceus cell phone. Apollo leaned back in his golden throne with his shades on. He had iPod headphones on, so I wasn't sure he was even listening, but he gave me a thumbs-up. Dionysus looked bored, twirling a grapevine between his fingers. And Ares, well, he sat on his chrome-and-leather throne, glowering at me while he sharpened a knife.

On the ladies' side of the throne room, a dark-haired goddess in green robes sat next to Hera on a throne woven of apple-tree branches. Demeter, Goddess of the Harvest. Next to her sat a beautiful grey-eyed woman in an elegant white dress. She could only be Annabeth's mother, Athena. Then there was Aphrodite, who smiled at me knowingly and made me blush in spite of myself.

All the Olympians in one place. So much power in this room it was a miracle the whole palace didn't blow apart.

'I gotta say,' Apollo broke the silence, 'these kids did okay.' He cleared his throat and began to recite: '*Heroes win laurels* –'

'Um, yes, first class,' Hermes interrupted, like he was anxious to avoid Apollo's poetry. 'All in favour of not disintegrating them?'

A few tentative hands went up – Demeter, Aphrodite.

'Wait just a minute,' Ares growled. He pointed at Thalia and me. 'These two are dangerous. It'd be much safer, while we've got them here –'

'Ares,' Poseidon interrupted, 'they are worthy heroes. We will not blast my son to bits.'

'Nor my daughter,' Zeus grumbled. 'She has done well.'

Thalia blushed. She studied the floor. I knew how she felt. I'd hardly ever talked to my father, much less got a compliment.

The goddess Athena cleared her throat and sat forward. 'I am proud of my daughter as well. But there is a security risk here, with the other two.'

'Mother!' Annabeth said. 'How can you –'

Athena cut her off with a calm but firm look. 'It is unfortunate that my father, Zeus, and my uncle, Poseidon, chose to break their oath not to have more children. Only Hades kept his word, a fact that I find ironic. As we know from the Great Prophecy, children of the three elder gods . . . such as Thalia and Percy . . . are dangerous. As thickheaded as he is, Ares has a point.'

'Right!' Ares said. 'Hey, wait a minute. Who you callin' –'

He started to get up, but a grapevine grew round his waist like a seat belt and pulled him back down.

'Oh, please, Ares,' Dionysus sighed. 'Save the fighting for later.'

Ares cursed and ripped away the vine. 'You're one to talk, you old drunk. You seriously want to protect these brats?'

Dionysus gazed down at us wearily. 'I have no love for them. Athena, do you truly think it safest to destroy them?'

'I do not pass judgement,' Athena said. 'I only point out the risk. What we do, the Council must decide.'

'I will not have them punished,' Artemis said. 'I will have them rewarded. If we destroy heroes who do us a great favour, then we are no better than the Titans. If this is Olympian justice, I will have none of it.'

'Calm down, sis,' Apollo said. 'Jeez, you need to lighten up.'

'Don't call me *sis*! I will reward them.'

'Well,' Zeus grumbled. 'Perhaps. But the monster at least must be destroyed. We have agreement on that?'

A lot of nodding heads.

It took me a second to realize what they were saying. Then my heart turned to lead. 'Bessie? You want to destroy Bessie?'

'Mooooooo!' Bessie protested.

My father frowned. 'You have named the Ophiotaurus Bessie?'

'Dad,' I said, 'he's just a sea creature. A really *nice* sea creature. You can't destroy him.'

Poseidon shifted uncomfortably. 'Percy, the monster's power is considerable. If the Titans were to steal it, or –'

'You can't,' I insisted. I looked at Zeus. I probably should have been afraid of him, but I stared him right in the eye. 'Controlling the prophecies never works. Isn't that true? Besides, Bess– the Ophiotaurus is innocent. Killing something like that is wrong. It's just as wrong as . . . as Kronos eating his children, just because of something they *might* do. It's wrong!'

Zeus seemed to consider this. His eyes drifted to his daughter Thalia. 'And what of the risk? Kronos knows full well, if one of you were to sacrifice the beast's entrails, you would have the power to destroy us. Do you think we can let that possibility remain? You, my daughter, will turn sixteen on the morrow, just as the prophecy says.'

'You have to trust them,' Annabeth spoke up. 'Sir, you have to trust them.'

Zeus scowled. 'Trust a hero?'

'Annabeth is right,' Artemis said. 'Which is why I must first make a reward. My faithful companion, Zoë Nightshade, has passed into the stars. I must have a new lieutenant. And I intend to choose one. But first, Father Zeus, I must speak to you privately.'

Zeus beckoned Artemis forward. He leaned down and listened as she spoke in his ear.

A feeling of panic seized me. 'Annabeth,' I said under my breath. 'Don't.'

She frowned at me. 'What?'

'Look, I need to tell you something,' I continued. The words came stumbling out of me. 'I couldn't stand it if . . . I don't want you to –'

'Percy?' she said. 'You look like you're going to be sick.'

And that's how I felt. I wanted to say more, but my tongue betrayed me. It wouldn't move because of the fear in my stomach. And then Artemis turned.

'I shall have a new lieutenant,' she announced. 'If she will accept it.'

'No,' I murmured.

'Thalia,' Artemis said. 'Daughter of Zeus. Will you join the Hunt?'

Stunned silence filled the room. I stared at Thalia, unable to believe what I was hearing. Annabeth smiled. She squeezed Thalia's hand and let it go, as if she'd been expecting this all along.

'I will,' Thalia said firmly.

Zeus rose, his eyes full of concern. 'My daughter, consider well –'

'Father,' she said. 'I will not turn sixteen tomorrow. I will never turn sixteen. I won't let this prophecy be mine. I stand with my sister Artemis. Kronos will never tempt me again.'

She knelt before the goddess and began the words I remembered from Bianca's oath, that seemed like so long ago. 'I pledge myself to the goddess Artemis. I turn my back on the company of men . . .'

Afterwards, Thalia did something that surprised me almost as much as the pledge. She came over to me, smiled and, in front of the whole assembly, she gave me a big hug.

I blushed.

When she pulled away and gripped my shoulders, I said, 'Um . . . aren't you supposed to not do that any more? Hug boys, I mean?'

'I'm honouring a friend,' she corrected. 'I *must* join the Hunt, Percy. I haven't known peace since . . . since Half-Blood Hill. I finally feel like I have a home. But you're a hero. You will be the one of the prophecy.'

'Great,' I muttered.

'I'm proud to be your friend.'

She hugged Annabeth, who was trying hard not to cry. Then she even hugged Grover, who looked ready to pass out, like somebody had just given him an all-you-can-eat enchilada coupon.

Then Thalia went to stand by Artemis's side.

'Now for the Ophiotaurus,' Artemis said.

'This boy is still dangerous,' Dionysus warned. 'The beast is a temptation to great power. Even if we spare the boy –'

'No.' I looked around at all the gods. 'Please. Keep the Ophiotaurus safe. My dad can hide him under the sea somewhere, or keep him in an aquarium here in Olympus. But you have to protect him.'

'And why should we trust you?' rumbled Hephaestus.

'I'm only fourteen,' I said. 'If this prophecy is about me, that's two more years.'

'Two years for Kronos to deceive you,' Athena said. 'Much can change in two years, my young hero.'

'Mother!' Annabeth said, exasperated.

'It is only the truth, child. It is bad strategy to keep the animal alive. Or the boy.'

My father stood. 'I will not have a sea creature destroyed if I can help it. And I *can* help it.'

He held out his hand, and a trident appeared in it: a six-metre-long bronze shaft with three spear tips that shimmered with blue, watery light. 'I will vouch for the boy, and the safety of the Ophiotaurus.'

'You won't take it under the sea!' Zeus stood suddenly. 'I won't have that kind of bargaining chip in your possession.'

'Brother, please,' Poseidon sighed.

Zeus's lightning bolt appeared in his hand, a shaft of electricity that filled the whole room with ozone storm smell.

'Fine,' Poseidon said. 'I will build an aquarium for the creature here. Hephaestus can help me. The creature will be safe. We shall protect it with all our powers. The boy will not betray us. I vouch for this on my honour.'

Zeus thought about this. 'All in favour?'

To my surprise, a lot of hands went up. Dionysus abstained. So did Ares and Athena. But everybody else . . .

'We have a majority,' Zeus decreed. 'And so, since we will not be destroying these heroes . . . I imagine we should honour them. Let the triumph celebration begin!'

There are parties, and then there are huge, major, blowout parties. And then there are Olympian parties. If you ever get a choice, go for the Olympian.

The Nine Muses cranked up the tunes, and I realized the music was whatever you wanted it to be: the gods could listen to classical and the younger demigods heard hip-hop or whatever, and it was all the same soundtrack. No arguments. No fights to change the radio station. Just requests to crank it up.

Dionysus went around growing refreshment stands out of the ground, and a beautiful woman walked with him arm in arm – his wife, Ariadne. Dionysus looked happy for the first time. Nectar and ambrosia overflowed from golden fountains, and platters of mortal snack food crowded the banquet tables. Golden goblets filled with whatever drink you wanted. Grover trotted around with a full plate of tin cans and enchiladas, and his goblet was full of double-espresso latte, which he kept muttering over like an incantation: 'Pan! Pan!'

Gods kept coming over to congratulate me. Thankfully, they had reduced themselves to human size so they didn't accidentally trample party goers under their feet. Hermes started chatting with me, and he was so cheerful I hated to tell him what had happened to his least-favourite son Luke, but before I could even get up the courage, Hermes got a call on his caduceus and walked away.

Apollo told me I could drive his sun chariot any time, and if I ever wanted archery lessons –

'Thanks,' I told him. 'But, seriously, I'm no good at archery.'

'Ah, nonsense,' he said. 'Target practice from the chariot as we fly over the U.S.? Best fun there is!'

I made some excuses and wove through the crowds that were dancing in the palace courtyards. I was looking for Annabeth. Last time I saw her, she'd been dancing with some minor godling.

Then a man's voice behind me said, 'You won't let me down, I hope.'

I turned and found Poseidon smiling at me.

'Dad . . . hi.'

'Hello, Percy. You've done well.'

His praise made me uneasy. I mean, it felt good, but I knew just how much he'd put himself on the line, vouching for me. It would've been a lot easier to let the others disintegrate me.

'I won't let you down,' I promised.

He nodded. I had trouble reading gods' emotions, but I wondered if he had some doubts.

'Your friend Luke –'

'He's not my friend,' I blurted out. Then I realized it was probably rude to interrupt. 'Sorry.'

'Your *former* friend Luke,' Poseidon corrected. 'He once promised things like that. He was Hermes's pride and joy. Just bear that in mind, Percy. Even the bravest can fall.'

'Luke fell pretty hard,' I agreed. 'He's dead.'

Poseidon shook his head. 'No, Percy. He is not.'

I stared at him. 'What?'

'I believe Annabeth told you this. Luke still lives. I have seen it. His boat sails from San Francisco with the remains of Kronos even now. He will retreat and regroup before assaulting you again. I will do my best to destroy his boat with storms, but he is making alliances with my enemies, the older spirits of the ocean. They will fight to protect him.'

'How can he be alive?' I said. 'That fall should've killed him!'

Poseidon looked troubled. 'I don't know, Percy, but

beware of him. He is more dangerous than ever. And the golden coffin is still with him, still growing in strength.'

'What about Atlas?' I said. 'What's to prevent him from escaping again? Couldn't he just force some giant or something to take the sky for him?'

My father snorted in derision. 'If it were so easy, he would have escaped long ago. No, my son. The curse of the sky can only be forced upon a Titan, one of the children of Gaia and Ouranous. Anyone else must *choose* to take the burden of their own free will. Only a hero, someone with strength, a true heart, and great courage, would do such a thing. No one in Kronos's army would dare try to bear that weight, even upon pain of death.'

'Luke did it,' I said. 'He let Atlas go. Then he tricked Annabeth into saving him and used her to convince Artemis to take the sky.'

'Yes,' Poseidon said. 'Luke is . . . an interesting case.'

I think he wanted to say more, but just then Bessie started mooing from across the courtyard. Some demigods were playing with his water sphere, joyously pushing it back and forth over the top of the crowd.

'I'd better take care of that,' Poseidon grumbled. 'We can't have the Ophiotaurus tossed around like a beach ball. Be good, my son. We may not speak again for some time.'

And just like that he was gone.

I was about to keep searching the crowd when another voice spoke. 'Your father takes a great risk, you know.'

I found myself face to face with the grey-eyed woman who looked so much like Annabeth I almost called her that.

'Athena.' I tried not to sound resentful, after the way

she'd written me off in the council, but I guess I didn't hide it very well.

She smiled dryly. 'Do not judge me too harshly, half-blood. Wise counsel is not always popular, but I spoke the truth. You are dangerous.'

'You never take risks?'

She nodded. 'I concede the point. You may perhaps be useful. And yet . . . your fatal flaw may destroy us as well as yourself.'

My heart crept into my throat. A year ago, Annabeth and I had had a talk about fatal flaws. Every hero had one. Hers, she said, was pride. She believed she could do anything . . . like holding up the world, for instance. Or saving Luke. But I didn't really know what mine was.

Athena looked almost sorry for me. 'Kronos knows your flaw, even if you do not. He knows how to study his enemies. Think, Percy. How has he manipulated you? First, your mother was taken from you. Then your best friend, Grover. Now my daughter, Annabeth.' She paused, disapproving. 'In each case, your loved ones have been used to lure you into Kronos's traps. Your fatal flaw is personal loyalty, Percy. You do not know when it is time to cut your losses. To save a friend, you would sacrifice the world. In a hero of the prophecy, that is very, very dangerous.'

I balled my fists. 'That's not a flaw. Just because I want to help my friends –'

'The most dangerous flaws are those which are good in moderation,' she said. 'Evil is easy to fight. Lack of wisdom . . . that is very hard indeed.'

I wanted to argue, but I found I couldn't. Athena was pretty darn smart.

'I hope the Council's decisions prove wise,' Athena said. 'But I will be watching, Percy Jackson. I do not approve of your friendship with my daughter. I do not think it wise for either of you. And should you begin to waver in your loyalties . . .'

She fixed me with her cold grey stare, and I realized what a terrible enemy Athena would make, ten times worse than Ares or Dionysus or maybe even my father. Athena would never give up. She would never do something rash or stupid just because she hated you, and, if she made a plan to destroy you, it would not fail.

'Percy!' Annabeth said, running through the crowd. She stopped short when she saw who I was talking to. 'Oh . . . Mom.'

'I will leave you,' Athena said. 'For now.'

She turned and strode through the crowds, which parted before her as if she were carrying Aegis.

'Was she giving you a hard time?' Annabeth asked.

'No,' I said. 'It's . . . fine.'

She studied me with concern. She touched the new streak of grey in my hair that matched hers exactly – our painful souvenir from holding Atlas's burden. There was a lot I'd wanted to say to Annabeth, but Athena had taken the confidence out of me. I felt like I'd been punched in the gut.

I do not approve of your friendship with my daughter.

'So,' Annabeth said. 'What did you want to tell me earlier?'

The music was playing. People were dancing in the streets. I said, 'I, uh, was thinking we got interrupted at Westover Hall. And . . . I think I owe you a dance.'

She smiled slowly. 'All right, Seaweed Brain.'

So I took her hand, and I don't know what everybody else heard, but to me it sounded like a slow dance: a little sad, but maybe a little hopeful, too.

20 I GET A NEW ENEMY FOR CHRISTMAS

Before I left Olympus, I decided to make a few calls. It wasn't easy, but I finally found a quiet fountain in a corner garden and sent an Iris-message to my brother Tyson, under the sea. I told him about our adventures, and Bessie – he wanted to hear every detail about the cute baby cow serpent – and I assured him that Annabeth was safe. Finally I got round to explaining how the shield he'd made me last summer had been damaged in the manticore attack.

'Yay!' Tyson said. 'That means it was good! It saved your life!'

'It sure did, big guy,' I said. 'But now it's ruined.'

'Not ruined!' Tyson promised. 'I will visit and fix it next summer.'

The idea picked me up instantly. I guess I hadn't realized how much I missed having Tyson around.

'Seriously?' I asked. 'They'll let you take time off?'

'Yes! I have made two thousand seven hundred and forty-one magic swords,' Tyson said proudly, showing me the newest blade. 'The boss says "good work!" He will let me take the whole summer off. I will visit camp!'

We talked for a while about war preparations and our dad's fight with the old sea gods, and all the cool things we could do together next summer, but then Tyson's boss started yelling at him and he had to get back to work.

I dug out my last golden drachma and made one more Iris-message.

'Sally Jackson,' I said. 'Upper East Side, Manhattan.'

The mist shimmered, and there was my mom at our kitchen table, laughing and holding hands with her friend Mr Blowfish.

I felt so embarrassed, I was about to wave my hand through the mist and cut the connection but, before I could, my mom saw me.

Her eyes got wide. She let go of Mr Blowfish's hand really quickly. 'Oh, Paul! You know what? I left my writing journal in the living room. Would you mind getting it for me?'

'Sure, Sally. No problem.'

He left the room, and instantly my mom leaned towards the Iris-message. 'Percy! Are you all right?'

'I'm, uh, fine. How's that writing seminar going?'

She pursed her lips. 'It's fine. But that's not important. Tell me what's happened!'

I filled her in as quickly as I could. She sighed with relief when she heard that Annabeth was safe.

'I knew you could do it!' she said. 'I'm so proud.'

'Yeah, well, I'd better let you get back to your homework.'

'Percy, I . . . Paul and I –'

'Mom, are you happy?'

The question seemed to take her by surprise. She thought for a moment. 'Yes. I really am, Percy. Being around him makes me happy.'

'Then it's cool. Seriously. Don't worry about me.'

The funny thing was, I meant it. Considering the quest

I'd just had, maybe I should have been worried for my mom. I'd seen just how mean people could be to each other, like Hercules was to Zoë Nightshade, like Luke was to Thalia. I'd met Aphrodite, Goddess of Love, in person, and her powers had scared me worse than Ares. But seeing my mother laughing and smiling, after all the years she'd suffered with my nasty ex-stepfather, Gabe Ugliano, I couldn't help feeling happy for her.

'You promise not to call him Mr Blowfish?' she asked.

I shrugged. 'Well, maybe not to his face, anyway.'

'Sally?' Mr Blofis called from our living room. 'You need the green binder or the red one?'

'I'd better go,' she told me. 'See you for Christmas?'

'Are you putting blue candy in my stocking?'

She smiled. 'If you're not too old for that.'

'I'm never too old for candy.'

'I'll see you then.'

She waved her hand across the mist. Her image disappeared, and I thought to myself that Thalia had been right, so many days ago at Westover Hall: my mom really was pretty cool.

Compared to Mount Olympus, Manhattan was quiet. Friday before Christmas, but it was early in the morning, and hardly anyone was on Fifth Avenue. Argus, the many-eyed security chief, picked up Annabeth, Grover and me at the Empire State Building and ferried us back to camp through a light snowstorm. The Long Island Expressway was almost deserted.

As we trudged back up Half-Blood Hill to the pine tree where the Golden Fleece glittered, I half expected to see Thalia there, waiting for us. But she wasn't. She was long gone with Artemis and the rest of the Hunters, off on their next adventure.

Chiron greeted us at the Big House with hot chocolate and toasted cheese sandwiches. Grover went off with his satyr friends to spread the word about our strange encounter with the magic of Pan. Within an hour, the satyrs were all running around agitated, asking where the nearest espresso bar was.

Annabeth and I sat with Chiron and some of the other senior campers – Beckendorf, Silena Beauregard and the Stoll brothers. Even Clarisse from the Ares cabin was there, back from her secretive scouting mission. I knew she must've had a difficult quest, because she didn't even try to pulverize me. She had a new scar on her chin, and her dirty blonde hair had been cut short and ragged, like someone had attacked it with a pair of safety scissors.

'I got news,' she mumbled uneasily. '*Bad* news.'

'I'll fill you in later,' Chiron said with forced cheerfulness. 'The important thing is you have prevailed. And you saved Annabeth!'

Annabeth smiled at me gratefully, which made me look away.

For some strange reason, I found myself thinking about the Hoover Dam, and the odd mortal girl I'd run into there, Rachel Elizabeth Dare. I didn't know why, but her annoying comments kept coming back to me. *Do you always kill people when they blow their nose?* I was only alive because so many people had helped me, even a random mortal girl like that. I'd never even explained to her who I was.

'Luke is alive,' I said. 'Annabeth was right.'

Annabeth sat up. 'How do you know?'

I tried not to feel annoyed by her interest. I told her what my dad had said about the *Princess Andromeda.*

'Well.' Annabeth shifted uncomfortably in her chair. 'If the final battle does come when Percy is sixteen, at least we have two more years to figure something out.'

I had a feeling that when she said 'figure something out', she meant 'get Luke to change his ways', which annoyed me even more.

Chiron's expression was gloomy. Sitting by the fire in his wheelchair, he looked really old. I mean . . . he was really old, but he usually didn't look it.

'Two years may seem like a long time,' he said. 'But it is the blink of an eye. I still hope you are not the child of the prophecy, Percy. But, if you are, then the second Titan war is almost upon us. Kronos's first strike will be here.'

'How do you know?' I asked. 'Why would he care about camp?'

'Because the gods use heroes as their tools,' Chiron said simply. 'Destroy the tools, and the gods will be crippled. Luke's forces will come here. Mortal, demigod, monstrous . . . We must be prepared. Clarisse's news may give us a clue as to how they will attack, but –'

There was a knock on the door, and Nico di Angelo came huffing into the parlour, his cheeks bright red from the cold.

He was smiling, but he looked around anxiously. 'Hey! Where's . . . where's my sister?'

Dead silence. I stared at Chiron. I couldn't believe nobody had told him yet. And then I realized why. They'd been waiting for us to appear, to tell Nico in person.

That was the last thing I wanted to do. But I owed it to Bianca.

'Hey, Nico.' I got up from my comfortable chair. 'Let's take a walk, okay? We need to talk.'

He took the news in silence, which somehow made it worse. I kept talking, trying to explain how it had happened, how Bianca had sacrificed herself to save the quest. But I felt like I was only making things worse.

'She wanted you to have this.' I brought out the little god figurine Bianca had found in the junkyard. Nico held it in his palm and stared at it.

We were standing at the dining pavilion, just where we'd last spoken before I went on the quest. The wind was bitterly cold, even with the camp's magical weather protection. Snow fell lightly against the marble steps. I figured outside the camp borders there must be a blizzard happening.

'You promised you would protect her,' Nico said.

He might as well have stabbed me with a rusty dagger. It would've hurt less than reminding me of my promise.

'Nico,' I said. 'I tried. But Bianca gave herself up to save the rest of us. I told her not to. But she –'

'You promised!'

He glared at me, his eyes rimmed with red. He closed his small fist round the god statue.

'I shouldn't have trusted you.' His voice broke. 'You lied to me. My nightmares were right!'

'Wait. What nightmares?'

He flung the god statue to ground. It clattered across the icy marble. 'I hate you!'

'She might be alive,' I said desperately. 'I don't know for sure –'

'She's dead.' He closed his eyes. His whole body trembled with rage. 'I should've known it earlier. She's in the Fields of Asphodel, standing before the judges right now, being evaluated. I can feel it.'

'What do you mean, you can feel it?'

Before he could answer, I heard a new sound behind me. A hissing, clattering noise I recognized all too well.

I drew my sword and Nico gasped. I whirled and found myself facing four skeleton warriors. They grinned fleshless grins and advanced with swords drawn. I don't know how they'd made it inside the camp, but it didn't matter. I'd never get help in time.

'You're trying to kill me!' Nico screamed. 'You brought these . . . these things?'

'No! I mean, yes, they followed me, but *no!* Nico, run. They can't be destroyed.'

'I don't trust you!'

The first skeleton charged. I knocked aside its blade, but the other three kept coming. I sliced one in half, but immediately it began to knit back together. I knocked another's head off but it just kept fighting.

'Run, Nico!' I yelled. 'Get help!'

'No!' He pressed his hands to his ears.

I couldn't fight four at once, not if they wouldn't die. I slashed, whirled, blocked, jabbed, but they just kept advancing. It was only a matter of seconds before the zombies overpowered me.

'No!' Nico shouted louder. '*GO AWAY!*'

The ground rumbled beneath me. The skeletons froze.

I rolled out of the way just as a crack opened at the feet of the four warriors. The ground ripped apart like a snapping mouth. Flames erupted from the fissure, and the earth swallowed the skeletons in one loud *CRUNCH!*

Silence.

In the place where the skeletons had stood, a six-metre-long scar wove across the marble floor of the pavilion. Otherwise there was no sign of the warriors.

Awestruck, I looked to Nico. 'How did you –'

'Go away!' he yelled. 'I hate you! I wish you were dead!'

The ground didn't swallow *me* up, but Nico ran, down the steps, heading towards the woods. I started to follow but slipped and fell on the icy steps. When I got up, I noticed what I'd slipped on.

I picked up the god statue Bianca had retrieved from the junkyard for Nico. *The only statue he didn't have,* she'd said. A last gift from his sister.

I stared at it with dread, because now I understood why the face looked familiar. I'd seen it before.

It was a statue of Hades, Lord of the Dead.

Annabeth and Grover helped me search the woods for hours, but there was no sign of Nico di Angelo.

'We have to tell Chiron,' Annabeth said, out of breath.

'No,' I said.

She and Grover both stared at me.

'Um,' Grover said nervously, 'what do you mean . . . no?'

I was still trying to figure out why I'd said that, but the words spilled out of me. 'We can't let anyone know. I don't think anyone realizes that Nico is a –'

'A son of Hades,' Annabeth said. 'Percy, do you have *any idea* how serious this is? Even Hades broke the oath! This is horrible!'

'I don't think so,' I said. 'I don't think Hades broke the oath.'

'What?'

'He's their dad,' I said, 'but Bianca and Nico have been out of commission for a long time, since even before World War II.'

'The Lotus Casino!' Grover said, and he told Annabeth about the conversations we'd had with Bianca on the quest. 'She and Nico were stuck there for decades. They were born before the oath was made.'

I nodded.

'But how did they get out?' Annabeth protested.

'I don't know,' I admitted. 'Bianca said a lawyer came and got them and drove them to Westover Hall. I don't know who that could've been, or why. Maybe it's part of this Great Stirring thing. I don't think Nico understands who he is. But we can't go telling anyone. Not even Chiron. If the Olympians find out –'

'It might start them fighting among each other again,' Annabeth said. 'That's the last thing we need.'

Grover looked worried. 'But you can't hide things from the gods. Not forever.'

'I don't need forever,' I said. 'Just two years. Until I'm sixteen.'

Annabeth paled. 'But, Percy, this means the prophecy might *not* be about you. It might be about Nico. We have to –'

'No,' I said. 'I choose the prophecy. It will be about me.'

'Why are you saying that?' she cried. 'You want to be responsible for the whole world?'

It was the last thing I wanted, but I didn't say that. I knew I had to step up and claim it.

'I can't let Nico be in any more danger,' I said. 'I owe that much to his sister. I . . . let them both down. I'm not going to let that poor kid suffer any more.'

'The poor kid who hates you and wants to see you dead,' Grover reminded me.

'Maybe we can find him,' I said. 'We can convince him it's okay, hide him somewhere safe.'

Annabeth shivered. 'If Luke gets hold of him –'

'Luke won't,' I said. 'I'll make sure he's got other things to worry about. Namely, me.'

I wasn't sure Chiron believed the story Annabeth and I told him. I think he could tell I was holding something back about Nico's disappearance, but, in the end, he accepted it. Unfortunately, Nico wasn't the first half-blood to disappear.

'So young,' Chiron sighed, his hands on the rail of the front porch. 'Alas, I hope he was eaten by monsters. Much better than being recruited into the Titans' army.'

That idea made me really uneasy. I almost changed my mind about telling Chiron, but I didn't.

'You really think the first attack will be here?' I asked.

Chiron stared at the snow falling on the hills. I could see smoke from the dragon guardian at the pine tree, the glitter of the distant Fleece.

'It will not be until summer, at least,' Chiron said. 'This winter will be hard . . . the hardest for many centuries. It's best that you go home to the city, Percy, try to keep your mind on school. And rest. You will need rest.'

I looked at Annabeth. 'What about you?'

Her cheeks flushed. 'I'm going to try San Francisco after all. Maybe I can keep an eye on Mount Tam, make sure the Titans don't try anything else.'

'You'll send an Iris-message if anything goes wrong?'

She nodded. 'But I think Chiron's right. It won't be until the summer. Luke will need time to regain his strength.'

I didn't like the idea of waiting. Then again, next August I would be turning fifteen. So close to sixteen I didn't want to think about it.

'All right,' I said. 'Just take care of yourself. And no crazy stunts in the Sopwith Camel.'

She smiled tentatively. 'Deal. And, Percy –'

Whatever she was going to say was interrupted by Grover, who stumbled out of the Big House, tripping over tin cans. His face was haggard and pale, like he'd seen a spectre.

'He spoke!' Grover cried.

'Calm down, my young satyr,' Chiron said, frowning. 'What is the matter?'

'I . . . I was playing music in the parlour,' he stammered, 'and drinking coffee. Lots and lots of coffee! And he spoke in my mind!'

'Who?' Annabeth demanded.

'Pan!' Grover wailed. 'The Lord of the Wild himself. I heard him! I have to . . . I have to find a suitcase.'

'Whoa, whoa, whoa,' I said. 'What did he say?'

Grover stared at me. 'Just three words. He said, "*I await you.*"'

Find out what happens next!

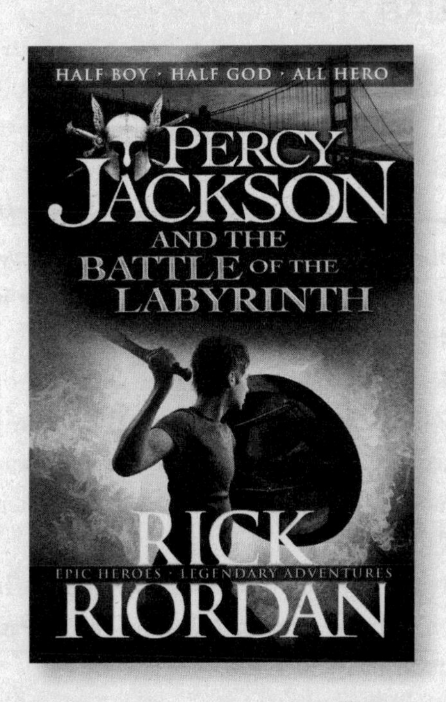

Turn over to read the thrilling opening of

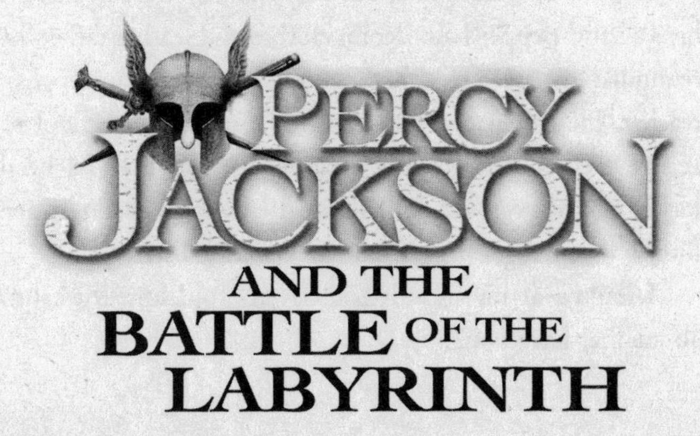

I I BATTLE THE CHEERLEADING SQUAD

The last thing I wanted to do on my summer break was blow up another school. But there I was Monday morning, the first week of June, sitting in my mom's car in front of Goode High School on East 81st.

Goode was this big brownstone building overlooking the East River. A bunch of BMWs and Lincoln Town Cars were parked out front. Staring up at the fancy stone archway, I wondered how long it would take me to get kicked out of this place.

'Just relax.' My mom didn't sound relaxed. 'It's only an orientation tour. And remember, dear, this is Paul's school. So try not to . . . you know.'

'Destroy it?'

'Yes.'

Paul Blofis, my mom's boyfriend, was standing out front, greeting future ninth graders as they came up the steps. With his salt-and-pepper hair, denim clothes and leather jacket, he reminded me of a TV actor, but he was just an English teacher. He'd managed to convince Goode High School to accept me for ninth grade, despite the fact that I'd been kicked out of every school I'd ever attended. I'd tried to warn him it wasn't a good idea, but he wouldn't listen.

I looked at my mom. 'You haven't told him the truth about me, have you?'

She tapped her fingers nervously on the wheel. She was dressed up for a job interview – her best blue dress and high-heeled shoes.

'I thought we should wait,' she admitted.

'So we don't scare him away.'

'I'm sure orientation will be fine, Percy. It's only one morning.'

'Great,' I mumbled. 'I can get expelled before I even start the school year.'

'Think positive. Tomorrow you're off to camp! After orientation, you've got your date –'

'It's not a date!' I protested. 'It's just Annabeth, Mom. Jeez!'

'She's coming all the way from camp to meet you.'

'Well, yeah.'

'You're going to the movies.'

'Yeah.'

'Just the two of you.'

'Mom!'

She held up her hands in surrender, but I could tell she was trying hard not to smile. 'You'd better get inside, dear. I'll see you tonight.'

I was about to get out of the car when I looked over at the steps of the school. Paul Blofis was greeting a girl with frizzy red hair. She wore a maroon T-shirt and ratty jeans decorated with marker drawings. When she turned, I caught a glimpse of her face, and the hairs on my arms stood straight up.

'Percy?' my mom asked. 'What's wrong?'

'N-nothing,' I stammered. 'Does the school have a side entrance?'

'Down the block on the right. Why?'

'I'll see you later.'

My mom started to say something, but I got out of the car and ran, hoping the redheaded girl wouldn't see me.

What was *she* doing here? Not even *my* luck could be this bad.

Yeah, right. I was about to find out my luck could get a whole lot worse.

Sneaking into orientation didn't work out too well. Two cheerleaders in purple-and-white uniforms were standing at the side entrance, waiting to ambush freshmen.

'Hi!' They smiled, which I figured was the first and last time any cheerleaders would be that friendly to me. One was blonde with icy blue eyes. The other was African American with dark curly hair like Medusa's (and, believe me, I know what I'm talking about). Both girls had their names stitched in cursive on their uniforms, but with my dyslexia, the words looked like meaningless spaghetti.

'Welcome to Goode,' the blonde girl said. 'You are *so* going to love it.'

But as she looked me up and down, her expression said something more like, *Eww, who is this loser?*

The other girl stepped uncomfortably close to me. I studied the stitching on her uniform and made out: *Kelli.* She smelled like roses and something else I recognized from riding lessons at camp – the scent of freshly washed horses. It was a weird smell for a cheerleader. Maybe she owned a horse or something. Anyway, she stood so close I got the feeling she was going to try to push me down the steps. 'What's your name, fish?'

'Fish?'

'Freshman.'

'Uh, Percy.'

The girls exchanged looks.

'Oh, Percy Jackson,' the blonde one said. 'We've been waiting for you.'

That sent a major *Uh-oh* chill down my back. They were blocking the entrance, smiling in a not-very-friendly way. My hand crept instinctively towards my pocket, where I kept my lethal ballpoint pen, Riptide.

Then another voice came from inside the building: 'Percy?' It was Paul Blofis, somewhere down the hallway. I'd never been so glad to hear his voice.

The cheerleaders backed off. I was so anxious to get past them I accidentally kneed Kelli in the thigh.

Clang.

Her leg made a hollow, metallic sound, like I'd just hit a flagpole.

'Ow,' she muttered. 'Watch it, *fish.*'

I glanced down, but her leg looked like a regular old leg. I was too freaked out to ask questions. I dashed into the hall, the cheerleaders laughing behind me.

'There you are!' Paul told me. 'Welcome to Goode!'

'Hey, Paul – uh, Mr Blofis.' I glanced back, but the weird cheerleaders had disappeared.

'Percy, you look like you've seen a ghost.'

'Yeah, uh –'

Paul clapped me on the back. 'Listen, I know you're nervous, but don't worry. We get a lot of kids here with ADHD and dyslexia. The teachers know how to help.'

I almost wanted to laugh. If only ADHD and dyslexia

were my biggest worries. I mean, I knew Paul was trying to help, but if I told him the truth about me, he'd either think I were crazy or he'd run away screaming. Those cheerleaders, for instance. I had a bad feeling about them . . .

Then I looked down the hall, and I remembered I had another problem. The redheaded girl I'd seen on the front steps was just coming in the main entrance.

Don't notice me, I prayed.

She noticed me. Her eyes widened.

'Where's the orientation?' I asked Paul.

'The gym. That way. But –'

'Bye.'

'Percy?' he called, but I was already running.

I thought I'd lost her.

A bunch of kids were heading for the gym, and soon I was just one of three hundred fourteen-year-olds all crammed into the stands. A marching band played an out-of-tune fight song that sounded like somebody hitting a bag of cats with a metal baseball bat. Older kids, probably student-council members, stood up in front modelling the Goode school uniform and looking all, *Hey, we're cool.* Teachers milled around, smiling and shaking hands with students. The walls of the gym were plastered with big purple-and-white banners that said WELCOME, FUTURE FRESHMEN, GOODE IS GOOD, WE'RE ALL FAMILY, and a bunch of other happy slogans that pretty much made me want to throw up.

None of the other freshmen looked thrilled to be here, either. I mean, coming to orientation in June is not cool when school doesn't even start until September, but at

Goode, 'We prepare to excel early!' At least that's what the brochure said.

The marching band stopped playing. A guy in a pinstripe suit came to the microphone and started talking, but the sound echoed around the gym so I had no idea what he was saying. He might've been gargling.

Someone grabbed my shoulder. 'What are you doing here?'

It was her: my redheaded nightmare.

'Rachel Elizabeth Dare,' I said.

Her jaw dropped like she couldn't believe I had the nerve to remember her name. 'And you're Percy somebody. I didn't get your full name last December when you tried to *kill* me.'

'Look, I wasn't – I didn't – What are *you* doing here?'

'Same as you, I guess. Orientation.'

'You live in New York?'

'What, you thought I lived at Hoover Dam?'

It had never occurred to me. Whenever I thought about her (and I'm *not* saying I *thought* about her; she just, like, crossed my mind from time to time, okay?), I always figured she lived in the Hoover Dam area, since that's where I'd met her. We'd spent maybe ten minutes together, during which time I'd accidentally swung a sword at her, she'd saved my life and I'd run away, chased by a band of supernatural killing machines. You know, your typical chance meeting.

Some guy behind us whispered, 'Hey, shut up. The cheerleaders are talking!'

'Hi, guys!' a girl bubbled into the microphone. It was

the blonde I'd seen at the entrance. 'My name is Tammi, and this is, like, Kelli.' Kelli did a cartwheel.

Next to me, Rachel yelped like someone had stuck her with a pin. A few kids looked over and snickered, but Rachel just stared at the cheerleaders in horror. Tammi didn't seem to notice the outburst. She started talking about all the great ways we could get involved during our freshman year.

'Run,' Rachel told me. 'Now.'

'Why?'

Rachel didn't explain. She pushed her way to the edge of the stands, ignoring the frowning teachers and grumbling kids she was stepping on.

I hesitated. Tammi was explaining how we were about to break into small groups and tour the school. Kelli caught my eye and gave me an amused smile, like she was waiting to see what I'd do. It would look bad if I left right now. Paul Blofis was down there with the rest of the teachers. He'd wonder what was wrong.

Then I thought about Rachel Elizabeth Dare, and the special ability she'd shown last winter at Hoover Dam. She'd been able to see a group of security guards who weren't guards at all, who weren't even human. My heart pounding, I got up and followed her out of the gym.

I found Rachel in the band room. She was hiding behind a bass drum in the percussion section.

'Get over here!' she said. 'Keep your head down!'

I felt pretty silly, hiding behind a bunch of bongos, but I crouched beside her.

'Did they follow you?' Rachel asked.

'You mean the cheerleaders?'

She nodded nervously.

'I don't think so,' I said. 'What are they? What did you see?'

Her green eyes were bright with fear. She had a sprinkle of freckles on her face that reminded me of constellations. Her maroon T-shirt read HARVARD ART DEPT. 'You . . . you wouldn't believe me.'

'Oh yeah, I would,' I promised. 'I know you can see through the Mist.'

'The what?'

'The Mist. It's . . . well, it's like this veil that hides the way things really are. Some mortals are born with the ability to see through it. Like you.'

She studied me carefully. 'You did that at Hoover Dam. You called me a mortal. Like you're not.'

I felt like punching a bongo. What was I thinking? I could never explain. I shouldn't even try.

'Tell me,' she begged. 'You know what it means. All these horrible things I see?'

'Look, this is going to sound weird. Do you know anything about Greek myths?'

'Like . . . the Minotaur and the Hydra?'

'Yeah, just try not to say those names when I'm around, okay?'

'And the Furies,' she said, warming up. 'And the Sirens, and –'

'Okay!' I looked around the band room, sure that Rachel was going to make a bunch of bloodthirsty nasties pop out of the walls, but we were still alone. Down the hallway, I heard a mob of kids coming out of the gymnasium. They were starting the group tours. We didn't have long to talk.

'All those monsters,' I said, 'all the Greek gods – they're real.'

'I knew it!'

I would've been more comfortable if she'd called me a liar, but Rachel looked like I'd just confirmed her worst suspicion.

'You don't know how hard it's been,' she said. 'For years I thought I was going crazy. I couldn't tell anybody. I couldn't –' Her eyes narrowed. 'Wait. Who are you? I mean *really*?'

'I'm not a monster.'

'Well, I know that. I could *see* if you were. You look like . . . you. But you're not human, are you?'

I swallowed. Even though I'd had three years to get used to who I was, I'd never talked about it with a regular mortal before – I mean, except for my mom, but she already knew. I don't know why, but I took the plunge.

'I'm a half-blood,' I said. 'I'm half human.'

'And half what?'

Just then Tammi and Kelli stepped into the band room. The doors slammed shut behind them.

'There you are, Percy Jackson,' Tammi said. 'It's time for your orientation.'

'They're horrible!' Rachel gasped.

Tammi and Kelli were still wearing their purple-and-white cheerleader costumes, holding pom-poms from the rally.

'What do they really look like?' I asked, but Rachel seemed too stunned to answer.

'Oh, forget her.' Tammi gave me a brilliant smile and started walking towards us. Kelli stayed by the doors, blocking our exit.

They'd trapped us. I knew we'd have to fight our way out, but Tammi's smile was so dazzling it distracted me. Her blue eyes were beautiful, and the way her hair swept over her shoulders . . .

'Percy,' Rachel warned.

I said something really intelligent like, 'Uhhh?'

Tammi was getting closer. She held out her pom-poms.

'Percy!' Rachel's voice seemed to be coming from a long way away. 'Snap out of it!'

It took all my willpower, but I got my pen out of my pocket and uncapped it. Riptide grew into a metre-long bronze sword, its blade glowing with a faint golden light. Tammi's smile turned to a sneer.

'Oh, come on,' she protested. 'You don't need that. How about a kiss instead?'

She smelled like roses and clean animal fur – a weird but somehow intoxicating smell.

Rachel pinched my arm, hard. 'Percy, she wants to bite you! Look at her!'

'She's just jealous.' Tammi looked back at Kelli. 'May I, mistress?'

Kelli was still blocking the door, licking her lips hungrily. 'Go ahead, Tammi. You're doing fine.'

Tammi took another step forward, but I levelled the tip of my sword at her chest. 'Get back.'

She snarled. 'Freshmen,' she said with disgust. 'This is *our* school, half-blood. We feed on whom we choose!'

Then she began to change. The colour drained out of her face and arms. Her skin turned as white as chalk, her eyes completely red. Her teeth grew into fangs.

'A vampire!' I stammered. Then I noticed her legs. Below the cheerleader skirt, her left leg was brown and shaggy, with a donkey's hoof. Her right leg was shaped like a human leg, but it was made of bronze. 'Uhh, a vampire with –'

'Don't mention the legs!' Tammi snapped. 'It's rude to make fun!'

She advanced on her weird, mismatched legs. She looked totally bizarre, especially with the pom-poms, but I couldn't laugh – not facing those red eyes and sharp fangs.

'A vampire, you say?' Kelli laughed. 'That silly legend was based on *us,* you fool. We are *empousai,* servants of Hecate.'

'Mmmm.' Tammi edged closer to me. 'Dark magic formed us from animal, bronze and ghost! We exist to feed on the blood of young men. Now come, give me that kiss!'

She bared her fangs. I was so paralysed I couldn't move, but Rachel threw a snare drum at the *empousa*'s head.

The demon hissed and batted the drum away. It went rolling along the aisles between music stands, its springs rattling against the drum head. Rachel threw a xylophone, but the demon just swatted that away, too.

'I don't usually kill girls,' Tammi growled. 'But for you, mortal, I'll make an exception. Your eyesight is a little *too* good!'

She lunged at Rachel.

'No!' I slashed with Riptide. Tammi tried to dodge my blade, but I sliced straight through her cheerleader uniform, and with a horrible wail she exploded into dust all over Rachel.

Rachel coughed. She looked like she'd just had a sack of flour dumped on her head. 'Gross!'

'Monsters do that,' I said. 'Sorry.'

'You killed my trainee!' Kelli yelled. 'You need a lesson in school spirit, half-blood!'

Then she, too, began to change. Her wiry hair turned to flickering flames. Her eyes turned red. She grew fangs. She loped towards us, her brass foot and hoof clopping unevenly on the band-room floor.

'I am senior *empousa*,' she growled. 'No hero has bested me in a thousand years.'

'Yeah?' I said. 'Then you're overdue!'

Kelli was a lot faster than Tammi. She dodged my first strike and rolled into the brass section, knocking over a row of trombones with a mighty crash. Rachel scrambled out of the way. I put myself between her and the *empousa*. Kelli circled us, her eyes going from me to the sword.

'Such a pretty little blade,' she said. 'What a shame it stands between us.'

Her form shimmered – sometimes a demon, sometimes a pretty cheerleader. I tried to keep my mind focused, but it was really distracting.

'Poor dear.' Kelli chuckled. 'You don't even know what's happening, do you? Soon, your pretty little camp in flames, your friends made slaves to the Lord of Time, and there's nothing you can do to stop it. It would be merciful to end your life now, before you have to see that.'

From down the hall, I heard voices. A tour group was approaching. A man was saying something about locker combinations.

The *empousa*'s eyes lit up. 'Excellent! We're about to have company!'

She picked up a tuba and threw it at me. Rachel and I ducked. The tuba sailed over our heads and crashed through the window.

The voices in the hall died down.

'Percy!' Kelli shouted, pretending to be scared. 'Why did you throw that?'

I was too surprised to answer. Kelli picked up a music stand and swiped a row of clarinets and flutes. Chairs and musical instruments crashed to the floor.

'Stop it!' I said.

People were tromping down the hall now, coming in our direction.

'Time to greet our visitors!' Kelli bared her fangs and ran for the doors. I charged after her with Riptide. I had to stop her from hurting the mortals.

'Percy, don't!' Rachel shouted. But I hadn't realized what Kelli was up to until it was too late.

Kelli flung open the doors. Paul Blofis and a bunch of freshmen stepped back in shock. I raised my sword.

At the last second, the *empousa* turned towards me like a cowering victim. 'Oh no, please!' she cried. I couldn't stop my blade. It was already in motion.

Just before the celestial bronze hit her, Kelli exploded into flames like a Molotov cocktail. Waves of fire splashed over everything. I'd never seen a monster do that before, but I didn't have time to wonder about it. I backed into the band room as flames engulfed the doorway.

'Percy?' Paul Blofis looked completely stunned, staring at me from across the fire. 'What have you done?'

Kids screamed and ran down the hall. The fire alarm wailed. Ceiling sprinklers hissed into life.

In the chaos, Rachel tugged on my sleeve. 'You have to get out of here!'

She was right. The school was in flames and I'd be held responsible. Mortals couldn't see through the Mist properly. To them it would look like I'd just attacked a helpless cheerleader in front of a group of witnesses. There was no way I could explain it. I turned from Paul and sprinted for the broken band-room window.

I burst out of the alley onto East 81st and ran straight into Annabeth.

'Hey, you're out early!' She laughed, grabbing my shoulders to keep me from tumbling into the street. 'Watch where you're going, Seaweed Brain.'

For a split second she was in a good mood and everything was fine. She was wearing jeans and an orange camp T-shirt and her clay bead necklace. Her blonde hair was pulled back in a ponytail. Her grey eyes sparkled. She looked like she was ready to catch a movie, have a cool afternoon hanging out together.

Then Rachel Elizabeth Dare, still covered in monster dust, came charging out of the alley, yelling, 'Percy, wait up!'

Annabeth's smile melted. She stared at Rachel, then at the school. For the first time, she seemed to notice the black smoke and the ringing fire alarms.

She frowned at me. 'What did you do this time? And who is this?'

'Oh, Rachel – Annabeth. Annabeth – Rachel. Um, she's a friend. I guess.'

I wasn't sure what else to call Rachel. I mean, I barely knew her, but after being in two life-or-death situations together, I couldn't just call her nobody.

'Hi,' Rachel said. Then she turned to me. 'You are in *so* much trouble. And you still owe me an explanation!'

Police sirens wailed on FDR Drive.

'Percy,' Annabeth said coldly, 'we should go.'

'I want to know more about half-bloods,' Rachel insisted. 'And monsters. And this stuff about the gods.' She grabbed my arm, whipped out a permanent marker and wrote a phone number on my hand. 'You're going to call me and explain, okay? You owe me that. Now get going.'

'But –'

'I'll make up some story,' Rachel said. 'I'll tell them it wasn't your fault. Just go!'

She ran back towards the school, leaving Annabeth and me in the street.

Annabeth stared at me for a second. Then she turned and took off.

'Hey!' I jogged after her. 'There were these two *empousai*,' I tried to explain. 'They were cheerleaders, see, and they said camp was going to burn, and –'

'You told a mortal girl about half-bloods?'

'She can see through the Mist. She saw the monsters before I did.'

'So you told her the truth.'

'She recognized me from Hoover Dam, so –'

'You've met her *before*?'

'Um, last winter. But, seriously, I barely know her.'

'She's kind of cute.'

'I – I never thought about it.'

Annabeth kept walking towards York Avenue.

'I'll deal with the school,' I promised, anxious to change the subject. 'Honest, it'll be fine.'

Annabeth wouldn't even look at me. 'I guess our afternoon is off. We should get you out of here, now that the police will be searching for you.'

Behind us, smoke billowed up from Goode High School. In the dark column of ashes, I thought I could almost see a face – a she-demon with red eyes, laughing at me.

Your pretty little camp in flames, Kelli had said. *Your friends made slaves to the Lord of Time.*

'You're right,' I told Annabeth, my heart sinking. 'We have to get to Camp Half-Blood. *Now.*'

PERCY JACKSON IS BACK!

Join Percy and his friends from Camp Half-Blood as they face off against rival Roman demigods of Camp Jupiter, and set out on a deadly new mission: to prevent the all-powerful Earth Mother, Gaia, from awakening from her millennia-long sleep to bring about the end of the world.

The Heroes of Olympus series:

THE LOST HERO
THE SON OF NEPTUNE
THE MARK OF ATHENA
THE HOUSE OF HADES
THE BLOOD OF OLYMPUS

THE DEMIGOD DIARIES

MAGNUS CHASE

THE GODS OF ASGARD ARISE!

Magnus Chase has always run away from trouble, but trouble has a way of finding him. After being killed in battle with a fire giant, Magnus finds himself resurrected in Valhalla as one of the chosen warriors of the Norse god Odin. But now isn't a good time to be joining Odin's army. The gods of Asgard are preparing for Ragnarok – the Norse doomsday – and Magnus has a leading role . . .

The Magnus Chase series:

THE SWORD OF SUMMER

RICK
EPIC HEROES · LEGENDARY ADVENTURES
RIORDAN

www.rickriordan.co.uk